BURY MY HEART AT REDTREE

BY PATRICK CHALFANT

HAWK
PUBLISHING
GROUP

TULSA

LIBRARY OF CONGRESS CATALOG IN PUBLICATION DATA

Bury My Heart at Redtree / Patrick Chalfant

[1. Chalfant, Patrick - Fiction-United States.]

Cover photo credit www.freestockphotos.com.
Author photo by Carl Rambo.

ISBN 1-930709-53-6
Library of Congress Control Number: 2004112701

Published in the United States by HAWK Publishing Group.

HAWK Publishing Group
7107 South Yale Avenue #345
Tulsa, OK 74136
918-492-3677
www.hawkpub.com

HAWK and colophon are trademarks belonging to the HAWK
Publishing Group. Printed in the United States of America.
9 8 7 6 5 4 3 2 1

BURY MY HEART AT REDTREE

BY

PATRICK CHALFANT

Also by
Patrick Chalfant

WHEN THE LEVEE BREAKS

For Drake

May the mountains of your dreams
never extend beyond the reach
of your imagination.

Chapter 1

*S*urvival is the psyche's sole responsibility in times of danger. When life becomes threatened, emotion supersedes logic; the ability to maintain and exploit rational judgment to resolve the conflict is dwarfed by the overpowering emotional responses, ranging from intense hostility to extreme fear. Under these conditions, human beings are most often controlled by either the id or the superego. In either instance, rationality is abandoned and instinct reigns.

Taylor glanced at the carnage of snack food. Fragments of everything from Twinkies to motor oil to cheap domestic beer splattered the walls and floor of the convenience store, all blasted by shotgun fire. As he examined the scene of destruction, an innocent smile began to form. Pulling out a pocket camera, he snapped a picture. A photo of such madness would enthrall even the most ardent critic of surreal art, for it was corporate America that lay before him, shattered and scattered all over the floor. The art students back at school would love it.

Reality quickly subdued the lipstick-covered smile on Taylor's face as more blasts roared from across the store. Taylor was in no danger, however. Due to extensive injuries and blood loss, the storeowner's vision was seriously impaired, rendering his aim practically futile. Although he was making a valiant effort, his bullets kept striking the shelves far from where Taylor stood. While laughing at the wounded man's marksmanship, Taylor wiped the sweat from his brow, smearing the caked makeup.

Across the aisle, Elijah stroked the long black hair that fell down his low-cut dress onto his fake breasts. With a nod to Taylor, he charged toward the wounded store owner exercising no caution. Taylor took a deep breath, pumped the 12 gauge, and turned the corner at full speed. More shotgun blasts rattled the walls as he unloaded his weapon.

In an instant, the gunfire ceased. When the haze of smoke settled, he saw the owner lying on the floor behind the counter.

"Did you make your mark?" Taylor asked.

Elijah merely nodded. He had often remarked that he was the reincarnation of the great chief Crazy Horse—an Indian born a hundred years too late. Judging from his warlike instincts, Taylor agreed.

"Good, then let's go."

Elijah kicked aside debris on his way to the microwave, turned the dial, and hit the start button. Before the raid, they had planned to use the microwave as a signal. When Elijah placed the burrito inside the oven and turned the knob, they would remove the sawed-off shotguns from their duffle bags and begin the attack. Although Taylor had estimated the shootout would be over very quickly, he had been wrong. When his first shot missed, the storeowner pulled his weapon. By the time it was all over, the burrito sat cold in the microwave.

"Do you really think we have time to wait on the burrito?" he asked.

"Just as well," Elijah replied. "I can't stand cold burritos."

While Elijah waited, he grabbed some packets of salt and pepper and stuffed them in his pockets. Moments like these stretched Taylor's patience. The law could arrive any minute, yet they were waiting on Elijah to heat a snack. All that stood between them and a life behind bars was bean dip, cayenne peppers, and hamburger wrapped in a flour tortilla. That was Elijah, though. He never failed to surprise.

When the microwave's bell finally rang, Elijah grabbed the burrito and happily headed for the cash register. As he passed it, he tossed two crumpled dollar bills on the counter.

Taylor waited impatiently outside, scanning the surrounding area for activity. Even though the job took much longer than anticipated, the small town showed no signs of life. The convenience store was located on the outskirts of town, but that really didn't matter. Even if it had been on Main Street not a soul would have noticed. Like every other Sunday night, the small town was dead.

Taylor and Elijah left the store and strolled to the car, where Keith was waiting in the passenger's seat.

"Where in the bloody hell have you been!" Keith screamed the moment Taylor jumped behind the steering wheel.

After Elijah crawled into the back seat, Taylor slammed the car into drive and sped out of the parking lot.

Elijah sprinkled some salt on his burrito. "My dinner got cold," he replied, before taking a huge bite.

"Don't tell me that we've been waiting on a burrito! The burrito was just a signal, not something to fatten that rock gut of yours!" Keith shouted in his native British dialect.

"I was hungry," Elijah beamed.

"You could have gotten us all killed! Don't you remember the plan? We were to be in and out with no hesitations," Keith fumed. "Once again, you've acted like a jackass and risked everyone's lives."

"Whatever you say, Limey," said Elijah.

"Piss off," Keith growled.

"Everybody calm down," Taylor mediated. "We got out alive. That's the important thing." He expelled a deep breath and looked at the ceiling of the old Plymouth. "We were lucky today, though. Very lucky."

Elijah rolled his eyes. "I thought it went pretty smooth."

"I'm afraid he was expecting us," Taylor said.

"Why's that?" asked Elijah.

"'Cause he had his piece nearby. Business owners in small towns don't usually stock weapons. No need for it."

"Perhaps we should rethink our plan then," Keith said. "Maybe they're onto us."

"No way!" Elijah shouted. "We're not stopping until we're finished."

"Maybe they know," Keith surmised. "Maybe our luck's runnin' thin."

Taylor reached into a duffel bag to retrieve a small pocket mirror. "Here," he said, handing the mirror to Keith.

"What do you want me to do with this?" Keith asked.

"Your afro's uneven," Taylor laughed.

"Bloody hell!" Keith bellowed. "You two are acting like children.

Have you no idea what we're up against?"

"Absolutely," Taylor stated as his smile dissolved. "I understand the danger of our quest, but remember, we know what we're doing. As long as our minds stay clear, they're no match."

Keith was silent. "No hope," he finally said. "That's all you two wankers leave me with. No hope and no confidence."

"Just trust me," Taylor said.

"That's becoming increasingly difficult," Keith replied. Slipping off his afro wig, he wiped away the brown makeup that covered his face and arms. "And this makeup is absurd. Do you really think anyone's going to buy into these costumes?"

"It's worked so far," Taylor replied.

"Correct, but if we are spotted, it's doubtful that we'll fool anyone."

"You never know," Elijah said.

"Come on now, I don't resemble a proprietor of prostitutes any more than you two look like cheap white whores. These hideous costumes don't conceal our identities at all. The police will know to look for two Caucasian males and an Indian barbarian, all in their early twenties."

"Forget about it," Taylor replied. "I think you make a fine pimp."

"I think so, too, sweet daddy," Elijah added.

"We've got a long drive," Taylor replied, smashing the gas pedal. "You guys might as well get some sleep."

Chapter 2

Refusing to be veiled by the passing dark clouds, the full moon dimly illuminated the sky as the Plymouth sped down the interstate. With the others fast asleep, Taylor kept his head tilted out the window to combat the weariness settling in his bones.

"Keith, it's your turn to drive," Taylor mumbled. "I'm getting sleepy."

"Afraid I'm not really up to it at the moment," Keith muttered without opening his eyes. "Perhaps the pinhead could be of use."

"I know preschoolers who drive better than him."

"Give the radio a go. It'll help to keep you awake."

"We're out in the boonies, remember? I doubt there's any music at this hour."

"Suit yourself."

Desperate, Taylor turned on the radio and switched the frequency to AM. Surfing for a station, he stopped on a news report.

Another town has felt the wrath of the recent string of bizarre murders. Around eight o'clock this evening, a convenience store in Little Chief was robbed, leaving one man seriously injured or dead. It is believed that it could be related to the spree of murderous assaults that have occurred in the last month. A witness reportedly saw a man dressed in women's clothing in the vicinity. Police aren't certain if the assault was committed by the same perpetrators, or if this was a copy-cat crime...

"We're becoming famous," Elijah said, suppressing a yawn.

"Try infamous," snapped Keith.

Taylor smiled and turned off the radio. In the distance, he spotted a man alongside the road.

"Look, a hitchhiker!"

"Absolutely not!" Keith declared. "You guys promised!"

"Come on, pick him up," said Elijah.

"I don't know. It's awful late," Taylor replied.

"I'll be nice, I promise. Let's hear his story, just like in the old days," Elijah reassured. "Besides, there's no cars out at this hour. The poor bastard will never get a ride and it's supposed to rain tonight."

To Keith's dismay, after a few moments of contemplation, Taylor swerved onto the shoulder of the interstate and said, "Under one condition—get in the back and be quiet. We've had enough excitement today."

"I'll agree, but only so I can get back to sleep," Keith said. "If you ask me, it's barbaric the way you fools ridicule these poor hitchhikers."

Keith jumped over the seat and crawled under a blanket beside Elijah to hide from view.

The hitchhiker opened the passenger door, threw in his duffle bag and climbed inside. He was a middle-aged man with filthy long hair, ragged clothes, and an awful stench.

As Taylor sped back onto the road, he extended his arm to shake the hitchhiker's hand.

"The name's Taylor."

The hitchhiker ignored Taylor's welcoming gesture, so he awkwardly drew it back. "What's your name?"

"Satchel Evans," he replied with a cold stare. "My friends call me Satch."

"All right Satchel. Where are you headed?"

"Nashville. I hear there's lots of work out there."

"Oh yeah? What's your occupation?"

"I ain't got no occupation. I just work hard."

Taylor laughed. "Work hard doing what?"

"I'm a roofer," the hitchhiker said. "Where are you going?"

"To a reservation," Taylor replied.

"An Injun reservation?" the hitchhiker asked with a raised eyebrow.

"Yeah."

"You live there?"

"Sometimes. When I'm not going to college."

"I've heard stories 'bout them Injuns," the hitchhiker remarked. "Ever shoot one of 'em?"

Still crouched in the backseat, Elijah's face grew red.

"Actually, I've never shot anybody," Taylor responded curtly.

"Yeah, them Injuns is hard to hit, I bet, what with their cacklin' and runnin' around," the hitchhiker laughed. "Ever had you a squaw?"

Uncertainty swirled in Taylor's mind. His first instinct was to silence the hitchhiker's foolish babble, but after giving it some thought he decided that another altercation on the road this close to home would be foolish. Besides, he'd seen enough violence for one night.

"Have you ever been in a situation when you feel that perhaps you've said something that could possibly offend the other members of your listening party?" Taylor politely asked.

The hitchhiker sat in silence with a baffled look on his face.

"After all, it's only your opinion. You shouldn't try to impose it on anyone else," Taylor continued.

The hitchhiker remained silent for a moment, then stated, "You're talking that college-boy bullshit, ain't ya?"

"I'm just making an observation. It's merely an objective statement and I don't mean for it to be offensive."

The hitchhiker pulled a large knife from his coat and thrust it at Taylor's neck. "Object this, smart ass!"

"I see that you came prepared," Taylor said, remaining calm.

"Damn right I did. Now, pull this sum-bitch over!"

"I don't think I can do that."

Shocked by Taylor's lack of fear, he pressed the knife firmly against Taylor's throat. "I think you will, boy!"

To the hitchhiker's dismay, Taylor increased the speed of the vehicle.

"I ask you to stop for a moment and analyze the situation that you have created," Taylor said in a calm voice. "Upon my harmless invitation, you have exploited my generosity and are threatening me with violence. Now we shall have a duel."

"Damn right we will!" the hitchhiker said with a crazed look in his eye.

"Next I ask you to review your options under these circumstances," Taylor methodically said. "You have a butcher knife. I am seemingly unarmed, but if you would cast aside your blurred vision and embrace the reality of the moment, analyzing the two roles we play in this confrontation, you will find that your weaponry is useless."

"That's all bullshit," said the hitchhiker. "You's trying to trick me."

"Oh yeah? You do believe in the laws of physics, don't you?"

"Physics ain't got a goddamn thing to do with me and you right now!" the hitchhiker screamed.

Taylor sensed his guinea pig was weakening, about to break. "Oh, but I'm afraid it does," he said with growing confidence. "Your fate was sealed the moment you lunged at me. I will keep increasing the speed until the engine redlines. Even if your knife penetrates my neck, by sheer willpower I will make certain my foot remains pressed against the floorboard. If that doesn't persuade you, I'll simply steer into the nearest solid object." Pointing ahead, he added, "Like the railing on that bridge in the distance."

The hitchhiker eased his grip on the handle of the knife as the words sank in.

Taylor smiled. "Unless you reconsider immediately, we shall both meet our grizzly demise."

The hitchhiker sat speechless as sweat beaded on his face. Taylor pegged the arrow on the RPM gauge near the red line.

"Not convinced? Or is that sawdust brain of yours baffled by all the variables?"

In a motionless trance, the hitchhiker stared at the rapidly approaching bridge.

"Put the knife on the dash," Taylor demanded. When the dumbfounded man didn't retract the knife, Taylor increased the speed until the cab shook.

"All right, damn it!" the hitchhiker shouted, throwing the knife on the dash.

"Well, well, we have a semi-educated man after all," Taylor said as he grabbed the knife.

After the car passed the bridge, Taylor took his foot off the gas pedal and pulled to the side of the road.

"Get the hell out."

Still shaking, the hitchhiker jumped from the car before it

completely stopped, then watched it return to the interstate and resume speed.

Elijah and Keith were quick to crawl into the front seat.

"Now you two see how logical reasoning solves problems," Taylor said confidently.

"No thanks to me holding down Elijah back there," Keith barked.

"I was nice," Elijah proclaimed. "I didn't hurt him, did I?"

"It's a bloody miracle."

While yawning, Taylor wiped his tired eyes. "You guys shut up."

Wearing a wicked smile, Elijah slapped Taylor on the knee. "How far are we from home?"

"A couple of hours," Taylor replied.

"Are you still sleepy?"

"Even more so."

"Then why don't you and the girl crawl in the back and get some sleep?" Elijah said.

Keith was angered by Elijah's comment, but was too tired to respond.

"Will you drive carefully?" Taylor asked.

"You have my word," said Elijah.

"Promise?"

"I promise."

Taylor exited the interstate and drove to a nearby roadside convenience store. As the vehicle stopped, he and Keith stepped into the backseat and Elijah jumped in behind the wheel.

"Don't do anything stupid," Taylor muttered while lowering his head against the corner of the backseat.

"Wouldn't dream of it," Elijah replied as he drove away. A quick glance in the rear-view mirror confirmed that Keith and Taylor's eyes were already closed. A maniacal grin swelled as he slowly turned the vehicle around and drove toward the on ramp of the westbound interstate, the direction from which they came.

Elijah floored the gas and sped into the night. Rain coated the windshield, a preview of the violent storm looming ahead. The highway was completely barren as lightening cracked the sky. In a moment of radiant light, Elijah spotted the object of his quest. He quickly steered across the flat median, traveling west on the eastbound lane.

The hitchhiker was dumbfounded when he saw the approaching car. As if he knew what had come for him, he turned to seek refuge, but the Plymouth's furious speed left little time for evasive action. Elijah stuck his head out the window and howled as the car engulfed the wandering man.

"Remember Wounded Knee!"

A bolt of lightening struck nearby and the sound of thunder loudly rolled through the air. Elijah thrust his fist out the window of the Plymouth, then threw the hitchhiker's bag onto the pavement.

The car slowed and quickly turned, resuming the journey east.

"What the hell's going on?" Taylor muttered groggily.

"Oh, nothing. I hit a badger in the road. Go back to sleep."

Taylor wiped the sleep from his eyes and inspected the surroundings. His senses dulled from sleep, he failed to notice anything abnormal, so he resumed his nap.

As the vehicle roared eastward, the falling rain washed the blood from the front bumper.

Chapter 3

Stan Jennings often envisioned himself as a sheriff in the Old West rounding up criminals, trying them in court, then, if found guilty, immediately serving swift and severe punishment. However, modern law didn't always see it Jennings' way. Fast-talking attorneys sometimes swayed jurors, ruining cases that he had worked on for months.

As a detective, he'd seen his fair share of disappointment with the justice system. He'd sat in the courtroom on numerous occasions, listening to overpaid lawyers exploiting insignificant technicalities to ultimately win acquittals for their clients. Each time he saw a guilty man go free, a piece of himself slipped away.

In his twenty-three years with the State Bureau of Investigations, he had strived to accept the corrupt system of justice on its terms—not his. By the time he was forty-eight years old, he had successfully prosecuted hundreds of criminals. Even though lawyers would sometimes slip a guilty man through the cracks, more often than not, he put the bad guys away.

Over time, balancing his resentment toward the justice system became more difficult, but his ethics never faltered. The system wasn't perfect, that much was for certain, but he still respected it and vowed each day to uphold every law. He'd been a detective so long that he could retire any time he wanted, but the life of a lawman was his destiny.

Jennings breathed a sigh of aggravation as he sat at the head of the conference table and stared at his wristwatch. As usual, the detectives were late for the 8:30 Monday morning meeting. He didn't look up as they strolled leisurely into the room. Out of the corner of his eye, he saw Carol walk in and close the door. Raising his head, he watched her take a seat. Lost in time by the beauty and warmth of her presence, he smiled.

"Yo, Sheriff Dillon, what're you grinnin' about?" Detective Jenkinson asked.

Startled by the comment, Jennings instantly seized the role of meeting leader. "There was another murder out west."

"Well, that's nothing to be grinnin' about," one of the ten detectives joked, as the room filled with laughter.

"No, I was thinking about something else," Jennings announced, then paused. He stared at his notebook, trying to re-familiarize himself with his notes.

"I didn't think you thought about anything else, Sheriff Dillon," Jenkinson commented.

Jennings pushed down a wave of anger, resolving not to let it show. Because he loved old western movies and television shows, the detectives had nicknamed him Sheriff Dillon after the character on *Gunsmoke*. Of course it was harmless fun, but at times like this it seemed to burn with disrespect.

"The latest murder was similar to the others in the last month," Jennings said. "A witness spotted a man walking out of the convenience store around the time of the crime, dressed in women's clothes. He didn't get the tag, but thought it was an old model sedan."

"Were there any accomplices?" a detective asked.

"He thought there might be others inside the vehicle, but the back glass was tinted and dirty so he didn't get a head count."

"That doesn't help much," Carol said.

"No it doesn't. People, we have got to establish a pattern for these goons and stop them. The death toll is up to three now, and the boys upstairs are getting really pissed." With a glance toward Carol, he asked, "Any related reports?"

"Possibly. A hitchhiker was run down last night on the interstate a few hours from the crime scene. I doubt it's related, but I'll check it out."

"Good. Everyone be alert and remember, we've got to establish a pattern."

"Are you testifying today in the Finken case?" asked Jenkinson.

"No. I won't be called until later in the week."

"Do you think we'll get a conviction?"

Jennings thought for a moment. "If there's any rule of order in the universe, then yes, we'll get a conviction. However, he's hired some big-gun lawyers and I wouldn't be surprised if..."

"I've got an uncle who lives in that part of the world and knows Finken. He says he's a snake that'd sell his own mother for money," said Jenkinson.

"I know he's trouble. He and his nephew single-handedly ruined the farming industry in that part of the state."

Jenkinson laughed. "What goes around, comes around."

"What happened?" a detective asked.

"Albert Finken pissed off the wrong farmer. A guy named Carlyle. Remind me and I'll tell you about it sometime," Jenkinson said.

"I'm confident we'll get him. We've got a strong case."

"I hope so," replied Jenkinson. "I'm gettin' tired of seeing rich people stand above the law."

"Don't worry, there's lots of compelling evidence—we've got him dead to rights."

"We've had loads of evidence in cases before and didn't get a conviction," said Carol.

"I have a good feeling about this one. We'll get our man. Now, let's get to work."

As the detectives left the room, Jennings took a deep breath and loudly voiced: "And would it be too much for you people to make it to at least one meeting on time this year?"

Detective Rolds laughed, walked to the head of the table, and put his hand over Jennings' heart.

"Careful, Sheriff Dillon," he joked, "you might upset your ticker and I'll have to holler at Doc."

"Thanks, Rolds," he said with a smirk. "I'll keep that in mind."

Only Carol remained as Rolds strolled out the door.

"You've become quite the jolly old fellow," she said with a smile.

"Why do you say that?"

"Well," she said as she walked seductively toward him, "Sheriff Dillon doesn't seem so rough around the edges anymore." Curling her arms around his waist, she added, "He's becoming quite a softie."

Jennings shook his head. "Just because I don't scream at them doesn't mean that I'm satisfied with their work ethics."

Carol laughed. "Like it or not, you're getting mellow in your old age. I think it's nice that they feel they can joke with you. You've really come a long way."

"Yeah, a long way, goin' the wrong way."

"No, really, you're so much easier to get along with now. They trust you. What more can you ask?"

"How 'bout a little respect?"

"Stop takin' things so seriously. It's only a job."

"Yeah, I know it's only a job, but it's a damned important one."

"You're doing great," Carol replied.

"Yeah, I hope."

"How do you really feel about the Finken case?"

"Like I said, we've got him dead to rights. The evidence is overwhelming. But sometimes things like that don't matter."

"I know," replied Carol. "What lawyers did he hire?"

"A couple of sharks from California, Pinkus and Newman, I believe are their names."

"Do you know anything about them?"

"Only that they're feared throughout the land. They've been involved in some high profile cases for celebrities."

"Finken must be loaded with cash to be able to afford them."

"He's a drug dealer, Carol. He's got mountains of cash," said Jennings.

"Are we seeking the death penalty?"

"According to the prosecutor, yes. We should be able to get it, too."

"Any new evidence or witnesses?"

"No, but again, we don't really need them. We've got enough to prove it beyond a reasonable doubt."

"I hope," Carol replied.

"Me, too."

Jennings stood and gathered his notebook and pens. "Sorry, but I need to get back to my desk. I have tons of things to file."

"There's something we need to talk about."

He stopped cold. Turning pale, he scrutinized Carol. "That's usually not the kind of thing I like to hear from my girlfriend."

She gazed deep into his eyes. "You look like you need to get out of Carson for a while, and you've never met my parents..."

Relief washed over him. "Whew. I was afraid you were pregnant."

Carol rolled her eyes. "No, silly. I just want you to come with me to Ducotey."

"You know I have a history with in-laws. They destroyed both my marriages."

"My parents are different, Stan," she said and waved her left hand, "and remember, I don't have a ring. Besides, my dad is an outdoorsman. You two could go wander in the wilderness and, well, find yourselves."

"Not more of that Nirvana shit," he winced.

"I'm not asking you to discover your identity in the universe. I'm just asking you to do me a favor and meet them. We've been dating for three years. They're starting to ask questions. Please. For me?"

Jennings looked at his notepad, then boyishly asked, "Think your dad will let me ride one of his horses?"

She laughed. "Of course. You can do anything you want."

"Anything?" An evil smile accompanied his question.

"Within reason..."

"All right, but one cross word from an overprotective mother and I'm outta there."

Carol smiled and kissed him. "I wouldn't have it any other way."

Chapter 4

The dull clamor from the classroom's antique heater vents woke Taylor from his nap. He held much reverence for the psychology building's heating unit because it regularly roused him from his frequent lapses during class. Realigning his senses, he found Professor Heinrich scribbling incoherent passages on the chalkboard and babbling something about Freud. The other twenty-five students in the room seemed captivated by his words, but it was nothing new for Taylor.

"Before we leave today, I'd like to address an issue that's just come to my attention," the balding professor said. "It seems as though someone in our department has been having a laugh with the female interns down at the university's child development center."

The professor walked toward Taylor, who was seated on the back row of the classroom. "Let me just say that the university's president is very perturbed," he added, stopping next to Taylor. "The culprit was somewhat experienced in hypnosis. He managed to talk the interns into individually undergoing some, shall we say 'creative' hypnosis disguised as a harmless school experiment. At first, no one noticed anything unusual, but then whistles mysteriously appeared at the center for the children to play with."

The students were on the edges of their seats, gripped by the professor's words.

"What's so uncommon about that, you ask?" Professor Heinrich paused to look around the room. "Oh, nothing really, except that when the interns heard the children's whistles, they took off their shirts."

Taylor sensed every eye in the room fixed on him. As usual,

whenever tomfoolery surfaced in the psychology department, Taylor was automatically the first suspect.

"When the little boys discovered that they held the power to expose the interns, well, let's just say they whistled Dixie over and over again."

The room exploded with laughter. Taylor turned red as he quickly scanned the faces of his classmates and found that almost everyone in the room, including the professor, was in tears from laughing so hard. Only a small group of female students wore straight faces.

"I fail to see the humor in this crime," a voice cried from the group. "The perpetrator should be expelled from this department and from school, for that matter."

"That's not for us to decide," Professor Heinrich said. "I'm sure the university president will deal with the matter accordingly."

The professor stepped on Taylor's foot. "Let's just hope the mastermind behind this keeps his nose clean. After all, some of you will be graduating very soon and I'd hate for such an infraction to stand in the way of all the hard work you've done to obtain your masters degrees."

Taylor looked at the professor and slowly nodded.

"That's all for today," Professor Heinrich said. The students immediately gathered their belongings and shuffled toward the door.

"I've looked over the outlines of some of your dissertations and have been surprisingly disappointed," he added. "Remember, I do not want you to reconfirm previous research. Be bold. Reach beyond your horizons."

Since they were still snickering, most of the students didn't hear the professor's words.

"Make haste—papers will be due soon. Keep in mind that insane ideas can sometimes be refined and molded into brilliant theories."

The professor looked at Taylor. "Oh, and Taylor, I'll not accept a study of erotic hypnosis. Matter of fact, I'm expecting more from you."

Taylor smiled. "Oh, you won't be disappointed."

Chapter 5

K yle Gayland's mammoth stomach jiggled and rolled onto itself each time his green, four-wheel-drive Suburban hit one of the potholes littering the old state highway. The only passenger, Jonathan Peat, laughed to himself when he noticed Gayland's gut never seemed to stop its incessant movement. Like dropping a rock into a huge body of Jell-O, the waves rippled endlessly.

Gayland parked at the main entrance of the Redtree Indian Housing Unit complex. A few Native Americans conversed with each other in front of the houses, which were astonishingly dilapidated.

"My God!" Peat said. "I can't believe people actually live in such squalor."

"Oh, don't you worry, Mr. Peat," Gayland replied, chewing on an unlit cigar. "They won't for long."

"How do you figure?"

"Well sir, these nasty old Injun' homes are the essence of our prosperity. All we've got to do is pull our resources together and, above all, be covert. After that, it's all just money in the bank."

"But how are we gonna get 'em out? I've known a few Indians in my day. They can be rather stubborn," Peat said.

"Not in the event of a health crisis. Look over yonder."

On the other side of the complex, a man dressed in rubber boots and protective overalls was spraying chemicals around the perimeter of the houses.

"What's he doing?" asked Peat.

"He's supposed to be spraying the houses for spiders and ticks."

"Supposed to be?"

"Yeah," he laughed. "That's what he's supposed to be doing."

"Who is he?"

"Joe Escartes. He's our cleanup man. Me and the investors hired him to do the dirty work to these poor sons of bitches."

A wicked smile grew on Peat's face. "If I hadn't known you for thirty-five years, I'd say you were a maniacal, heartless man."

"Does that mean that I can count you in?"

Peat stared at Joe Escartes. "I do believe so. This looks to me like it could be a dangerous investment. You might need my help."

"Fine. Fine indeed," Gayland said as he lit his cigar. "I do believe that you've just made a very profitable decision."

Gayland turned the Suburban around and started for the highway. As he drove out of the complex, the Suburban passed a crimson-and-cream colored Studebaker with two Native Americans inside. The Indians stared intently at the bankers as they passed. The older Indian didn't bother to conceal his laughter.

"What's that old man laughin' at?" Peat asked.

"Who knows? Maybe he's already been hitting the fire water or took too much medication. I certainly would if I had to live here."

"If all goes as planned, he won't have to put up with this place much longer," Peat laughed.

"Amen."

"You don't suppose he recognizes us, do you? I mean, is it smart for us to be seen together right now?"

"Why, we're down here on business in Ducotey," Gayland said, as if he'd been rehearsing the alibi. "We were just passing through and wanted to take a look at the houses our tax money built."

"Kyle Gayland, you are a mastermind. It sounds to me like you've got it all worked out."

"I certainly do."

"What about the police down here? Will they be a problem?"

"I wouldn't worry too much 'bout the law in these parts," Gayland said. "I contribute a great deal of money to the local yokels."

"Oh, the power of money," Peat laughed.

"It's a sweet thing. Ever eat an Indian meat pie?"

"Never," replied Peat.

"Well then, sir, you're in for a treat. There's a little dive here in Ducotey that makes a fantastic pie."

"When in Rome, do as the Romans."

"Indeed," Gayland laughed.

Chapter 6

Loud knocks on the apartment's front door woke Taylor from his mid-afternoon nap. He was still in a daze when he opened the door, but his senses quickly sharpened when he saw Wendy.

"Been taking a nap, I see," she said.

"Yeah, I had a long night."

"Did you and your buddies get drunk and pull another all-nighter?"

"Well, sort of," he mumbled.

She walked into the apartment. "Were you with Elijah and Keith?"

"Yeah, they were there, along with some others," he replied, closing the door.

Wendy walked to the refrigerator, opened the door and peered inside. Finding only old lunchmeat, she opted for a soda. "You look rough. I bet you didn't make class this morning."

"I slept through most of it, but I was there. How 'bout you?"

"Yeah, and boy, oh boy was it invigorating," Wendy said, opening the soda as she sat on the couch. "I'm so ready to graduate and get the hell out of here. I've had my fill of this university and this town."

"I love the university," Taylor said. "And what's wrong with Carson? It's just the right size—not too big and not too small. There's plenty to do here."

Wendy grabbed the television remote. "I've just had enough. I'm burned out."

"I don't know why," Taylor said, sitting beside her. "Are you that anxious to get a job?"

She laughed. "As long as I don't have to study, I'd be happy sweeping the floors of the auditorium."

Taylor took her hand. "Look, we'll leave this place very soon. December is right around the corner. Trust me, you'll miss it after we're gone. These are the happiest days of our lives, so they say."

"God, I hope not." After a few moments of awkward silence, Wendy rubbed his thigh then took his hand in hers. "Speaking of our lives, have you given that subject much thought?"

"What do you mean? Our lives together?"

"Right. What are our plans?"

Warning sirens blared in his head. Be careful where you tread, he thought. She's about to bring up marriage.

"Why do you ask?"

"I've been thinking about it a lot lately."

"What have I told you about thinking?" laughed Taylor.

She jabbed him in the ribs. "Be serious."

"Yeah, I've thought about it. After all, we graduate on the same day and I'm not planning to hang around after that. Are you?"

"That's not what I mean," Wendy said.

Even though she smiled to mask it, Taylor felt her vulnerability. "Do you mean marriage?"

"I know we've never talked about it, but it would be the next logical step. After all, we've been dating for three years. After we graduate and find jobs, our relationship might be difficult to maintain if we live in separate cities. I don't even know where I'll be. Do you?"

"I have no idea, but if worse comes to worst, we can sweep the auditorium floors together. I'm sure they could use a couple more hands. It's an awfully big auditorium," he laughed.

"Would you be serious for a moment?"

"Sorry. I assumed we would."

"Would what?" asked Wendy.

"Get married."

She smiled, squeezing his hand as she leaned her head on his shoulder.

"Does that make you happy?"

"It does. I've wanted to talk to you about it for some time."

"I feel that it's the next thing to do, but I don't think that logic has anything to do with it. Love's an emotional thing, you know."

"That it is," she replied with a smile.

"Anything else bothering you?"

"Not anymore. How's your experiment going?"

"I'm almost finished with the dissertation."

"When are you going to tell me about it? Not that I would fully understand…"

"At the awards banquet."

"Awards banquet?"

"Yeah, the psychology department recognizes the top five students in the masters program every year. The students give a synopsis of their projects in the auditorium. You'll find out about it then."

"So you've already won?"

"No, but I will."

"I do like confidence in a man."

"It's not confidence, my dear. I'm simply that good," Taylor said, trying to imitate a snobbish scholar. "Remember, ol' girl, I do have a four point."

"How could I forget?" Wendy asked sarcastically.

Taylor's demeanor turned serious. "What makes you say that? I never talk about my grades."

"I know you don't, but I hear about it all the time when I'm at parties and I run into your classmates from the Psych Department. They think you're a genius."

"They think that because they're nerds and they care about that sort of thing. Trust me, most people don't care much about grades. I sure as hell don't."

"I wish I loved my major as much as you love yours."

"What are you talking about? You apply yourself better than I do."

"But it's easy for you," she snapped. "I don't know how you hold such a deep fascination with psychology."

"It's really not that difficult. The funny thing about it is, the more I learn about the human psyche, the more disturbing I find it to be."

"How's that?"

Taylor thought for a moment. "We'll get into that sometime later. Sorry to change the subject, but have you seen much of Kyle Gayland lately?"

"What's with this sudden interest in Mr. Gayland? This is the third time this week you've asked about him."

Taylor searched for a plausible answer. "I've always been

fascinated by bankers…You know, their power…Besides, I think he's interesting. Have you noticed anything different about the way he's been acting?"

"No," Wendy sternly replied. "He hasn't been flirting with me if that's what you're implying."

"That's not what I mean. Have you seen any new faces in the office? Anything unusual?" Taylor asked.

"No, but I'm just his part-time secretary. I don't pay much attention to who's coming in and out of his office. Besides that, he's the bank president. If I went snooping around his place I'd get fired on the spot."

"Not if you don't get caught."

"He's a nice man, Taylor," she said with sincerity. "Without him, I wouldn't be at school. He's paying me very well and he's even said that he'd help pay my tuition if I decide to get my doctorate."

"All that just because you're a nice girl?"

"He could have ulterior motives, I don't know."

"Just keep your eyes open for anything peculiar, okay?"

"There has been a strange man calling lately."

The statement peaked Taylor's interest. "What's his name?"

"Humphry, or something like that."

"It's not Hempshaw, is it?"

"Yeah, yeah it is. John Hempshaw. Why, do you know him?"

"What does he want?"

"He wants to talk to Gayland, but Gayland always avoids him. It seems like Hempshaw's more belligerent each time he calls. He's an ass."

Taylor stared at the ceiling as his mind raced.

"Is something wrong?" Wendy asked.

"Be leery of him."

"What do you care?" she asked with suspicion.

"I don't care. Just watch out for him."

"Do you know him?"

"I know of him. He's from my hometown."

"I'll start watching, I promise." Weary of the conversation, she changed the subject. "You want to go get something to eat?"

"No, I've got other business tonight. I'll call you when I get back."

Chapter 7

By the time Taylor, Elijah and Keith made their way to the back seats of the auditorium, the ceremony had already begun. Around two hundred guests in suits and dresses had gathered to pay homage to the man of the day, Kyle Gayland. From preachers to politicians, everyone's proud smiles showed their eagerness to hear a few words from the distinguished banker.

Gayland was seated at a long table next to the podium with the university's president and other distinguished alumni, listening to the mayor's remarks about the honored guest.

"Kyle Gayland has proven to be a valuable asset to the City of Carson for many years. The thing I most admire about him is his compassion. He's earned the trust of both the private sector and various government entities by aiding minorities and the less fortunate. He's been instrumental in the construction of housing units for low income citizens and he's also given a great deal of his time and money to those in need. It is with great honor that on behalf of the City of Carson, I present this award of recognition to him for his valiant efforts."

Beaming a counterfeit smile, Gayland walked to the podium and shook hands with the mayor.

"I feel honored to be recognized by such a fine group," he said. "A long time ago, when I was a young man, I vowed to make not only my life better, but also the lives of my fellow citizens."

"Bullshit!" Elijah yelled as he jumped from his seat and shot past Keith to rush the stage.

Taylor grabbed his arm and threw him back in his seat. "This is not the place!" he seethed. "You'll blow everything if you don't sit still and shut up!" After a few seconds, he released his hold on

Elijah's arm and sat back in his chair. Elijah's cold stare remained focused on the banker.

"Let's get outta here," Keith whispered to Taylor. "We've already drawn too much attention to ourselves."

"Shut up!" he muttered.

Either Gayland didn't hear Elijah's interruption or he simply chose to ignore it. He continued, "It has been my goal since childhood to fulfill that promise, but it hasn't been easy. I haven't done it alone, though. Since I've received so much help from the community, I feel that I must share this award with all of you."

To thunderous applause, Gayland bowed with the elegance of a classical pianist. After the clapping subsided, he left the stage to mingle with his audience.

As Gayland walked to the floor of the auditorium, he was congratulated by townspeople gathered in a reception line to shake his hand and pat his back. They adored Gayland as if he were a rock star.

The sight of him posing for pictures with a congressman was more than Taylor could take. "Mindless sheep," he snapped as he stood to leave. "It's time to go. I'm getting sick."

"He's got all of 'em snowballed," Taylor said as the Plymouth soared through the night.

"You got that right," Elijah responded from the backseat.

Taylor looked across the front seat to Keith, who was applying the final touches of brown makeup.

"Quit messing with your makeup. It looks fine," Taylor said. "We're not going to a beauty contest."

"Got to make it right," Keith replied. He looked in the mirror and made a few more adjustments.

"He's getting pretty good at puttin' on that makeup," Elijah said. "I reckon he likes it."

"Oh shut up!" Keith shouted. "Look at you! It looks as if someone rolled your face in flour, then smeared shit underneath your eyes, it does!"

"Elijah, your makeup does leave much to be desired," Taylor said.

"You're both more than welcome to come back here and straighten it up, if you dare."

Taylor shot Elijah a menacing gaze via the mirror. Catching his own reflection, he noticed mascara streaked down one side of his face. He briefly considered fixing it, then decided that the streaked makeup gave him more of a frightening, surreal look.

"I couldn't believe the line of shit that was spewing from his mouth. Aiding the minorities, my ass. If he's recognized for anything, it should be for killing the minorities," Taylor said.

"The banker spread lies tonight like the white man spread disease to my people," spouted Elijah.

"Easy on the white man analogies, Elijah," Keith warned. "And need I remind you that we're trying to keep a low profile? Please keep that in mind the next time you have the impulse to behave like a buffoon in public."

Elijah reached forward and slapped Keith on the back of the head.

"Stop it, you two," Taylor said. "Keith's right. No more outbursts. This thing is far from over."

"I say we kill him now," said Elijah. "The longer we wait, the more time he has to slip away."

"He won't slip away," Taylor confidently said. "Too much money is at stake. Remember, he's a greedy bastard."

"Or we could cease this now and allow the police to hand him his justice," Keith said with a flare of hope.

"He's too powerful and too smart for the police," Taylor replied. "He won't leave them a clue. Besides, Gayland owns too many people."

"No harm in trying," Keith replied.

"I'm afraid there is. If we sit around and wait, he'll kill more and more. This is the only solution," Taylor said.

"Agreed," said Elijah. "So why are we waiting?"

"We will destroy them all," said Taylor. "Don't worry; he'll get his turn."

"I dream of the day," said Elijah.

"Forget him for now. Focus on tonight."

"Tonight sounds rather simple," Keith said. "You've been watching Mr. Johnson, so you know his routine. He closes the store at nine o'clock, opens a bottle, then retreats to a room at the back of the store until after midnight."

"Imagine that, a drunk running a liquor store," Elijah said.

"And don't forget, there's a camera right inside the front door," Taylor said.

"It'll be a piece of cake," Elijah bragged.

"Don't be so sure. The last one acted like he knew we were coming. He was ready."

"He's not acting like anything now."

Chapter 8

*T*he id's domination of the psyche is evident when the helpless victim is overcome with anger and rages against the aggressor. The desire to compromise is abandoned; the victim's focus is not merely to survive, but to disarm and kill.

Standing over the sink in his office, Ray Johnson cracked open a sixteen-ounce bottle of soda and poured half the drink down the drain. He filled the soda bottle with Crown Royal, gave the elixir a firm shake, then sat on his six-hundred dollar leather office chair and propped his feet on the antique oak desk.

Remote in hand, he surfed the TV channels. When no programs held his interest, he settled for a news station and lowered the volume. Slipping off his shoes, he sipped his whiskey while watching his favorite sexy anchorwoman deliver the daily news.

Ray's senses were dull as he drifted into a fantasy world with the auburn-haired anchor. Scantily dressed, they were running down a sandy beach with crystal blue water crashing ashore. She didn't seem to mind his beer gut or his body odor. All she wanted was to be exploited by a real man like Ray, a man who took charge and did things his way, no matter what the cost.

As Ray's imagination ran wild, he reached for the anchorwoman. The fantasy ceased abruptly when the cold steel of a pistol touched his temple. His eyes flew open as he shouted, "Who the hell are you?"

"I'm the medicine man," said Taylor. "I've come to stop the sickness."

"I ain't sick," Ray said, growing angry. "Now get the hell outta here!"

"I'm afraid that's impossible. May I ask you a question?"

"Do I have a choice?" Ray snarled.

"What would you most like to do right now?"

Ray remained silent, his eyes heavy with a mixture of panic and loathing.

"I need to know," Taylor said. "Would you like to run away, to escape?

"Taylor!" Elijah yelled.

Taylor could hear Elijah in the front of the store.

"How's it going in there?" Elijah asked.

"No problems," Taylor replied.

"You'd better come in here."

"I'm rather busy."

"Get in here. You gotta see this," replied Elijah.

Keeping an eye on Ray, Taylor backed to the office door, turned slightly and looked toward Elijah.

"What?" he barked.

"Check out all this booze. This is high dollar stuff."

"We're not taking any of it, so put it back."

With Taylor's attention diverted, Ray quickly reached inside his desk drawer to grab his .44 Magnum, and tucked it between his legs.

"And stay out of the cash register, too," Taylor ordered before turning back to Ray.

"Let me ask you a question," said Ray.

"All right."

"If you ain't gonna take that booze or any of the money, why the hell did you come here?"

"Like I said, I'm here to stop the sickness."

"And like I said, I ain't sick."

"No, but you've caused a great deal."

"I don't know what the hell you're talking about, boy." He looked over Taylor's drag outfit. "You are a boy, ain't ya?"

"Tell me, Mr. Johnson, what emotion is controlling your instincts at this moment? Is it fear, indifference, or rage?"

Ray's expression was unreadable. He had learned years ago in the military that apathy was the best response to interrogation. "Not real sure," he finally replied.

"Now, Mr. Johnson, I know there must be thousands of impulses flashing through your mind."

"Finish the job!" Elijah yelled from the front room.

Taylor glanced at his watch. "We are running short on time. Tell me, what is the one thing right now that you'd like to do?"

"I reckon I can think of something," Ray said with an evil smile.

"Do tell."

Ray slowly reached between his legs. "I'd like to paste your nuts to that wall."

"So, it's anger that you're feeling?"

Ray nodded slowly.

"Finish the job, Taylor," said Elijah, bursting into the room.

Ignoring Elijah's remark, Taylor continued: "It's fight or flight, and if you had my gun, you'd choose fight. Am I correct?"

"Maybe I've got my own gun," replied Ray.

"Maybe you should go ahead and shoot his ass," Elijah said.

A sound near the front of the liquor store caught their attention. He and Elijah quickly moved to the office door to check for signs of life.

"Hurry guys!" Keith shouted. "Hurry before we get caught."

As Taylor and Elijah turned to face the old antique desk, a shot blasted through the room. Taylor turned and saw smoke rising from the barrel of Ray's .44 Magnum. The bullet struck Elijah in the right leg, sending him to the floor. While Ray continued firing, Taylor dropped to his knees and crawled out of the office with Elijah. The two rested in an aisle in the wine section. Still inside his office, Ray reloaded his pistol then walked into the store's open area.

Reacting to the latest round of gunfire, Keith bolted out of the building and jumped into the car.

"You're a coward!" Elijah stood and screamed.

"Get down!" Taylor yelled.

More shots rang out. Broken glass and wine rained down on them.

Suddenly, the shooting stopped.

"Was that six shots?" asked Elijah.

"I think it was five," answered Taylor. "But I'm not sure."

While Taylor pondered their next move, Elijah pumped his shotgun and hobbled into the open area of the store. Limping, he blasted everything in sight—beer cans, whiskey bottles, even the posters of gin models. It wasn't until he ran out of shells that he finally noticed Ray hiding behind several cases of Mexican beer.

Elijah turned toward Taylor. Ray jumped up, pointed his pistol at Elijah's back, and fired. The bullet narrowly missed Elijah but shattered the front glass of the store into thousands of pieces.

Relatively certain Ray's ammunition was spent, Taylor pumped his shotgun, stood and began firing.

As Ray ran in a crouched position toward his office, Taylor honed him in his sights. However, before he could fire, two loud blasts from Elijah's shotgun shattered the silence. Buckshot rippled through Ray's body, sending him crashing into a wine rack. Chardonnay and broken glass covered Ray's blood-soaked shirt as he slumped to the floor.

Elijah reloaded as he walked to Ray's body.

"You can reload yours as fast as I can shoot mine," said Taylor. "I had him in my sights."

With a snarl, Elijah studied his prey like a proud hunter over a slain buffalo. "I was born for this," he declared.

"Let's get the hell out of here."

Elijah glanced at Taylor. "What happened to your leg?"

Taylor looked down. Blood covered one of his legs from the thigh down. "I must have cut it when I started shooting. I guess this means I'll have to buy more panty hose," he joked. "How's your wound?"

"Not bad," Elijah said. "The bullet nicked the side of my leg. I'm bleeding, but it didn't hit the bone." After reloading the shotgun, he blasted everything in sight.

Keith stuck his head through the gaping hole that used to be a window. "Hurry! We've got to get the hell out of here, now!"

"Rub everything down," Taylor said. "Pay special attention to spilt blood. We can't leave any of ours behind."

The three quickly wiped the doorknobs, then cleaned their blood spots from the floor. After they rushed to the car, Taylor jumped behind the wheel and quietly drove out of town.

"Were you safe here in the car?" asked Elijah with sarcasm. "I hope it wasn't too scary."

"Somebody has to keep watch," replied Keith. "I don't suppose you had a reason for destroying all the booze and everything else?"

"It just felt right."

"You two quit bickering," said Taylor. "I'm bleeding and I'm tired."

"You're not the only one," Elijah answered.

"Where are we headed?" Keith asked.

"To the doctor. I figure our wounds need some attention," Taylor said.

Campanow dressed the wounds on Taylor's leg. "This is pretty severe. You were lucky."

"I wrapped it good and tight," Taylor replied, looking at his leg. In spite of the gruesome horrors that he, Elijah, and Keith had recently caused, the sight of his own blood made his stomach quiver.

"If not, you'd be dead," replied Campanow.

Even though Campanow's house was miles from civilization, Keith was still gripped by paranoia. He paced nervously, keeping an eye on the window.

"Had it not been for me, they'd all be dead," Keith said.

"Your contribution was essential," Elijah said. "You kept the car warm. What would we have done without you?"

"Don't forget, I was the one watching your back. Had it not been for me, we might all be in jail."

"Hand me a fresh rag," said Campanow. Taylor picked up a clean towel and handed it to the old Indian. Since the bleeding had stopped, he used a rag to daub yellow ointment on the wound.

"Did you stop the sickness?" asked Campanow.

"Yes," Taylor responded. "It wasn't easy, though. He fought hard."

"Was he prepared?"

"No, but he was hostile. He had a gun stashed in his desk. I only turned my back on him for a second and all hell broke loose. But luck was on our side—he was either very drunk or a terrible shot."

Campanow wrapped his leg with gauze. "Maybe both. You must be very careful as there is much more work to do. Beware, the white man is very smart. Your smallest mistake could be your worst."

"Don't worry. Everything's under control," Taylor said and paused. "I'm anxious to get to Gayland."

"Aren't we all," Elijah said.

"Have you spoken to Kacey recently?" asked Taylor.

"Yes," Campanow replied.

"Is he getting closer to Gayland?"

"Not yet."

"That banker is a slippery one," replied Taylor. "He's never alone. He never leaves himself vulnerable."

"No. Kacey is smart. He'll get to him."

"And you're sure we can trust Kacey?"

Campanow taped the gauze on Taylor's leg. "Yes," he said. "He's an Indian. I've known him for a very long time. Our blood is the same."

"If we get caught, will he talk?" Taylor asked.

"No. He has spent much time investigating the crimes that the banker and his fools have committed against our people. Don't worry about him. Our blood is the same."

"It's too bad the police won't help, especially since Kacey has evidence."

"He tried years ago, but their ears turned deaf when he mentioned the banker. They will not stand in the way of a powerful white man. The banker has many friends in high places. He is immune to justice."

Elijah's face turned red. "We shall give him justice."

Taylor walked to the east wall of the shack. He lifted a blanket, which hid several boxes of ammunition. He picked up a box and walked to the door, where Elijah and Keith waited.

"So far, it's been easy to stay ahead of the local police in each town," Taylor said to Campanow, "but the state and federal investigations will soon begin. I'd like to finish as fast as possible."

Campanow nodded. "It will end soon enough, warrior. Soon enough."

Chapter 9

Remnants of absolute chaos greeted Detective Jennings when he entered the liquor store. It was like stepping into a battle zone—practically every bottle of booze in the place had been blasted.

"Must have been one hell of a shootout," Jennings said to the only uniformed officer at the scene.

The policeman was oblivious to Jennings' comment. His eyes were fixed on a pool of caked blood.

"Judging by all the shells on the floor, I'd say the assailants had enough ammo to stock a third world army," Jennings said.

The officer remained silent. Jennings waved a hand in front of the young man's face. Unmoving, he stared blankly ahead with sweat beading on his forehead.

"We figure they struck shortly after midnight," a voice behind Jennings declared.

"Is that when it was reported?" he asked as he turned to face a middle-aged Native American dressed in plain cloths. "Are you the detective working the case?"

"The boy who cleans the joint found him this morning and no, I'm retired."

"Retired? Then what are you doing here?"

"Just helping out."

"Can't find anything better to do?" Jennings asked with a smile.

"I guess not," the man laughed.

"Pretty messy robbery."

"I've seen worse."

"Oh? You must not be from around here. Crimes like this are

scarce in this part of the state. The whole town is on edge."

"I grew up here but moved after I graduated from high school. I ended up in Kansas City where I was a detective for twenty years. My wife and I moved out here a couple of years ago to get away from this sort of thing. It must have followed us. Are you from the State Bureau?"

"Yeah. I'm Stan Jennings."

"Nice to meet you, Stan."

An awkward moment of silence hung in the air.

"Do you have a name?"

"Quana Smith."

"You're from Ducotey, huh?"

"I sure am," Quana replied.

"My girlfriend is from Ducotey."

"Really. What's her name? I might know her."

"Carol Parker."

"You're kidding!"

"From the expression on your face, I'm guessing you know her."

"Hell, I was practically raised with her. She and my kid sister were best friends. I spent a great deal of my childhood with her."

Jennings chuckled. "It's a small world, eh?"

"That it is," replied Quana. "Her parents still live here. I see them from time to time. She comes from a great family."

Jennings looked at the blood stains on the floor, which reminded him that he had work to do. "Do you know where the sheriff is?"

"He's trying to calm the townspeople. They're all a bit shaken right now."

"Who's in charge?"

"I hope it's not him," Quana laughed and pointed at the young officer who was still entranced by all the blood.

"Hey, Robertson!"

The officer was unresponsive.

"Robertson!" Quana called again.

"I'm all right, I'm fine, I'm fine..." he weakly replied.

"You need to take a break. Get out of here for a while. Go buy us all some sodas."

Robertson's legs barely carried him out the door.

"What's his problem?" Jennings asked. "Is he related to the victim?"

"No, he's a local boy and hasn't been on the job long. This is the first time he's seen anything like this."

"I'm sure it's a first for most of the people here."

"Almost. A few years ago, we lost a few folks at some Indian houses just down the road."

"Was it this gruesome?"

"In a different way," Quana said.

"What do you mean?"

"Some Indians died. Some think they were murdered."

"What happened?"

"No one really knows. They lived at the Kickingbird Housing Unit. Something made everyone who lived there sick, not sure what it was. Some of them died. A lot of folks think they were intentionally poisoned."

"That's odd," Jennings said. "I would have thought that we would have been called in to investigate. I don't remember hearing anything about it."

"It was kept rather quiet, which lent credibility to the theory that they were murdered."

"What do you think?"

"Everyone's always looking for a conspiracy, especially around here," Quana said, then paused. He breathed deeply and looked into Jennings' eyes. "I think that a bunch of Indians got sick and died. Nothing more."

Detective Jennings looked to the ceiling and immediately spotted a camera above the door. "Has anyone got a look at the tapes from the camera yet?" he asked.

Quana laughed. "There's no film. It was just for show."

Jennings sighed. "What do you know about the victim?"

"His name is Ray Johnson. He's had this store for as long as I've been back, probably a lot longer. I don't know why, though. He had loads of money. Been that way for a long time. I've known him since grade school."

"Any enemies?"

"Lots of enemies. He wasn't very well liked around here, kind of a tyrant. Rumor is that he's been involved in lots of shady business deals through the years. It's doubtful anybody'll miss him."

"Married?"

"No. Like I said, he wasn't very well liked."

Jennings scanned the destruction. "It's just like the others," he muttered to himself.

"Pardon?" Quana asked.

"I'll bet no money was taken from the cash register."

"Yeah, how'd you know?"

"I've seen it before. These perpetrators aren't out for money. They're out for blood."

As Jennings backed his car out of the liquor store parking lot, his cell phone rang.

"Find anything?" asked Carol.

"Not really. It's very similar to the others—another bloodbath."

"The case is gaining notoriety. It made the morning news."

"What'd they report?"

"Nothing new. They interviewed the county sheriff and he said that it could be related to the others. He wasn't saying much, though."

"I ran into an old friend of yours."

"Oh yeah? Who?" asked Carol.

"Quana Smith."

"Really? I thought he was in Kansas City."

"He's back," Jennings said. "Said he'd had enough of city life."

"I'd love to see him. He's a dear friend and a helluva guy. He was like a brother to me growing up."

Jennings smiled. "He told me lots of stories about you. You have some explaining to do when I get back."

Carol laughed. "I can't wait to hear them."

As Jennings drove out of town, he looked at the faces of the children who were standing by the side of the road. Even though they were too young to understand what had happened, they looked as though they understood that their town had been soiled.

"Everyone here is in shock. You wouldn't believe it."

"The whole state is talking about it."

"That's not a good thing," Jennings replied.

"I know. I hope we get a lead soon."

"The crime scenes are very clean. If we're lucky, they'll make a mistake."

Chapter 10

Barbecue sauce flew in every direction as Kyle Gayland annihilated the pork ribs like a school of piranha tearing through a wounded ox. The napkin tucked into his starched white collar did little to shield his expensive three-piece suit. Across the booth, Jonathan Peat watched in awe. He'd known Gayland for years and was always amazed by his rather bizarre eating habits.

The sheer amusement of watching him eat like a pig quickly grew old. There were bigger issues at hand, much bigger issues, and they didn't sit well with Peat. "I heard on the morning news that there was another murder last night at a liquor store in Ducotey. You might want to slow Joe Escartes down a little," Peat's voice trembled.

Gayland stopped eating and scanned the café for patrons close enough to be within earshot. "Keep your voice down and stop worrying. Escartes knows what he's doing."

"Have you talked to him lately?"

"Not since I paid him the first installment. He should be contacting me soon, though. I'm waiting on him to page me."

Peat's hands twitched nervously on the table. "I'm afraid people are going to make a connection to us."

"How could they possibly do that?"

"I don't know, I'm just afraid they will," Peat muttered. Now that people were dying, he felt the heavy burden of guilt and it weighed far more than he'd ever imagined. "I'm thinking that maybe I shouldn't have gotten into this."

"Damn it, Peat, I assumed that being a banker, you had the stomach for this sort of thing."

"Well, sometimes I think I do. But not always. Like now, for instance."

"People aren't going to suspect anything with these unrelated deaths out in the middle of the boonies," Gayland said with ease. "Trust me, we've got nothing to worry about."

"Well then explain the cross-dress thing. Have you read the newspapers? Why is Escartes dressing up like a woman?"

"Perhaps he's nurturing the angry female inside him," laughed Gayland. "I don't give a damn, though. It's probably just something his kind does, as a disguise."

"Maybe this sumbitch is crazier than you thought. Maybe he'll come after us next!"

Gayland looked hard and deep into Peat's eyes. His first reaction was to strike him down, but he knew that Peat was weak and fragile. Any sudden tension might give him a heart attack.

"Now listen," Gayland said, as if he were speaking to a juvenile, "I've used Escartes on other occasions. He's been in the business for a long time and he knows what he's doing. Stop worrying so much."

Peat looked at the barbecue sauce covering the table, then expelled a long breath. "The next time you see him, tell him to slow down a little, okay? I'm afraid someone is going to find out about this."

"Our little partnership is quite covert. Only the two of us, the surviving investors, and the attorneys know."

"What about your lawyers? They won't become righteous and turn us in, will they?" Peat asked.

"Come on, boy, they're lawyers. What do you think? Besides, Ratcliff's the only attorney left and I trust him like a brother," said Gayland.

"What happened to the other lawyer?"

"Ratcliff asked him to join our venture. We needed the money, so I accepted, but I never really trusted the beady-eyed little shit."

"So what'd you do?"

"Escartes took care of him a couple of weeks ago."

"Oh."

"Can't have too many variables. That's the way this game is played. Desperate men cut deals with prosecutors."

Peat felt the cold chill of Gayland's indifference to human life. He knew better than to show his fear and disgust, since Gayland would read it as weakness. Peat had no desire to be next on the list.

"I worry that someone might talk," Peat said.

"Don't bother. I bought that land under an alias, using the cash from the investors. No one else knows anything about this. So, you see, there are no traces. After they're gone, it's all ours. It'll just be me, you, and Ratcliff."

"What about the other investors who are still alive? What if they've told someone about doing business with us?"

Gayland's patience was wearing thin. He stopped eating and leaned close to Peat. "Do you really think that the investors will tell anyone that they've hired a hit man to poison Indians to get them out of their homes? And do you think they'll admit that they bought land with a banker who has enough political stroke to sell the land to the government at an inflated price for new Indian housing?"

"Of course not," Peat replied. "But they might have mentioned your name to someone. Come on, Gayland, you're a well-known man."

He leaned back in the booth. "Then I'll deny it. Remember, it was cash and there's not a trace."

"All right, then," Peat said, somewhat relieved. "I have another question."

"Shoot."

"Will I share the same fate as the other investors?" Peat's nervous body language denied his attempt to mask the fear raging through his body.

"Peaty, ol' boy, I'm surprised you would ask such a thing," Gayland said with an exaggerated smile. "I would never do anything to harm you. We've been through too much together. I only brought you into this because in the past, you've told me that you were interested in business opportunities. I asked you about this venture, you accepted, and here we are. I can assure you that there's nothing to be worried about."

"The remaining investors worry me."

"They'll never talk. There's only a handful left. Besides that, Escartes will take care of 'em soon enough."

"All right," Peat said.

"And by the way, when can you pay me?"

Peat felt his stomach turn. "I'm having problems with that," he said.

"Problems? What kind of problems?"

"I have the money, it's in a safe in our house. I'm just having some problems getting it out."

"I don't understand," Gayland said, perturbed. "Just take it out. What's so hard about that?"

"My wife and my kids know about that money. They'll miss it."

Incensed, Gayland firmly grasped Peat's hand and pulled it toward him. "Make up something. Tell them you're putting it in some kind of no-load mutual fund. You're a banker, for God's sake! Tell them you've found a big investment deal."

Terrified, Peat placed his hands over his face and sobbed gently. "I'm sorry," he moaned. "I'm not a strong man like you."

Gayland knew he was dealing with emotional dynamite. "Don't be sorry. It's me who should be apologizing. I didn't mean to scare you."

"I'm doin' the best I can," said Peat, still sobbing. "It's not easy. You don't know my wife and my kids. They can be animals."

"It's okay, it's okay, just do the best you can." Gayland looked around the restaurant and noticed several patrons staring at the misty-eyed Peat. "It's okay, folks," said Gayland with a smile, his mind racing. "It's okay. My friend here is having some marital issues."

Peat rolled his eyes and grabbed a napkin from the dispenser. He wiped his face, then drank some water.

Gayland began devouring the ribs once again. "There is one other issue," he said with his mouth full.

"What's that?"

"Hempshaw's beginning to be a problem."

"Hempshaw?"

"Yeah, Hempshaw."

"I don't know who he is," Peat said.

"He's one of the investors. A real pain in the ass. He's been calling a lot. I guess he's getting nervous."

"So what do we need to do?" Peat asked.

"We need to get rid of him," Gayland said while shoveling potato salad in his mouth. "That's why I need your money."

"I thought my money was going toward buying the land where the houses will be rebuilt."

"I've already paid for that," said Gayland.

"So you're telling me that my money will be used to kill

people?"

"Yep."

"Dear God. Oh, dear God."

"Forget about it," Gayland said. "Don't get high and mighty on me now."

Gayland raised his glass of tea to a nearby waitress. After she refilled his cup, he slapped her on the butt as she walked away. She turned and gave Gayland a smile.

"Cute girl," he said.

Peat tried to eat but was overwhelmed by Gayland's nonchalant manner about death.

"How can you be so damned calm about all this? Aren't you at least a little nervous?" he asked.

Gayland smiled. "'Cause this ain't my first rodeo, dear Peaty. This ain't my first rodeo."

Chapter 11

W hy do we need to ride horses? Can't we just drive to this place?" Wendy asked as Taylor cinched the saddle.

"We could drive, but the terrain is very rough," he replied, helping Wendy up onto the saddle.

"Did you have horses on your dad's farm growing up?" he asked.

"We did, but I was always too busy doing other things to ride much. I've always loved it, though. It's such a peaceful way to experience nature."

"There's nothing like it," Taylor responded as they rode out of the corral and into the pasture.

"How far is this place?" Wendy asked.

"Just a couple of miles. We could walk it if we had to, but I just thought it would be more fun to ride. Besides, these horses need the exercise."

"Whose horses are they, anyway?"

"They belong to an older man named Richmond. He lives in the house back by the barn. He and I used to ride together. It doesn't look like he's home today, but he told me that I could ride the horses anytime I wanted."

"I have to admit, it's been awhile, but this feels pretty good," Wendy said. "It's all coming back to me."

Taylor loosened his hold on the reins and nudged his horse with his feet.

"Try to keep up," he said with a smile as his horse galloped past Wendy. Not to be outdone, Wendy followed in hot pursuit.

The afternoon sun stretched tall shadows along the canyon's towering white walls. Wendy was dumbstruck by the raw beauty of the canyon and the pristine river flowing lazily through its base.

"This is incredible," she said, sliding off the horse's back. As she walked to the edge of the cliff, she added, "I never knew a place so beautiful existed."

"Few do," Taylor said. "It's called Running Bear Cliff. All this land is owned by the tribe, so the public doesn't have access to it."

Taylor stepped off the horse and led him to an old tree. He wrapped the bridle's reins around a branch, then joined Wendy. Together, they stood on top of Running Bear Cliff and watched the river flow, some two hundred feet below.

"It's like something out of a movie," Wendy said. She pulled her .35-millimeter camera from its case and began taking pictures. "I can't believe you haven't shown this to me. My instructor will love these pictures."

"Are they for an assignment?"

"Yes," Wendy replied, carefully focusing each shot. "We're supposed to find something inspirational in nature."

"This is a very special place. As a matter of fact, you're the only outsider I've ever brought here."

"Really? I thought you grew up nearby."

"I did, close to Ducotey. It's just a couple of miles away."

"Surely you brought girls up here when you were in high school."

"No. Like I said, you are the first outsider. The only other people who've seen this place are Elijah, Keith, and a friend of mine from Ducotey. And that's only because we all grew up here."

"How long have you known them?" asked Wendy.

"Keith and Elijah?"

"Yeah."

"A very long time. I met Elijah first, just after I moved here. Keith came along a year or so later," Taylor said.

"It sounds like you guys are pretty close."

"Like family."

Wendy lowered the camera to look at Taylor. "Am I really the first girl you've shown this to?"

"You're the only girl I've brought here. And if you don't shut up," he added with a smile, "you're going to be the only girl I've ever thrown off the ledge."

"You would never throw me over," Wendy laughed. "You wouldn't know what to do without me. Let's face it, Taylor, we're soul mates and you're hopelessly in love with me."

"Maybe I am."

"How did you find this place?" Wendy asked while scanning the area.

"I'm not sure. I just always remember coming up here and playing with Elijah and Keith. I suppose we just happened upon it."

"Why's it called Running Bear Cliff?"

"I don't know," Taylor said with a blank look. "We just came up with it when we were kids."

"It's truly fantastic. Where exactly is the house you grew up in?"

"It's on the far end of the reservation in the old Kickingbird Housing Unit—not too far from here—about a fifteen minute walk."

In the distance, a screech echoed in the canyon walls.

"What's that?" Wendy asked.

Taylor searched the area, then pointed toward the water far below. "Can you see her?"

"Where? What is it?"

"Down by the river. It's an eagle, flying just above the water."

Wendy finally spotted the majestic bird and immediately began taking pictures. "It's like she owns this place and she's letting us know that she's aware of our presence. Why does she squawk so much?"

"She's looking for something," Taylor said, then paused. "When I was little, my grandmother, my adopted grandmother, used to tell me stories about eagles. She said that eagles are an extension of our psyche and that they are one of the purest symbols of mother earth. She used to always say that if she ever came back, she'd rather return as an eagle."

"Is your grandmother still alive?"

"No."

"Think that's her?"

Entranced by the sound and sight of the eagle, Taylor didn't reply.

"Do you think it would be okay if I brought some people from my class here to take more pictures?"

"No!" Taylor shouted. "This place is sacred to me! I don't want anyone to know about it!"

Taken aback, she softly said, "I'm sorry. I won't bring anyone, I promise."

Taylor walked to the canyon's edge to regain his composure.

"Are you all right? I'm sorry, I didn't mean to..."

"Since I brought you here, there's something you must know. You are now within the circle. There's no going back."

"I don't want to go back. I want to be here. I want to be with you." She walked to Taylor and wrapped her arms around him.

"I just don't want anyone to know about this place. It's very special."

"Don't worry. It's safe with me."

Sensing both vulnerability and the security of their bond, Wendy took a deep breath to bolster her courage, then asked, "Up until now, you've shut me out of your past. Now that we're here, within the circle, please tell me what happened to your parents."

"I've never met my real parents," Taylor said. "I don't know who they were, or even if they're alive."

"So, you were adopted?"

Taylor stared at the horizon. "You know I don't like to talk about this."

"If you can't trust me, who can you trust?"

He stood in silence.

"You were adopted?"

"Not at first. I lived at an orphanage until I was ten."

"That must have been a difficult life."

"It's not as bad as you'd think. When you're young, you don't know any better. It was the only world I knew, so I wasn't aware of what I was missing."

"When you turned ten, you were adopted?"

He nodded. "That's when I first met my mom and dad."

"What were their names?"

"Rosemary and Paul Runningbear."

"What was that like, I mean coming from an orphanage into a home? I'll bet it wasn't an easy transition."

"It wasn't. In the orphanage I lived in a world of chaos—a world with no rules. My adopted parents brought me into a very structured environment, rich in Native American culture."

"But you were a white kid. Was it easy to accept their culture?"

"I didn't at first. I was at a rebellious age. But I understand it now. I've embraced their heritage with all my heart."

Taylor paused, studying the rocks far below before continuing. "When you boil it down, it's all the same anyway."

Wendy snickered. "Are you telling me that all cultures are the same?"

"No, I'm just saying that the people within the cultures are the same and generally, people are corrupt. The exploitation that existed in the adoption agency was rampant in the reservation and is rampant throughout the whole world."

"Maybe so, but there's a strong counterbalance of love in this universe, too."

"Love hasn't done anything to bring my parents back," Taylor said.

"Do you think of them a lot?"

"Of course."

Wendy proceeded cautiously, knowing she stood at a crossroads in their relationship. She hoped that after all they'd been through together, he was finally ready to be honest with her. "I wish we could talk about them sometime, when you feel like it."

"My adopted mom and dad were murdered."

Wendy was shocked. "What?"

"They were murdered."

"By whom?"

"Businessmen."

"I'm sorry," she replied. "When did it happen?"

"About four years ago. Right after I started college."

"I'm sorry, honey."

"Yeah, me too," he muttered.

"Are you all right without them?"

"Well, I have to be. Even though I was adopted, we were very close."

"I'll bet you were. Where did it happen?"

"In their own home—the place they should have been safest."

"Were they robbed?"

Taylor fought to conceal his rage. "No," he said. "They were poisoned."

"My God! How? Who would do such a horrible thing?"

"It doesn't matter now. All that matters is that they're gone. Everything's gone, except the house."

"Do you ever go back and visit?"

"Of course. That's where Elijah and Keith live. When I'm in town, I usually go by and visit them."

"I'll bet you have lots of good memories there."

Taylor smiled. "I sure do. My parents and I did have our share of conflict, though."

"Such as?"

"Well, they didn't want me to go to college."

"Why's that?"

"They didn't see the need. They wanted me to buy a farm around here and raise cattle. That was their world—living on the land."

"And now you've almost earned your masters degree. Talk about a change. I wonder how they'd feel about it."

"They'd be proud, but they probably wouldn't understand. My pursuit of a life in psychology would be foreign to them."

"It's a different world, that's for sure."

He smiled. "I live in several worlds, but to me, it's all the same."

The sun was slipping behind the canyon walls, casting long shadows that muted the vibrant colors. "It's getting dark. We should probably go."

"I reckon we should," he responded and walked to his horse. As he unwrapped the reins from the tree branch, Wendy took pictures of the horses and Taylor.

As he mounted the horse, she noticed a dark stain on his pant leg. "What happened to your leg?" she asked. "Is that blood?"

"Actually it is. I accidentally cut myself yesterday."

"Doing what?"

"I was out running and fell on an old whiskey bottle. It cut me up pretty bad."

"Did you go to the doctor?" she asked, very concerned.

"Yeah, I had someone look at it. Don't worry, it's all right."

"Maybe you need to cut back your activities and let it heal," Wendy said.

Taylor softly shook his head. "Can't slow down now. I can never slow down."

Chapter 12

Fred Parker parked his crimson and cream Studebaker a few hundred yards downhill from Campanow's house. Cedar branches slapped his face as he walked slowly through the darkness to the old Indian's one-room shack. The branches reminded Fred how much he disliked visiting the remote woodland area.

Like most people on the reservation, Fred visited Campanow to seek his wisdom and advice. As the oldest of the tribe elders, he was revered by all. He led the lifestyle of his forefathers—living off the land while shunning most modern conveniences. Only a battery-powered AM radio, which he listen to religiously, especially at night, separated him from his ancestors.

Campanow lived in the most secluded part of the reservation. His house stood atop a hillside blanketed with thick brush and cedar trees. The moon was obscured by heavy cloud coverage from an incoming autumn storm, forcing Fred to rely on his sense of touch to navigate the wilderness. The darkness and high winds increased the challenge.

Fred trudged diligently through the brush until he reached a clearing and spotted an auburn glow radiating through the shack's two windows. He walked to the door and knocked several times before Campanow answered. After greeting each other, Fred joined his friend beside a fire burning on a circular stone foundation in the middle of the room.

Fred immediately noticed a blanket covering several boxes on the interior east wall of the shack. Since he had never seen them before, he asked, "What's with the blanket?"

Campanow stared deep into Fred's eyes. "It is uncivilized for you to come here with questions that mean nothing."

"Excuse me. I'm sorry to be the bearer of such, but I have some bad news."

"Tell me." Campanow replied as he placed some papers into a manila envelope. After sealing the envelope, he slid it across the floor.

"Many are sick. Some of them very bad."

"From where did this sickness come?"

"Not sure, but I have a theory. All who are sick live in the Redtree Housing Unit."

"And you?"

"I do not live there. I am not sick."

Campanow simply stared at the fire's glowing embers.

"A few days ago, when you and I were at Redtree, I saw two white men. I think they might be responsible for the sickness."

Campanow listened, still staring at the coals.

"I've seen one of them before—the fat man with white hair. I believe he is a banker."

"I saw them, too," he replied. "The banker's name is Gayland. He's from Carson and is no stranger to our land, nor to the evil that men do."

"Do you think he is responsible?"

Campanow didn't respond.

"Maybe we should call the police."

"I have little faith in the police. They've failed us before, many times."

Fred was disheartened by his elder's apathy. "We could tell the Bureau of Indian Affairs," he suggested. "Maybe they could..."

"Do you know what happens," Campanow interrupted, "if you throw a bullfrog into a pot of boiling water?"

Fred carefully considered the cryptic question. Speaking in riddles was nothing new for the old man. "I imagine that the frog jumps out."

Campanow nodded. "If you place a bullfrog in a pot of cool water, then heat the water up slowly to a boil, do you know what happens to the frog?"

"He jumps out?"

For the first time in their meeting, Campanow looked directly at

Fred. "No," he said. "He boils to death."

Fred suddenly felt ill. He was certain he knew more than he was saying. "So, what should I do?"

"When you feel the water becoming warmer beneath your feet, free yourself and free your people."

Campanow reached into one of the pockets of his shawl and removed what appeared to be a handful of small pebbles. He then began chanting in the ancient tribal language that was foreign to Fred. Although Fred was forty-three years old and had lived on the reservation his entire life, like most of his people he wasn't fluent in his native language. As with almost all other aspects of their lives, they'd grown accustomed to the conveniences of the white man's ways.

Fred knew to remain silent during Campanow's chant, so he stared at the fire and waited. As Campanow's voice grew louder, he waved the handfuls of pebbles around his head, then crashed his hands onto the hardwood floor. He then ended the chant, looked directly to the ceiling, and cast the pebbles into the fire.

The fire crackled and radiated brilliant flashes of red, blue, and emerald flames. Although Fred had seen Campanow perform this ritual countless times, he always felt an overwhelming sense of awe at the old world ceremony.

When the fire returned to normal, Fred was surprised that Campanow was no longer at his side. After scanning the room, he found him lying on the floor in a corner, fast asleep.

Although Fred wasn't sure which ritual Campanow had performed, he knew that it must have been significant because it had completely drained the old man of his energy. After most ceremonies, he remained animated and explained the hidden nuances of the chant and the other minute details. Campanow's exhaustion could only mean one thing—a great ugliness had surfaced in the tribe—an ugliness that would test the physical and spiritual strength of them all.

Chapter 13

Taylor sighed, then clicked the save icon on his word processor. A glance at the digital clock on his desk confirmed that four hours had flown by in what had seemed like only minutes.

Rereading his dissertation's latest passage several times to check for grammatical errors, he was pleased with the way everything was coming together. Soon, his graduate degree, Gayland and the investors, and perhaps even his marriage to Wendy would all be resolved. Life was exactly the way he'd envisioned it.

In response to a knock on the front door, he quickly closed the document, shut down the computer, then made his way through the apartment. As he entered the living room, he found Elijah sitting on the couch.

"How goes it?" Taylor asked.

"I've been better," Elijah replied.

"How's your leg?"

"It, too, has been better. How's yours?"

"Very sore. It hurts a little to walk, but it should be all right. Campanow did a nice job."

"I'm not sure we should go to that crazy old bastard anymore. I felt like a chicken being cut on by a witch doctor."

"We didn't have much choice. Going to the hospital could've alerted the police. We just need to be more careful next time."

"Keith's becoming more and more of a problem. I'm tired of dealing with him."

Taylor was mildly surprised. "What brought all this on? Everything seems to be going fine," he said.

"In my opinion he's a liability. A risk."

Taylor shook his head. "The same could be said about you."

"Why do you say that?" Elijah shouted as he jumped from the couch.

"We're all liabilities to each other if we don't act as a team," Taylor replied calmly.

"That sounds all well and good, coach, but sitting in the car while you and I do the dirty work is not contributing."

"He keeps a watch outside each time we go in. That's his purpose."

"But we're becoming more and more efficient," Elijah claimed. "We're fast enough now that we don't need a person to stand watch anymore."

"We always need someone to watch. Besides that, we're almost finished. It'll be over soon."

"That's what bothers me."

"That this is almost over?" Taylor asked, puzzled.

"No, that we're not finished. There are more investors. We have more work to do. Bringing him along is a, uh, well, it's a huge disadvantage."

"I disagree. We need him. Remember, this is a collective effort. We've been successful so far because we've worked as one. Each of us does his role."

Elijah shook his head in disagreement.

"He's a good man and he's reliable," Taylor said. "That trait is difficult to find in people. We've known him practically our entire lives. He's never let us down before."

"I can think of plenty of times he's let me down."

"When?"

"Back in school, even now. Hell, he's always been nothing but a problem."

"But you've been roommates ever since we graduated from high school," Taylor said. "Why are these problems surfacing now?"

"Maybe it's just that we're all changing. You've got to admit, what we're doing isn't easy to stomach. You and I are drawing strength from our mission; Keith is growing weaker and more paranoid with each hit. Face it, Taylor, he's always been a nuisance."

"I don't see it that way at all. He's never bothered me."

"That's because you don't remember the way it was before he

came along."

"That was long ago and I was a kid, so my memory's kind of fuzzy."

"You were getting your ass kicked by a couple of thugs on the playground because you were the only white kid at the Indian school. I pulled the bullies off of you, then together we beat the hell out of them."

"Yeah. I remember that. We whipped their asses proper. But what does that have to do with Keith?"

"As kids, you and I fought the bullies, same as we're fighting them now. After we beat the shit out of those guys, nobody ever messed with either of us again."

"So?"

"The following year, when Keith came to our school, everything changed. As soon as we became friends with him, our intimidation and domination died," Elijah said. "He made us soft because he was always standing between us and the punks, telling us that violence wasn't the answer."

"Big deal. It was school. Who cares?"

"I care because it's the same now. Nothing has changed. God knows what we could have stolen in all these past hits. Think of the money we'd have. We'd be rich, Taylor."

"Our crusade isn't about money, it's about justice," Taylor said in a stern voice. "Justice that the authorities are too afraid to dispense. We're removing the investors because they are murderers."

"And who's idea was it not to take the money?"

Taylor was slow to answer. "It was Keith's idea."

"Bingo! You do exactly what he wants you to do. You're completely under his control."

"It makes the hits more mysterious. It's harder for the police this way because they don't have a motive. And besides, I made the decision, not Keith."

"But he suggested it and you listened."

"But I listen to you, too. Wearing the women's clothing, that was your idea. Keith didn't like it but I insisted and he gave in."

Elijah stared silently at Taylor.

"Forget about it. Just stick to the plan. Everything will be fine."

"For the record, I don't like the idea of him finishing this with us. These jobs are not for the weak."

"We're doing fine, Elijah," Taylor said as the phone rang. "Don't sweat the small stuff."

"You'd better be right."

Taylor talked on the phone for a few seconds, then hung up. "That was Wendy. She wants me to stop by the bank."

"Are you going to the safe?"

"Definitely."

"Can I come?"

"No," Taylor answered abruptly. "No need for you to meet Wendy."

"Are you afraid that I'll sweep her off her feet?"

He laughed. "No, that thought hadn't entered my mind."

"Then what has?"

"If we get caught, I don't want her involved in any of this."

"You should have more confidence in your team, coach."

"It's for her protection. Just in case."

"I'm not planning to get caught."

"Neither am I."

"But in the event that we do, they won't take me alive."

"That's what worries me about you," Taylor replied.

Chapter 14

The cold wind blew a chill down the neck of Fred Parker's short sleeve shirt as he walked toward the Indian hospital's main entrance. Fred chuckled to himself when he felt the bitter cold and remembered that he'd left his jacket in his Studebaker. All things considered, he decided, forgetting a jacket wasn't so bad. Many of his lifelong friends were barely clinging to life. Catching a cold was the least of his worries.

As Fred walked through the front doors, he spotted a nurse down the hall. "Excuse me, ma'am," he called.

When the nurse turned, Fred recognized his old friend, Linda Jackson. From her solemn expression, he knew that she was deeply troubled.

"Hi," Fred said. "How's your husband?"

"He's gonna pull through, I think," she replied in a frail voice. "Everyone between the ages of six and sixty-six is gaining ground."

"And the others?" Fred asked, removing his ball cap.

"Not good. The infants and the old people were hit hard. I don't think some of them will make it." With a downcast look, she sighed.

"Do the doctors know what's wrong?"

"Not yet."

"Do they have any ideas?"

"They're running IV's and doing tests. They think they were exposed to something."

"This is like what happened a few years ago at Kickingbird."

"I remember."

"Do you think this is as bad?"

"It looks like it could be. We lost five people then. This time there are eight in bad shape."

"Damn."

"I'll say."

"Do you need anything from your house? I'll be passin' that way."

"Yes, I do, but you can't go there."

"Why's that?"

"The Redtree Housing Unit has been quarantined."

"Quarantined? If the doctors haven't pinpointed what's wrong, then why are the houses quarantined?"

"Because that's where all the sick people live. Makes sense that the problem is there."

"This is all too familiar."

"And nothing was resolved last time."

"Yeah, but houses just don't poison the people living inside them."

"Maybe it's not the houses. I'm not sick and I live there, too," said Linda.

"Even so, my gut is telling me that something stinks about all this."

"I agree, but the solution four years ago was to pack us up and move us out. I really doubt this time will be any different."

"Take care of them, Linda. They need all our strength."

"I will." As he turned to leave, she asked, "Where are you going?"

"I've got to do some thinking. I can feel the water warming beneath my feet."

Chapter 15

Even though it was after 9:30 p.m., Wendy was still toiling away at the bank. Everyone else was gone, even the janitors. Due to her demanding curriculum, she'd found herself falling farther and farther behind at work. Her only option was to stay late each day to catch up on all the meaningless work that Gayland stacked on her desk while she attended her morning classes.

"It's awful late for a pretty girl like you to be here working," someone in the dark hallway outside Wendy's office whispered.

Startled, she said, "Hello? Who's there?"

"You should be home with your boyfriend. It's getting late and I'm sure he's lonely."

Wendy smiled. Even though she couldn't see the mysterious person, she recognized the voice.

"Maybe I don't have a boyfriend," said Wendy.

"Then maybe I should give you a visit."

"Maybe you should," said Wendy.

Wendy chuckled when she saw the man's hand slowly slide into the room to dim the lights. He entered the room walking seductively and singing, "I'm in the mood for love..."

Wendy laughed. "You're a nut!"

"That I am," Taylor replied. "Does that excite you?"

"It certainly does. But unfortunately, I'll be here all night if I don't get this work done."

"I wish you'd stop saying that ugly word."

"Work?"

"Yeah. You're young and beautiful. You shouldn't be so consumed with work. It isn't natural."

"Well, it pays the bills."

"To each his own."

"How did you get through the front door? Is it unlocked?"

Taylor smiled, then held up Wendy's keys. "No, but I know people on the inside."

"You do realize that you could get me into a lot of trouble doing that."

"I haven't been caught yet."

Wendy turned to her keyboard and began typing. "What have you been doing?"

As Taylor inspected the small office, he replied, "Working on my dissertation."

"How's the research going?"

"Fine. It's coming right along." He stopped outside the door to Gayland's office. "Say, you don't mind if I snoop around in there, do you?"

Wendy stopped typing and thought for a moment. "No, but leave everything exactly the way it was. Heads will roll if he finds out that someone's been snooping around his office."

"Don't worry."

"It's hard not to," Wendy said as she began typing again. "What are you looking for in there?"

"Oh nothing, just keeping up on my favorite banker's activities."

Taylor walked straight to Gayland's desk and opened the top drawer, which was filled with notebooks. After he removed the drawer, he emptied the spiral notebooks, turned the drawer over, then placed it on the desk. Since the office was only moderately lit, he turned on the desk lamp.

A series of numbers written in pencil were on the underside of the drawer. Retrieving a pen and piece of paper from his pocket, he copied them then replaced the notebooks and returned the drawer to its proper place.

"Is everything going all right?" Wendy asked while she typed.

"It's fine. Just about finished," Taylor replied.

Taylor approached the large portrait of the fat banker, which hung on the wall behind the desk. He removed the portrait and found Gayland's combination safe. Using the numbers that he'd just copied, he unlocked the safe and removed a folder titled "Project Redtree."

Taylor quickly inspected the list of investors who contributed money to Gayland for the deadly chemicals at the Redtree Indian Housing Unit. He noticed that new names had been added. After jotting down the details of the latest partners, he closed the safe and returned the picture to the wall.

As Taylor turned off the lamp, he thought about one of the new names, Joe Escartes. Since he'd grown up in the area, he knew most of the names of the wealthy people within a hundred mile radius of Carson. But he didn't recognize Joe Escartes. Even more puzzling was the note next to his name—$15,000.00 – PAID.

"Find anything?" Wendy asked.

"Nothing that would interest you," Taylor said, smiling. "By the way, I'd like to meet Gayland."

"Why? I thought you didn't like him."

"I don't. I'd still like to meet him though. I think he's interesting. Maybe we could have lunch or something."

"I'll see what I can do, but he's always busy."

"Just try, okay?"

"All right. I'll try," Wendy said, then turned off the monitor to her computer. "Let's lock up and go. Where are you headed tonight?"

"The dissertation went well today, so I'm yours."

"Sounds great. Let's get out of here."

Chapter 16

Jennings entered the room and immediately knew that Carol was immersed in her work as usual. She didn't even notice his presence until he placed a hand on her shoulder.

"Good morning," he said. "Can I get you some coffee?"

"I just uncovered something interesting," Carol replied without looking up.

"What's that?"

"All the robberies have occurred in towns with less than three thousand people."

"Murders, not robberies," Jennings corrected. "Remember, they didn't take anything. This would be easier to solve if they did. At least we'd know it was just people being robbed at random. I think there's more to it than that."

"Agreed. But there's another connection. Every victim has been a prominent businessman with a lot of money."

Jennings shook his head. "This gets more insane by the minute. If these victims have lots of money, but none of it is taken during the crime, what's the motivation? Looks to me like..."

"It's not about money," Carol interrupted.

"Right, it's driven by something emotional. Could be fear, greed, revenge, who knows."

"None of that matters until we catch them."

"No, but if we're going to establish a profile, we've got to think like they think."

Carol asked. "How common is it for very wealthy people to live in small towns?"

"I'd say it's pretty rare, but it definitely happens. Usually, they own several businesses. In small towns, a few moderately wealthy people often control the town, some residents are in the middle class, but most are poverty level."

"But we're not talking about people who are just well off. The victims were people with extreme wealth. Two of them practically monopolized their towns. Don't you find that a little strange?"

"What's strange is that wealthy men from one-story towns are dying the same way. It's odd enough for people in that part of the state to be rich, even odder that they're meeting the same fate."

"Maybe you're right—it could be an emotional thing. If the assailants grew up in poverty and learned at an early age to hate rich people they might be out for revenge."

"Hating them is one thing, killing them is quite another. Let's look at the map."

Carol opened her desk and removed a map of the crime scenes.

Jennings studied the seemingly random red marks on the paper. "There's no apparent order, no link. As you said, the only thing that they have in common is that they've occurred in small towns in the western part of the state. Are any of the victims related?"

"No. I already checked."

"One was in a convenience store, two were in liquor stores, and one was in a lawyer's office." Jennings scratched his head. "Have we interviewed people who knew the victims?"

"Yes, and they all say the same thing. The victims were all people of affluence and weren't very well liked."

"At least that supports our theory that they're driven by emotion rather than need. The convenience and liquor stores are easy targets—quick in, quick out. To assassinate a lawyer in his office is different."

"Right. The lawyer was the first one hit, too. They must have known he would be there after hours."

Detective Jennings stared at the map intently. "We really have nothing to go on," he said.

"Just that wealthy people in small towns should be very cautious."

"I'll start calling the sheriffs of each county out west to ask them if they know of anyone who has a lot of money and is especially hated by the townspeople." Jennings sighed and looked at Carol. "We'd better figure out a way to speed this investigation up a notch."

Chapter 17

"W e've got ourselves a bona fide problem," Ratcliff said while he held the 12 gauge. Pointing the shotgun to the sky, he nodded.

Gayland responded by stepping on the button that released two clay pigeons. Ratcliff fired both barrels of the shotgun, easily destroying both targets. "Nice shooting," he said as he reloaded the throwing device. "What kind of problem?"

"A damned severe one," replied Ratcliff.

"That's not the kind of thing I like to hear from my attorney," Gayland said, forcing a smile.

"And that's not the kind of thing I like to tell my clients."

Gayland looked over both shoulders to make certain he and Ratcliff were alone. "Do tell."

"It appears as though your boy took our contracts."

Gayland was confused. "What boy and which contracts?"

"The Yankee."

"The Yankee?" Gayland asked, puzzled.

"The cleanup man."

"You mean Joe Escartes?"

"Yep," replied Ratcliff. "When he killed my partner at our offices in Strong City, he took the contracts."

Gayland was baffled. "What in the name of Jeremiah are you talking about?"

"My law partner. The beady-eyed little shit who was involved in our little business venture."

"Yeah, yeah, what about him?"

"Evidently Escartes did a little snooping after the hit."

"Yeah, so?"

"It seems as though Escartes went through his desk and found the contracts that link us all together."

"Hold on a minute! I don't remember signing any contracts. What the hell are you talking about?"

"A few of the investors wanted something in writing, so I drew up contracts. And yes, you did sign them; I just didn't tell you what they were."

"My God! That means their families have copies! We'll have to kill 'em all."

"That's the beauty of it," a calm Ratcliff replied. "The investors didn't get a copy. Each time one of them wanted a contract, I'd make them sign a copy. I then told them that I needed to make copies and what not, then I'd mail them the originals when I could."

"And you never mailed the original contracts?"

"Of course not," said Ratcliff. "We've hired Escartes to kill them all. No need in them havin' contracts."

"Did you sign the contracts, too?"

"Absolutely. We all did."

"As long as they don't have a copy, I suppose it was good thinkin'," a somewhat relieved Gayland said. "But I don't understand why they're missing."

"Again, someone took them from my partner's desk."

"I don't know why in the hell Escartes would take them. He has no need."

"Maybe he's going to blackmail us," Ratcliff replied.

"Impossible. I've used him many times before. Believe you me, I know enough about him to have him locked up forever."

"That doesn't help us much if we're in jail for the rest of our lives."

"That's out of the question," a confident Gayland replied. "He would never do such a thing. Maybe the contracts were thrown away by accident."

"That's a possibility, but doubtful. They were under lock and key," Ratcliff said, then paused. "I think you should talk to him. Find out if he's got anything brewing."

"It's not that easy. He spends most of his time in New York. He only comes down to do his business for us."

"When are you scheduled to meet him again?"

"I'm not. He told me he'd contact me."

Ratcliff reloaded his shotgun. "I don't like this one bit," he said. "This complicates matters."

"He'll be callin' soon. I owe him the second installment of the money, which I haven't collected from Jonathan Peat yet," Gayland said. "I'll start working on ol' Peaty boy, or figure something out."

"You'd best. There's a vulgar odor in the air and it stinks like a turd," Ratcliff said, then nodded.

"A turd indeed," Gayland said as he stepped on the button to release more clay pigeons.

Chapter 18

*I*f *the individual is ruled by submission, the superego governs the victim's emotional response and cedes control of the conflict. The helpless victim surrenders all resistance and relinquishes control of the circumstances to the aggressor. The superego's occupation of the psyche is no less dominating than the id's. However, the victim relies on faith, rather than might, to survive.*

The chill of the night air sent shivers through Lennie Perkins as he sped out of the Grayhorse High School Gymnasium's parking lot in his diesel pickup. Since he'd just served as scorekeeper at a high school girl's basketball game, his clinging, sweaty shirt magnified his discomfort, but not as much as the hollow feeling in the pit of his stomach that had plagued him since his mentor, Kyle Gayland, had left an urgent message calling for a meeting at 7:30 p.m. Since it was already 7:25 p.m. and he was fifteen miles from the secret meeting place, being late was a foregone conclusion.

At 43, Lennie had known Gayland most of his professional life. Gayland's influence had helped transform Lennie from a lowly loan officer to president of his own bank. Among the tricks he'd learned was the slow burn—a tactic used to gradually demand more collateral from starving farmers until they were completely upside down financially, then suddenly call their notes. Lennie had made big profits buying the farmer's land for pennies on the dollar at foreclosure auctions, making slight improvements, then reselling the land at market value. He owed his success to Kyle Gayland, and Gayland wasn't the type to let him forget it.

As Lennie turned down the old dirt and drove through the

countryside toward the secret meeting place, snow began to softly fall. The falling temperatures allowed it to quickly accumulate on the ground. After driving a few miles, he spotted tire tracks in the snow, prompting him to drive even faster since Gayland was probably already waiting.

It was 7:45 when Lennie finally reached the natural gas well. As Lennie drove onto the site, he spotted a parked car, but it wasn't Gayland's. Somewhat surprised, he grabbed his .45-millimeter handgun from the glove compartment and tucked it in his jacket. Leaving the headlights on, he parked his pickup several yards away. The brisk breeze sent shivers down his spine as he slowly walked toward the car.

"What're you doing out here, banker man?" someone called from inside the car.

Lennie wrapped his fingers around the gun's cold grip.

"And who might you be?" Lennie asked, moving closer.

Lennie was relieved when he recognized the old man who stepped out of the car. "Wallace Simonson, is that you?"

"It be."

No one knew much about Wallace Simonson. He lived alone on a farm not far from the abandoned well site. The only time he visited town was when he needed groceries or alcohol. He was rumored to have more money than any other man in the county, but he didn't believe in banks, so his money was reportedly buried on his place. He wore a heavy white beard and had a hearty taste for booze. It was easy to see why most of the townspeople considered him an outsider.

"What the hell are you doing out here?" Lennie asked, releasing his grip on the pistol.

"I asked first," replied Wallace.

Lennie shook his head in disbelief. "I'm meeting someone."

Wallace didn't respond. He merely looked into Lennie's eyes, then spit tobacco on the ground.

Lennie noticed empty beer cans lying on the ground.

"Are you just out having a drink?"

"Maybe," Wallace said. "Ain't no law against that is there?"

"No," Lennie said, growing impatient. "Look Wallace, I'm meeting someone here. You need to leave."

"Well, I need myself a loose woman, but you don't see me buggin' you about it."

Lennie knew that trying to reason with the old drunk was pointless. "I'm sorry. Please, could you move on? I really am meeting someone here."

"Well, maybe I am, too."

"No, waiting on a pink elephant doesn't count as meeting someone. I'm meeting a real person."

"Me, too. And he's as real as the snow that's fallin' on your head."

"Who might this person be?"

"He's a banker, same as you."

Lennie was floored by Wallace's response. "What?"

"He's a banker."

"What's his name?" Lennie asked, suspiciously.

"Gayland. Kyle Gayland."

"How do you know Kyle Gayland?"

"Let's just say we're in business together," Wallace snickered.

Lennie's mind raced as an overwhelming sense of paranoia swept over him. He removed the pistol from his coat pocket. "And he called you and told you to meet him here tonight?"

"Sure did."

Lennie breathed a sigh of relief.

Wallace looked down at the gun. "Is there something bothering you that I should know about?"

"I was getting worried there for a second," laughed Lennie. "There's been some strange things happen here lately and I was afraid that we'd been set up. But if you talked to Gayland yourself, then I'm sure..."

"I didn't talk to him," Wallace interrupted. "I talked to his assistant."

Lennie froze. "But he doesn't have an assistant, Wallace. Especially in the type of venture that we're involved."

"But he called you, right?"

"No," Lennie said, his voice trembling. He raised his pistol and scanned the area for signs of movement, but was blinded by the snow. "Someone left word with my secretary."

A series of loud roars echoed in the winter air. Wallace quickly sprawled on the seat of his car as Lennie dropped to the ground.

Shotgun blasts rang out again, this time closer. Pellets shattered the back glass of both vehicles.

"Dear God," Lennie cried, "what have we done?"

Still lying in his seat, Wallace reached to jerk the car into drive. When it moved forward, he sat up behind the wheel and floored the gas pedal.

"Don't leave me!" Lennie shouted.

"Save yourself," said Wallace as the car spun around and headed toward the entrance of the well site.

The car hadn't traveled more than one hundred feet before an arsenal of firepower was unleashed. Lennie watched in horror as Wallace's car slowed and veered into the fence line. The bullets had clearly made their mark. He knew his only hope was to make it back to his truck and drive like hell. Gun in hand, he ran toward the old reliable pickup.

The searing pain of hot lead tearing through his hand was followed by the sound of the shot. Shocked, he looked down to see his right hand bleeding and his gun in the snow. The unmistakable sounds of a shotgun pumping and reloading echoed from a spot just beyond his pickup. "What do you want from me?" he screamed.

"All that you took," replied Taylor, walking into Lennie's line of sight.

"I'll give you anything—money, drugs, whatever you want. I'm the president of a bank. I can do it. I swear."

"How 'bout those people that you poisoned? How 'bout you give their health back."

Lennie was dumbfounded. "That's what this is about? Them Injuns?"

"It certainly is."

"That was Gayland's idea, not mine. I only went along with it because he's very powerful. You don't say no to a man like Kyle Gayland."

Taylor smiled. "Of course you don't."

"I'm sorry, real sorry."

"I know," Taylor said. "I know."

Chapter 19

The fire crackled and hissed as Campanow sat next to its warmth and recited his incantations. As his chanting grew louder, he sprinkled a fine powder over the flames, causing the fire to dance high above him and his middle-aged Native American guest, Kacey, who sat nearby. Thrusting his arms into the air, he loudly bellowed the chant. As the roar of the winter wind whipped and howled outside the window, the fire soared to the cabin's ceiling as if the two forces of nature were performing in unison for the old man.

In an instant, Campanow ceased chanting and the room fell silent. With his legs crossed and his hands folded in his lap, he silently stared into the fire. The flames seemed captivated by his magic—alternately receding and dancing under his control. After a few moments, his strength faded. As his head slumped to his chest, the fire settled to a warm glow.

Although he'd seen it many times before, Kacey was always mystified by Campanow's magic. Each time he performed the ancient rituals they seemed to consume more and more of his physical strength. With a winter storm raging outside, Kacey moved closer to the fire to wait for the old man to return to consciousness.

"Have you stained more of your skin with the white man's ink?" asked Campanow, his eyes still closed.

Kacey was mildly surprised that Campanow was making small talk so soon after his ritual. Normally, he was so exhausted that he would remain silent for several minutes, sometimes hours.

"Of course not. I only have one and will never have another." Although Kacey smiled, he still felt slightly jaded by Campanow's reference to the tattoo he'd acquired years ago on a dare from a friend while he was drunk. The notorious tattoo of the initials KC quickly led everyone in the small town of Ducotey to dub him "Kacey." Even though the tattoo was rarely seen, each time Kacey encountered Campanow he consistently voiced his disapproval.

"Kids," said Campanow, then shook his head.

Kacey laughed. "I'm not that much younger than you."

"We are separated by many years. Much has changed in our culture during that time."

He grinned. "You're turning into a cranky old bastard."

Campanow opened his eyes, glared at Kacey for a moment, then closed them once again. "Are you getting closer to the white banker?"

"I'm making progress. I've been driving to Carson every day for the last couple of weeks to tail him. Yesterday, I stopped him on the street outside his office. I introduced myself and congratulated him on his recent award."

Campanow stirred the coals in the fire with a poker. "What were his words?" he asked.

"He gave me the usual bullshit about how it's better to give than receive. Just typical talk from a con man."

"Did you mention that you had a business proposition?"

"No. It was too soon. I need to get to know him better before I try to gain his trust."

"You must hurry. His time draws near."

"Don't worry. Did Taylor get the new list from Gayland's safe?"

"He did."

"How many are left?" asked Kacey.

"Besides the two in Grayhorse, only four remain—Gayland, Peat, Ratcliff, and Hempshaw."

"Hempshaw's store is just up the road in Ducotey."

"That is correct," said Campanow.

"It might be a good idea to bring Gayland to Hempshaw and take care of them both at the same time."

"Hempshaw thinks like a coyote. He'll be ready. For a white man, he has very keen senses."

Kacey thought for a moment. "I'll think about that."

"Taylor found another name on the list. A man named Escartes. Joe Escartes."

Kacey was puzzled. "I don't recognize that name."

"Nor do I. I think he's an outsider."

"Why would Gayland bring in an outsider? He knows plenty of investors in these parts."

"Could be an old friend. There's really no telling."

"I'll keep an eye out."

"Have you heard anything more from your circles?" asked Campanow.

"About the murders?"

He nodded.

"Nothing," said Kacey. "There's been very little chatter on the streets."

Campanow again stoked the coals in the fire. Kacey noticed that his eyes were growing tired.

"Have the two in Grayhorse been taken care of?"

"Not sure. Haven't heard yet," said Campanow.

"Was it set for tonight?"

"Yes."

"I doubt it was much trouble," said Kacey. "It was just a drunk and a small-time banker. Shouldn't be any problem for Taylor and…"

"The smallest of men can sometimes be courageous," interrupted Campanow. "Even bankers and drunks."

"I'm not worried."

Kacey realized that the hour had grown late. "I should go before the roads are covered in ice and snow. I'll be back in a couple of days."

"Can you bring more bullets?"

"Sure," Kacey replied. "What and how many?"

"Everything. As much as you can get."

Kacey shook his head. "As much as I can get? Do you realize that I can get my hands on cases of the stuff?"

"As much as you can get."

"All right. Anything you want."

Campanow's troubled expression grew more intense.

"Is something wrong?" asked Kacey.

"Fred Parker was here not long ago."

"So?"

"He talked about the fat banker. Suspicion resides in his mind."

"Do you think he knows what's going on?"

"I do not, but his daughter is with the State Bureau of Investigation."

Kacey thought for a moment. "It could work to our advantage, especially after we take care of Gayland. With him out of the picture, the police might actually discover the terrible things that he's done."

"And they could also find out what we've done."

"Not if all goes as planned."

Campanow sighed. "It never goes as planned."

"But you forget—justice is on our side."

Chapter 20

Taylor took a deep breath, then zipped up his jacket before stepping into the snow flurries whipping across the library's lawn. Backpack in hand, he turned into the wind to begin the eight block hike to his apartment.

He'd walked two blocks down the university's main street when he heard a car approaching. Since classes had been called off due to the snow, he thought it was slightly odd. The entire campus, with the exception of a few students at the library, seemed abandoned. The only vehicle he'd seen all morning was a four-wheel drive maintenance truck that was salting the university's streets.

Judging from the sound of the engine, Taylor estimated that the car was traveling moderately fast, too fast to be dispensing salt. When the tires skidded on the snow and ice, and the car began pacing him, he reached into his backpack to retrieve his .45-caliber pistol. Placing it in his coat pocket, he continued to walk without ever turning to face the vehicle.

As he passed a car parked on the side of the street, he glanced at the reflection of the vehicle. It was a green Suburban slowly gaining on him. The only green Suburban that Taylor was familiar with was the one he'd seen parked at the bank, owned by Gayland. This thought shot fear up Taylor's spine. He walked briskly past the parked car, then turned and knelt behind its right rear fender. Taylor threw down his backpack and retrieved his pistol from his pocket. Rolling in the snow, he slid on his back until most of his body was underneath the parked car.

Assuming the driver was one of Gayland's goons trying to even the score, Taylor jacked a round into the chamber. The Suburban's tires were only a few feet away, drawing closer, so he slid to the left, toward his backpack, until only his head and left arm were visible to the Suburban when it passed. With his left hand, he pointed the gun toward the rear of the parked car, providing him with a clean shot at the Suburban when it came into view.

Instead of continuing down the road, the Suburban stopped. Taylor watched the driver's snow boots touch the ground and cautiously approach. His heart raced, certain Gayland had hired a professional assassin. He certainly had the means and the disposition to do so.

As the driver walked toward the bumper of the parked car, Taylor kept him in his sights. The snow boots stopped at the car's right taillight, just inches away. After a moment, the red-soles began moving again.

Taylor's heart pounded in his ears. As soon as he confirmed that the stranger was armed, he would open fire.

The instant the stranger turned the corner to face Taylor, a loud scream sliced the icy air. He watched as the driver's red-soled snow boots rushed back to the Suburban. As soon as the driver's door slammed shut, the Suburban recklessly sped backward a few hundred feet.

"Taylor, is that you?" a female shouted.

Taylor closed his eyes in disgust. He immediately recognized Wendy's voice and realized she was wearing the snow boots he'd given her as a gift the previous winter.

"Holy shit," he muttered.

"Goddamn it, Taylor, is that you?" she shouted again.

Taylor slid out from beneath the car, unloaded the gun, and placed it in his backpack. "Yeah, honey, it's me," he said sheepishly.

Wendy drove the Suburban to him. "What in God's name is going on?" she asked.

At the sight of tears running down her face, he was speechless. "I uh..."

"You were going to shoot me!"

"No, no, no. It was just a little misunderstanding. Come on," he said with a smile, "I knew what I was doing."

"Wipe that smile off your face, damn it! This is nothing to joke about."

"I'm sorry, very sorry. I swear to God, I didn't know it was you. I didn't know who it was and I got scared."

Wendy grabbed a tissue from her purse and wiped her face.

"Is that Gayland's Suburban?"

"Yeah," Wendy replied.

"Why in the hell are you driving it?"

"'Cause it's four-wheel drive. My car won't get around in the snow and ice. Gayland called this morning and offered me a ride, so I took it.

"Oh."

"What in God's name are you doing with a gun?"

Taylor was slow to respond. "Well, I just carry it in case..."

"In case you decide to scare the shit out of your girlfriend?"

"Of course not. I just carry it with me in case I run into trouble."

"This is a small university, Taylor. There's not a lot of trouble here."

"Sure there is. People commit crimes every day."

"Bullshit! The biggest crime around here is someone stealing chips from the vending machine. And I don't think that warrants packin' heat."

Taylor knew he was busted. The only way to get out of this was to play hardball. "There have been some murders in this area lately," he said.

"On our campus? I haven't heard anything about them."

"No, not here. They've happened in small towns around Carson. Haven't you read about it in the newspaper?" After a long moment of silence he realized she was too angry to reply. He'd seen it before. It was time to change the subject. "So, what are you doing on campus? Didn't you hear that classes were called off?"

"Yeah, I heard," Wendy said. "I was looking for you. I went by your apartment not long ago and couldn't find you. I figured you'd be here."

"Yeah, I've been studying most of the morning. I was looking up a few things for my thesis."

"Do you remember how you're always telling me that you want to meet Gayland?"

"Yeah. So?"

"Now's your chance. I'm meeting him for lunch."

"Does he know I'm coming?"

"No," Wendy replied. "I told him I needed to run to my apartment to pick up something. When we get to the restaurant, I'll tell him that I just ran into you."

Taylor jumped into the Suburban. "This should be interesting."

Taylor and Wendy found Gayland sitting near the back of the Italian restaurant by the kitchen, puffing a cigar and sipping a martini. His eyes sparkled as he watched Wendy approach.

"Hello, Maria," Gayland beamed.

"Hello," replied Wendy as she took her seat.

The smile on Gayland's face disappeared when Taylor took the seat next to Wendy.

"Maria?" Taylor asked, looking at Wendy. "Who's Maria?"

"That's uh, what he sometimes calls me," Wendy replied, casting a wary look at the fat banker. "Gayland, this is Taylor."

Still seated, Gayland offered his hand. "Are you one of Wendy's friends from school?"

"You could say that," Taylor said, then shook his hand. "I've heard a lot about you."

"All good, I hope."

"Some of it."

"Well, boy, don't believe everything you hear."

"Don't worry," Taylor laughed. "I've heard a great deal about you, but I only believe the truth."

Gayland didn't know how to receive Taylor's remark. He tried to smile, but the gesture slowly melted from his face.

"I see," he muttered.

"Have you been waiting long?" asked Wendy.

Still distraught from Taylor's remark, Gayland was slow to answer. "Yeah, I've been here awhile."

"I'm sorry. The roads are very slick and..."

"No problem, my dear," Gayland interrupted. "Time flies when waiting on a pretty thing like you."

Taylor's rage burned inside him like a pool of liquid steel. Maintaining an innocent expression, he fought the impulse to jump over the table and end Gayland's poor, miserable life. Instead, he took a deep breath and forced a smile.

"Where are you from, college boy?" asked Gayland.

"A little town not far from here," Taylor replied.

"Does it have a name?"

Taylor noticed that Gayland's tone was progressively becoming more authoritative. "It certainly does. I come from Ducotey."

For an instant, Gayland paled.

"It's a small town located near an Indian reservation."

Gayland struggled for words. "I've uh, I've heard of it."

"Have you? I know a man who owns some land there and he's lookin' for a lawyer. Maybe you could recommend someone."

"I uh, I might know someone. Why does he need an attorney?"

"Evidently his land is fairly rich with oil and gas deposits. The petroleum companies are constantly badgering him. They tell him that he's sitting on an immense geological formation."

"Sounds interesting. Why does he need a lawyer?"

"He's tired of the petroleum companies calling him. He wants them to quit hassling him."

"Why doesn't he lease the mineral rights and let them drill the wells?"

"He's an old-school Indian. He thinks money is evil and doesn't want any part of it."

Gayland's face immediately reclaimed its color. "You don't suppose that he'd be willing to sell the mineral rights, do you?"

Taylor thought for a moment. "He'd do just about anything to keep those damn oil and gas companies away. They call him daily."

"How many acres does he own?"

"Around twelve hundred."

Gayland's eyes sparkled. "I'll bet I could help him. I do love to help people, especially minorities."

"Yeah, that's what I've heard."

Gayland pulled a card from his wallet and handed it to Taylor. "Give him this. Tell him to call me as soon as possible."

"Consider it done. His name is Kacey. He'll be in touch."

"Splendid," Gayland said as his eyes searched the restaurant. "Where's that damn waiter?" Suddenly, his color drained.

"Is something wrong?" asked Wendy.

"Oh, it's a…it's nothing."

Wendy and Taylor both followed his gaze to a dark-headed man with stone cold eyes sitting at a table across the restaurant.

"Who's he?" she asked.

"Him? I don't know. Never seen him before." Gayland pretended to read the menu as his face turned red. He was obviously unnerved.

Taylor noticed the stranger staring at him. After getting a good look, he turned to face Wendy and Gayland.

"Gayland, is that man bothering you?" asked Wendy.

Still thumbing through the menu, he replied, "Why would he bother me? I don't even know him. I'm just hungry," he said, then looked up. "Now, where is that waiter?"

As if on cue, the waiter made his way to their table.

"Can I take your order?" he asked.

"It's about time, boy," quipped Gayland. "What the hell do they pay you for around here? It sure as hell isn't for prompt service."

The waiter gave Gayland the standard go-to-hell look.

Gayland began, "I'll have the..." but stopped when the beeper tucked in his jacket pocket began to vibrate. "Son-of-a-bitch," he said. After reading the digital display, he tossed his napkin on his plate and stood. "I'm sorry, Wendy, my dear, but I'm afraid I have to leave. This is an emergency of sorts."

"Oh, no problem," Wendy said.

"I'll see you back at the office this afternoon. I suppose you'll need a ride home this evening?"

"That'd be fine. Do you need your Suburban now?"

"No, no, don't worry about that. I've got one of the bank's company cars. It gets along fine in these conditions," said Gayland, sweating profusely.

He walked over to Wendy, and, to Taylor's astonishment, kissed her on the cheek.

Taylor turned to locate the mystery man, but he was gone.

"It was interesting to meet you," said Taylor.

"And you as well. I hope to do some business with your friend."

"I hope so, too. I'll give him your number."

Gayland thought for a moment. "In my past dealings, I've found that Indians can be, well, shall we say, less prone to take care of business, if you know what I mean. Does this describe your friend?

"You'll be surprised. He's very proactive," Taylor said, trying not to laugh.

Gayland smiled. "Well, now, that's a good thing."

"Expect a call."

"I will. By the way, what's his name again?"

"Kacey," Taylor said. "At least that's what his friends call him."

Chapter 21

The wind whipped and rocked Gayland's car as he drove slowly through the snow-covered streets of Carson. Arriving at the dilapidated hotel on the edge of town, he immediately spotted Joe Escartes' car, complete with an old New York license plate. Over the past few days, he had made many failed attempts to contact Escartes, but at last, they would meet. The buzz of the martinis swirling in his head made him smile, but did little to halt the fear crawling up his spine. Even though the weather was miserable, he hoped his world was about to brighten.

Gayland's stomach rumbled from the lack of food as he waddled up to the hotel-room door and gave the secret knock. A few moments later Escartes cracked open the door. "Where the hell have you been?" Gayland asked.

Escartes briefly shut the door to remove the security chain. As soon as he reopened the door, Gayland stumbled inside the warm hotel room.

"I haven't heard from you in awhile," said Gayland. He removed his gloves and coat and sat on a shabby, putrid smelling chair.

"It's good to see you, too, you fat old bastard," Escartes said with a heavy Brooklyn accent.

Normally Gayland would have been incensed by the lack of respect that he so dearly thought he deserved from the world, but not with Escartes. Escartes could say or do anything without the slightest rebuttal from Gayland.

"Long time no see. How've you been, Killer?"

Escartes walked to the bathroom and retrieved a bottle of Jack Daniel's whiskey.

"You know, you shouldn't be callin' me that," he said. "Some freakin' jackass might overhear you and get wise to our affairs."

"Pardon me," said Gayland, gently. "Where have you been?"

"I swear, I don't understand you bankers. It's all business with you people. No time for small talk."

"I'm sorry. It's just that I haven't heard from you in a while and I've been getting a little nervous."

"Yeah, yeah, that's your freakin' nature. You wouldn't last a minute back in Brooklyn, pusbag."

Gayland forced a laugh. "You're probably right."

"You up for a little hooch?" Escartes asked while he poured himself a cup of straight Jack Daniel's.

"Well, actually I'm already a little lightheaded. That was my secretary that you saw me with down at the restaurant. We were having martinis and I've got a bit of a buzz going."

"Yeah, I saw her. She's a piece of work, that girl. As you rednecks say, 'I'd like to trot my pony around her track.'"

"Yes, I'm sure you would," Gayland said in a patronizing tone.

"Who was the jackass sitting next to her?"

"Oh, him, he's nobody. Just some punk she goes to school with."

"He was staring pretty hard, like he wanted a piece of me."

"I'm sure he was just lookin'. It probably didn't mean anything."

"And what was the deal with you? You were sweatin' and squirmin' like you were about to give birth to a freakin' rhino."

Gayland started sweating again. "Well, I don't like it when people see us together. I don't want us to be linked in any way."

Escartes was instantly offended. "What am I? An asshole?"

"Of course not," Gayland responded. "I just don't want us to be associated with one another."

"Are you's tellin' me where I can and can't go eat while I'm in this freakin' shithole town?"

"No, no, I'm not saying that at all," Gayland reeled. "It was just a mistake, my mistake, that's all, nothing more."

Escartes slammed his whiskey in one gulp and quickly refilled his cup. He lit a cigarette, then poured a shot of whiskey for Gayland.

"Are we good?" Gayland asked, extending his hand.

Escartes pulled a few drags on his cigarette and thought for a moment. "Yeah, we're good," he said and shook Gayland's hand. "You old bastard."

Escartes gave Gayland the glass of whiskey.

"I really shouldn't," Gayland said. "I'm already feeling woozy."

"Drink it," he demanded.

Gayland reluctantly sipped the whiskey.

"So, you been bangin' this broad or what?"

Gayland's face grew red. "Well, not yet," he said, "but I will be soon, rest assured."

Escartes reached for the bottle. After he finished pouring one for himself, he filled Gayland's cup. "What's her name?"

Gayland let out a deep breath and stared at his feet in silence.

"Maybe you can send her down here after you've had enough, huh?"

Still quiet, he barely managed a polite smile.

"What about it, huh?"

"Sure, sure, Escartes, anything you say."

With the courage of Jack Daniel's under his belt, Gayland decided it was safe to satisfy his morbid curiosity about Escartes' recent work. "I haven't seen you around in a while."

"Yeah, I went back home. I had some work to do."

Confused, Gayland said, "But Brooklyn's thousands of miles from here and most of the people that I hired you to take care of have been, well, taken care of."

Escartes took a sip from his whiskey. He could tell by Gayland's face and body language that he was serious. He thought for a moment. If most of the investors had been whacked and it wasn't by his hands, then he wouldn't get paid. That was definitely a problem since there was a great deal of money at stake.

"Just yankin' your chain, you freakin' shitwad. Of course I've been here. What do you think I am, a freakin' asshole?"

"Well, no, uh, I didn't think that at all."

"What do you think, that I got so much time on my hands that I can drive to Brooklyn and back just for giggles and shits?"

"Of course not," Gayland said, relieved. "Of course not."

Escartes lit a cigarette. He was elated that he'd pulled off the lie so flawlessly. He had no clue who'd removed the investors, and he didn't care.

Gayland paused momentarily. He needed answers, but asking Escartes anything was never easy. "I have a question about one of the hits…"

"Shoot," Escartes replied casually.

"Remember when you did Ratcliff's partner, down at the law offices in Strong City?"

"Sure."

"There were some contracts in his desk."

"Yeah," Escartes said. He walked to the table and poured some more whiskey.

"The contracts link all of us together."

"So?"

"Well, they're gone."

"So, what's the big deal?"

"Again, they link us and they're gone. We don't know where they are."

"I don't have your freakin' contracts, if that's what you're tryin' to imply."

"No, I'm not trying to imply anything. I just need to know where they went, in case you saw them."

While Escartes poured another cup of whiskey, he thought for a moment. Of course he didn't see any contracts at the lawyer's office; he was never there. But the disappearance of these contracts seemed to be a great burden to Gayland, possibly a reason to stop payment.

He stared at his whiskey glass and pretended that he was trying to recall the memory. "You know, now that I think about it, I did see some papers on his desk."

Gayland's eyes lit up. "You did?"

"Yeah, it was right after I whacked him. It was some legal mumbo jumbo with your name on it. Actually, there were several pages of legal stuff. Your name was on them."

Gayland felt a ray of hope. "Were other investors named, too?"

"Yeah, yeah," said Escartes.

"Good, good, that sounds like the right contracts."

"I'm sure they were," Escartes said. "So stop worrying, already."

Gayland sat on the edge of the old chair's seat. "What did you do with them?"

"Well," Escartes replied with the confidence of a seasoned liar, "I knew I couldn't leave them lying around the desk, you know, 'cause when the police came I didn't want them to know the lawyer was workin' for you."

Gayland was so excited he was about to pee on himself. "Yes, yes, then what'd you do?"

"So I folded them up and took them with me."

"Excellent. Where are they now?"

"Uhm, I guess they're in the same place I put 'em."

"And where's that?"

"On the street behind the lawyer's office."

Gayland jumped to his feet. "What?" he exclaimed.

Escartes smiled. "Yeah, I put them in the street."

"Holy shit!" shouted Gayland. "Then that means anyone could have found them!"

"I don't know 'bout that."

"What?"

Escartes walked to Gayland and grabbed his shoulder. "Relax, fat boy. I burned them. All's that left now are ashes, you asshole."

Gayland let out a huge sigh of relief. "Thank goodness. So there's no trace of them?"

"No traces."

"Whew," he said, then sat back down. "That calls for another drink."

"Sure, sure," Escartes responded and grabbed his cup. "You want a smoke, too?"

"Think I'll just stick with my cigars."

Escartes carried the fresh cup of whiskey to Gayland, who immediately took a big drink.

"You got some money for me?" Escartes asked as he pulled a deep drag off his smoke.

Gayland's relief was short lived. When the word money was mentioned, his hands began to shake, spilling whiskey onto the chair. "Oh, that, well, there's a bit of a hang-up with that."

"Come again?"

"There's uh, a little problem."

Escartes walked to Gayland. Looking squarely at him, he thrust a finger into Gayland's face. "Don't go makin' your problems into my problems, fat ass."

"Please don't be mad," said Gayland, reassuringly. "It's just a little hang-up."

"What kind of little hang-up?"

"Jonathan Peat hasn't paid me yet. He promised me that he has the money, he just can't get it out of his house."

"What's the problem?"

"It's his wife and kids. They know about the money and will miss it if it's gone."

"Tell him to be a man and take the freakin' money. What's he need their permission for?"

In an attempt to downplay the heat of the moment, Gayland nonchalantly closed his eyes and swallowed the entire glass of whiskey. When he opened his eyes, he found himself face down on the floor with Escartes on top of him, twisting his arm behind his back.

"Let's get a couple of things nice and straight, pig," said Escartes. "I'm not one of your freakin' country bumpkins who'll put up with your bullshit. You either get me my money or I'm gonna put you next on my list."

Escartes grabbed some hair and picked up Gayland's head, then slammed it down on the hard floor. "Am I makin' myself clear?" he shouted.

"Uh, huh."

"You best not be bullshittin' me. I've cut off people's nuts for less than this."

"I'm sure you have, but don't worry. I'll have it soon, I just don't have it right now."

To leave an added impression, Escartes pressed his knee hard into Gayland's back. He then stood and walked to the bathroom sink.

Gayland tried not to moan as he picked himself off the floor. He sat on the chair and forced a smile, as if nothing had happened. "Can I take a look at your list?"

"What list?"

"The list with the remaining investors."

Escartes thought for a moment. Since he'd been out of town for the last several days and hadn't actually performed any of the assassinations, he had no idea what he did with the list. For all he knew, it was back in Brooklyn.

"You didn't lose the list, did you, Escartes?" asked a concerned Gayland.

"Who are you, my freakin' mother?"

"No, it's just that the list has all the investors' names on it. If it were to fall in the hands of the police, it could be used as evidence."

Gayland took a big swig of whiskey.

"Quit your yappin', dough boy," said Escartes. "It's around here somewhere."

Gayland's patience was fleeting. Though he had maintained control of himself, his anger was about to erupt. He slammed the remaining whiskey in his glass and stared at Escartes. Every impulse in his body directed him to savagely strike Escartes down and work him over, but then a little voice in his head rang out a wake-up call. Escartes was an assassin, his assassin, and he had to finish the job. Without him, the whole scheme would break down. The completion of Gayland's elaborate plans depended on this punk from the ghetto that stood before him.

"Dear God," Gayland said, placing his hands over his face.

"Wait a minute," said Escartes. "I just remembered. I think it might be in the glove box of my car."

"Could you please go look?"

Escartes let out a moan of disgust, stood, then exited the apartment and walked barefooted through the snow to his car. After a few moments, he returned to the room.

"Here," he said, then threw the list on Gayland's lap. "Are you freakin' happy now?"

A relieved Gayland immediately retrieved a pen from his coat and began crossing out names.

"All that are left are Hempshaw and Jonathan Peat," Gayland said. "In order to remove any risks, I'm going to keep this piece of paper. We've been over these people. I've shown you pictures, you know where they live."

"Yeah, yeah, I know. Hempshaw's in that little shit town Ducotey and Peat lives here in Carson."

"That right. I want you to take care of Peat first, then Hempshaw, in that order. Peat is a coward and is very nervous about all this. He'll be easy. Hempshaw is mean and will be more difficult."

"Why are we doin' them in that order?" Escartes asked.

"I want Peat done first because he's drivin' me crazy and he owes me money. You've got to wait until he pays me, though. I'll let you know when he does."

"Understood."

"But listen, I want you to take a break for a while. Because you've taken them out so fast, the police are getting stirred up over this. If things don't slow down, they'll have the *federalies* here and trust me, we don't want that."

Escartes laughed. "I've dealt with those bastards before. I tell you, they're a ruthless bunch. They'll put your balls through a cheese grater."

"I know how they are."

"So what about Ratcliff?" asked Escartes while he finished off his whiskey.

Gayland was bewildered. "Ratcliff?"

"When am I gonna tag his ass?"

"You mean Ratcliff, my attorney?"

"Yeah, he's the only other person who knows about this, right?" Escartes said, then poured himself another drink.

Gayland's heart raced. "Oh no. No, no, we're not going to do anything to harm Counselor Ratcliff. I need him in case we get caught. He's a very powerful attorney."

"Whatever," Escartes said with a shrug.

Gayland looked him in the eye. "Listen, just focus on Hempshaw and Peat. That's all. First do Peat, then take care of Hempshaw, in that order. But wait 'till I get my money."

"Oh, don't worry, I'll wait."

"And remember, lay low for a few days. We don't need any attention drawn to us."

"Stop worrying already."

"And watch out for Hempshaw. He's always ready for anything."

"You're really acting like my freakin' mother."

Gayland tried to relax and breathe slowly. "I just want things to run smoothly."

"Don't worry, it's my freakin' job, ass wipe."

"Yeah, I know."

A moment of awkward silence filled the room. Lost in thought, Gayland stared at the dirty chair. "I have a question."

"Yeah?"

"On the way over here, I heard that they just found Wallace Simonson and Lennie Perkins at Grayhorse. How did you get them together on that old well site, which by the way, is where I always met Lennie."

Escartes had no answer. Speechless, he tried to think of a plausible excuse.

"It was simple, really," said Escartes. "I sent this hooker to them individually and she told them to meet her at the well site."

Gayland thought for a moment. "I can understand that with Wallace, but Lennie is a family man. He's really not into that type of thing."

"Guess you misjudged him," Escartes said with raised eyebrows.

"I must have. How did you know about the well site?"

"Oh that," Escartes said with confidence. "I was driving through the country one day and spotted it. I figured it would be a good place to do it."

"I see." Glancing at his watch, he added, "I've got to get back to the bank. I'll bring you the second installment of cash soon. Now that I have your hotel and room number I'll call when I..."

"About that," Escartes interrupted.

"Yes."

"Since I was a nice guy and didn't cut off your nuts for not havin' my money, I figure you owe me a favor."

"Okay," said Gayland, reluctantly. "Name it."

"What's the broad's name and where does she live?"

"You mean the one you saw at the restaurant?"

"Yeah."

"Are you sure you can't find somebody else?"

"Naw, I like her."

After a moment of contemplation, Gayland decided that his own safety was far more important than his secretary's chastity. "Her name is Wendy and she lives in the apartment complex just south of the university."

"I think I might pay her a visit," said Escartes.

With a weak nod, Gayland left.

Chapter 22

Detective Jennings pushed his chair over to the office window. Although clouds still obscured the afternoon sun, Jennings met the sight with enthusiasm. "Looks like the snow has finally let up," he said. "Times like these make me want to be a kid again. Too bad we don't have a tractor and a car hood. The snow looks just right for sledding."

Quana looked up from the state map he was studying. "I've got both back in Ducotey. Just say the word, and we'll go."

"I wish I could, but we'd better get to crackin' on this case."

After reviewing the murder locations marked on the map with a red highlighter, Quana commented, "These hits don't look random. They're all in small towns."

In frustration, Jennings pushed his chair back to his desk. He stared at the ceiling and let out a deep breath.

"I'm beginning to think that this guy is a professional hit man. He just doesn't make mistakes."

The statement caught Quana's attention. "This guy? What makes you think it's just one suspect?"

"I don't know for sure. At the convenience store, which was one of the first places hit, a witness thought he saw more than one suspect, but he didn't get a good look."

Quana thought for a moment. "I'm not so sure. After reviewing your reports today, it sure looks like there are two to three shooters, just by the sheer number and variety of shell casings found at the crime scenes. But then again, it's possible for one man to shoot different weapons multiple times, but that's fairly uncommon."

"I've thought of that and it makes sense. Did you take a look at that car and truck today at the well site? They were both blown to hell. Just brushing through the snow I found lots of 12 gauge shotgun shells and casings from a .45 pistol. Hell, I even found a couple of shells from a .243 rifle."

"I too saw tons of spent ammo," said Quana. He pushed his chair back from Jennings' desk. "I really doubt this is the work of just one man."

"You're probably right. Hell, for one man to do this, he'd have to have crates of ammunition."

Quana glanced at the map. "At the liquor store, there was no money taken. And that's consistent with the other crime scenes, right?"

"Oh yeah. They're definitely not after money."

"Then what's their motivation?"

"All we know is that all the victims are prominent white men living in small towns. The victims are reclusive people with money, power and none would win a popularity contest. The culprits are definitely leaving an enormous path of destruction behind them."

"Looking at your map, I can see that they haven't spread this out too much. I'd say that they probably live somewhere in this part of the state."

"I agree."

"So, what if you're right?" asked Quana.

"About what?"

"About them being professionals."

Jennings' curiosity was piqued. "Go on."

"These killers might be from somewhere else, some far away city not even close to here. They could have been hired and brought in by someone who lives in this area."

Jennings was intrigued. "Right, but why?"

"Could be lots of things. One thing all the victims have in common is money, right?"

"Right."

"Maybe these victims were getting in the way of someone's business plans."

Jennings placed his hands on top of his head and let out a sigh. "That's a possibility."

"And remember, these crimes are being committed in the heart of the Bible Belt. People around these parts don't normally resort to murder to resolve their disputes."

"No doubt. When people get mad, they tend to fight like cats and dogs and be done with it."

"Have you talked to any of the sheriffs in nearby counties?" asked Quana.

"Yeah, but they haven't helped much. We told them we had a victim profile, and they all promised to be on the lookout."

"If we're right and it is murder-for-hire, there are strangers in the area, people coming in and out of these small towns. They'll be noticed by the residents," said Quana.

"Right. These towns are so small that someone's probably already seen the killers and they just don't realize it yet."

"It could be someone new to the community with a flamboyant lifestyle. Someone who has money and goes to extremes to get what they want. People in small towns will notice. We just have to be patient."

He chuckled. "Imagine a group of hit men blending in around here."

"You should stay in contact with the sheriffs of each county. It might help," said Quana.

"We'll take whatever help we can get."

"Are you bothered by this case?" asked Quana.

Jennings was slow to respond. "A little."

"You look like something's buggin' you."

"I suppose something is."

"Feel like talking about it?"

"When did you know it was time to get out of the business?"

"Of police work?"

"Yeah."

Quana laughed, then reclined in his chair. "So you're thinking about retiring, eh?"

Jennings smiled. "Maybe."

"It wasn't a question of when I wanted to retire," he said. "I loved Kansas City. But I had my twenty years on the force and my wife wanted to come back home, so I walked away. It was her decision more than mine."

"Any regrets?"

"Absolutely. I miss it everyday."

"Really?" asked Jennings.

"Of course. That's why I'm here, trying to help you."

"I'm surprised that you miss it," said Jennings.

"I believe in justice. I miss righting all the wrongs, or should I say trying to right all the wrongs," he chuckled.

"I hear that. There's a lot of bureaucracy to deal with in this business."

"That's the only part of it that I didn't like. The more I worked, the more I found and subsequently hated the bureaucracy and political corruption in my department. People with enough money were impervious to the law, and it made me sick."

"It's the same here," replied Jennings. "There's lots of big money in this area. You can't touch those people. They're in tight with the mayor and the chief of police and are basically off limits to us. I'm working a case that deals with it right now."

"It's not the Finken case, by any chance, is it?"

"Yes. It's becoming more and more difficult to bring down these corrupt bastards. Sometimes the law gets stepped on and you just have to simply turn your back to it."

"But justice must be served," said Quana. "I guess that's why I'm here today."

"I keep hoping that we'll get it right and take the riffraff off the streets. I guess that's why I haven't retired. Besides, I doubt that I'll go far on the senior golf tour."

"I couldn't even make the junior league," Quana laughed.

"Quana Smith?" a voice called from the hall outside Jennings' office. "Quana Smith, is that you?"

Jennings looked toward the doorway where Carol was standing.

Quana stood and smiled. "Well, hello, Tiger. How's my favorite little sis'?"

"A lot better now," Carol said, then walked briskly to Quana with beaming smile. "It's been so long since I've seen you," she said as they hugged.

"Too long," Quana replied.

Jennings was happy to see Carol so excited. "I first ran into Quana at the liquor store killing in Ducotey," he said. "I saw him again today at the crime scene near Grayhorse. He had business to do in Carson, so he followed me here and we've been talking about the case."

Carol was ecstatic. "It's so good to see you," she said to him, then looked to Jennings. "When we were kids, my family lived right down the road from his family. His little sister and I were best friends. She and I used to play together every day. Quana did his best to make our lives miserable."

"They were harmless mud pies," Quana laughed.

"Harmless, my ass. They were anything but harmless."

Carol and Quana laughed until tears streaked their cheeks.

"Was Kansas City good to you?" Carol said after composing herself.

"Oh yeah. We really liked it. After a while, my wife got her fill of the big city, though. She wanted to come home, so here we are."

Carol smiled. "Well, it's fantastic to have you back. Have you seen much of my mom or dad?"

"Oh yeah, I see Fred all the time, although..."

"Yeah, I heard there was an incident," interrupted Carol.

Embarrassed, Quana shook his head. "Yeah, there was a little debacle that had to do with some paint."

"Is he still not speaking to you?" asked Carol.

"No, not for quite some time."

"Just hang in there. He can be bull-headed, but he'll come around eventually."

"Yeah, I hope so. After all, it's not like he didn't get even. You should have seen what he did to my car."

"I heard," laughed Carol. "He can be like that."

"You're not telling me anything I don't already know," said Quana. "Have you been down that way lately?"

"It's been awhile since I've been back home. I need to go."

"Maybe you two could come spend the weekend. Not much to do in Ducotey, but you could get out of the city for a while," said Quana.

"I've been working on him," Carol said and pointed to Jennings. "He's not very willing to leave his house when he's off work, though."

"We'll go, I promise," Jennings replied.

"I'm going to hold you to it," Carol said.

Quana looked at his watch. "Look, I'd better get going. I need to run a couple of errands, then get back home."

"Thanks for stopping by," said Jennings.

"What did you guys find today?" asked Carol.

"It looks like the same perpetrators," answered Jennings. "We have to run ballistics, but the casings look the same as the others we've collected."

"I heard it happened on a well site near Grayhorse."

"Yeah," Quana replied. "Probably around 7:00 p.m. last night. A farmer noticed the vehicles this morning and called it in."

"How about tire tracks?" Carol asked.

"We found none," said Jennings. "The perpetrators evidently parked down the road then walked to the well site to ambush them. A considerable amount of snow fell before we got to the scene, so we're not going to have much to go on."

"Know anything about the victims?"

"A banker and an introvert, both very wealthy," said Quana.

"Sounds familiar, doesn't it?" replied Carol.

"The county sheriff said that the introvert was shunned by just about everyone in town, but the banker was somewhat well liked," said Quana.

"It was the same sort of scene as the others. They blasted the hell out of everything, in this case the vehicles, they didn't take any money, and were smart enough not to leave clues."

"Lots of ammo," Quana said.

"And by the way, Quana thinks that we're dealing with more than one perpetrator," said Jennings.

"We've suspected the same," Carol replied.

"He also mentioned the strong possibility of them being hired guns."

"It wouldn't surprise me," said Carol. "They know where to hit, when to hit, and they leave little in the way of clues. It looks very professional."

"I'll let you two hash this out. I'd better get going," Quana said and walked to the door.

"Were the victims related?" asked Carol.

"I don't think so," Jennings replied.

"Wonder how the killers got a recluse and a banker together?" said Carol.

"Especially at an abandoned well site in the middle of nowhere," Jennings added.

"Any ideas, Quana?" asked Carol.

"All I know is that I've never seen anything like this before. You're dealing with people who know what they're doing. This isn't an amateur job. I've got to run. It was great seeing you."

Carol walked to Quana and hugged him. "It was very nice to see you, too."

"You folks come to Ducotey soon."

"We'll do it," Jennings said. "I promise."

Chapter 23

Louise Parker stood over the kitchen table, individually wrapping dough around small portions of seasoned meat mixed with kidney suet. She'd been preparing her famous dish for most of the evening, anxiously awaiting her husband's return.

Just as she finished wrapping the meat, she heard Fred's old Studebaker pull into the driveway of their country home. She set several pies on a cookie sheet then placed it inside the already preheated oven.

"I smell meat pies," Fred called as he opened the garage door and removed his snow-covered clothes.

"I'm in the kitchen," said Louise.

Dressed only in underwear and a long sleeved shirt, Fred walked into the kitchen, where Louise was cleaning dirty pots and pans.

"What's the special occasion?" he asked.

"No occasion. I just figured you might like it if I made your favorite."

Fred smiled. "Seriously, what'd you buy? A car? A new house? What?"

Louise began to blush. "Stop it, silly. Is it wrong to make a special dish for a special man?"

"Of course not. Who'd you invite?"

"Ha ha. You should become a comedian."

"Maybe I will. When do we eat?"

"As soon as you put on some clothes and wash up. Where have you been?"

"Down at the hospital, talking to Linda Jackson."

Louise's facial expression turned somber. "How are they?"

"It looks like they're all going to pull through. We're damned lucky, though. They must have had only minor exposure to the chemicals. The Lord has been with us."

"Amen to that."

Fred opened the oven door and grabbed a hot meat pie off the cookie sheet before he rushed upstairs to shower and change into fresh clothes. When he returned, Louise was sitting at the table, ready to eat.

"I've been waiting for this," he said, devouring more pies.

"What else did Linda have to say?" Louise asked casually.

Fred was enjoying the meal and hated to waste energy speaking. After he scarfed down two pies, he stopped to catch his breath. "Plenty," he mumbled.

"Oh really?"

"They're doing it again," Fred said, then wiped his face.

"Doing what again?"

"They're relocating everyone from Redtree."

"The housing unit?"

Fred nodded.

Louise was shocked. "You mean they're relocating everyone who lived in the housing unit?"

"Yep."

"Again?" Linda asked. "Why are they doing that?"

Fred drank some tea, then grabbed another meat pie.

"'Cause the whole area has been condemned. It's unsafe," he said.

"I don't understand," replied Louise.

"Whatever made those people sick might still be there and it could be hazardous. The government has done some tests to the water and the land. They found some sort of bad chemical residue. They're afraid that if people are exposed, it might be a health risk. They're going to move everyone to a temporary location until they can find some land and build new houses."

Louise dropped her fork. "Oh my God!" she exclaimed. "This is just like what happened four years ago at Kickingbird. They did it to us again!" she cried, then covered her face with her hands.

Fred was quick to react to his wife's distress. He put his arm around her shoulders to soothe her. "We don't know that, honey. That's all just speculation."

"Bullshit!" she yelled. "Somebody's trying to kill our people! Don't tell me that there's a logical explanation when you know there's not."

"I know it doesn't make any sense."

"Why is somebody doing this to us?"

"I don't know," Fred replied. "But it will be investigated."

"It was investigated at Kickingbird and they didn't find a thing. I can't believe this is happening again."

Fred stared at the plate of fresh meat pies and pondered whether he should tell his wife everything he knew. "Look, I've got a lead. Let the investigators do their thing, then I'll see what I can do," he said and finished off the meat pie.

Louise wiped her face and took a deep, calming breath. "What kind of lead?" she asked.

Fred shook his head. "It's such a long shot I hate to even mention it."

"I'd like to hear it anyway."

Taking the last two meat pies, he placed them on his plate and said, "I was at the housing unit not long ago and I saw someone there."

"Who?"

"A banker. A guy named Gayland. He had someone else with him. I'm not sure who it was."

Louise was confused. "So? What does that mean?"

"From what I hear, he's a very wealthy and powerful man. He's also quite a shithead."

"What's that got to do with the price of beans in China?"

"Because it's unusual. Why would he be out there in the middle of nowhere?"

Louise shook her head. "I don't know."

"There was also something else. I saw a man spraying."

The statement turned Louise's head. "Really? Spraying for what?"

"When I saw the guy spraying, I assumed it was for insects. I don't even remember his face that well, other than he was dark-headed and in his late thirties or early forties."

"Was he wearing a uniform?"

Fred started eating another meat pie. "I don't know," he said with a full mouth.

Louise thought for a moment. "Do you think he might have been spraying poison on some of the houses?"

Fred shrugged. "It's possible, who knows?"

"That would explain how the chemicals got there, wouldn't it?"

Fred had eaten so much, his stomach felt as though it were about to burst. "Yes, it would." His eyes quickly shifted to his plate. Only two bites remained.

"Can you remember anything in particular? What he was wearing, the van he was driving, anything at all?" asked Louise.

"He was driving a white van, but it didn't have any sort of company name on it." Fred greedily ate the last two bites.

"Can't you remember anything?"

As soon as he swallowed, Fred dropped his fork and fell back in his chair. "No," he said. "I wasn't paying attention. The only thing I remember about the man was that he had dark hair."

"That doesn't help much."

"That's a record, by the way," said Fred.

"What?"

"Five. Never before have five meat pies fallen to one man at this table."

Louise rolled her eyes. "You should be very proud," she sarcastically replied. "You're truly a hero."

He laughed. "I'd like to thank all the little people who helped me get this far and..."

"I think you should go talk to Quana about this," interrupted Louise. "You two need to put the past behind you and start acting like men again."

A snarl rose on Fred's face. "I don't think I'm ready to do that just yet."

Louise leaned close. "It was just a football game, honey. Nothing more. Just because his team beat yours doesn't mean a damn thing."

"He had no right to do what he did, no right at all. If you want me to talk to someone about his, I'll talk to our daughter. But Quana? Never!" Fred snapped.

"He might be able to help with this. After all, he's retired and he probably doesn't have anything better to do."

"Carol is just as good a detective as Quana."

"Yes, but she's busy. She's working on several cases as we

speak."

"Then I'll give her another one."

Louise sighed and sat back in her chair. "You're acting like a child. College football is supposed to be bring people together, not tear them apart."

"He painted our door orange and black, Louise! Countries go to war for less!"

"And you painted his car crimson and cream! A door is easy to repaint, honey. A car is a little bit different."

"I improvised, that's all."

"You acted like a child," remarked Louise. "There was no need to retaliate the way you did."

"I don't care. He's no longer my friend. I'm not talking to him and that's final!"

Louise placed her hands on Fred's lap. "Fred, you're being unreasonable. We've been friends with his family for years. We've known Quana since he was a child," she softly said. "How long are you going to let a stupid little thing like a football game stand in the way of years of good memories?"

Fred looked down to Louise's hands and smiled. "You're trying to seduce me, aren't you?"

"Would you make up with Quana if I said yes?"

"Under normal conditions I'd do anything if you said yes, but there are two things that stand in the way."

"And what exactly could they be?"

"He really hurt my feelings when he painted my door."

"But you ruined his car."

"True, but he started it."

Louise shook her head. "I'm married to a fifty-nine year old child," she said. "What's the other reason?"

Fred looked down at his stomach. "I've eaten so much, I really don't think I can stand up."

Louise shook her head and laughed.

Fred tested the table's strength by rocking it back and forth. "This table looks pretty steady, though."

"We're getting too old for that, Fred Parker."

"Yeah, you're probably right. Besides, I might keel over if I get too excited after that meal."

Louise chuckled, then turned serious. "You and Quana need to make up. It's ridiculous that your rift has lasted this long. It's time to put all this behind you."

"Maybe I'll think about it," Fred said after contemplating her words.

"Something's got to be done about the housing unit, too. This whole thing is just too strange for it to be coincidental. When it happened the first time at Kickingbird I thought it was just odd. Now I think somebody's behind it."

"I agree. I'll do some more snooping around, then I'll talk to Carol."

Louise grabbed Fred's hand. "Honey, this is serious. If this is related to what happened four years ago, it's murder," she said.

Fred looked at the floor, unable to mask the fear in his eyes. "I know," he said, "and it scares the hell out of me, too."

Chapter 24

A series of loud knocks abruptly awoke Taylor.

"Hello?" someone shouted from outside the window.

Taylor struggled to find his bearings. Although the clock's digital numbers clearly read 11:30 a.m., he was still confused as he called, "Who is it?"

"Unlock the door. It's freezing out here!"

Taylor stumbled to the front door to look through the peephole, but saw no one. "Who's there?"

"Who do you think it is?"

"I'd guess from the tone of voice that it must be Wendy."

"Let me in!"

Arctic blasts of cold air accompanied Wendy as she rushed inside. After removing her coat, she sat on the couch and cast him a scornful look. "What took you so long?"

Taylor immediately noticed that she was pale and had dark circles under her eyes. "Sorry, I was asleep," he said, sitting beside her. "How are things with you?"

"Do you know what time it is?" asked Wendy.

"Yeah, around 11:30," he shrugged.

"Why did you sleep so late? Don't you know that's not good for your body?"

"I do it all the time. I've never heard you say anything about it before."

"Well I'm telling you now. You can't go on drinking all night with Keith and Elijah, then sleeping 'till noon," Wendy said. "You're acting irresponsible."

"Because I've been sleeping late?"

"Yes. You should take better care of yourself."

Confused by Wendy's bizarre behavior, Taylor scratched his head. "What in the hell are you talking about?"

Wendy didn't reply. She simply crossed her arms and legs and stared blankly at the wall.

"The reason I stayed up late is because I saw on the news last night that school was called off again today. I thought I'd take advantage of it, so I paid a visit to some of my nerd friends. I got home around three this morning."

"What were you doing with your nerd friends?"

"Drinking and talking about Freud."

"Freud, huh?"

"Well, we were talking more about his life than his teachings."

Wendy's eyes rolled. "I'll bet that was a hoot."

"It wasn't so bad. I had a good time." Taylor smiled. "Remember, nerds are people, too."

Since Wendy found no humor in Taylor's words, he decided to change the subject. "Are the roads any better?"

"They're fine," Wendy said. "I don't know why they canceled classes."

"Lots of students drive in each day from other towns. I'll bet the back roads are still slick..."

"As usual, you're probably right. Always first with the right answer, aren't you?"

Taylor shook his head and looked deep into Wendy's eyes. "What's with this bug up your ass?"

"I don't have a bug up my ass, Mister summa cum freakin' laude."

Taylor moved closer. "Would it make you feel better if you hit me?"

"Of course not. Now you're just being stupid."

"Okay, then let's go eat lunch. You're not working today, right?"

She nodded.

"I liked that Italian place we went to yesterday. Mind if we go there again?"

Without responding, Wendy slowly walked to the kitchen sink and stood in silence. Taylor approached her. "I take it you're not in the mood for Italian?"

Wendy didn't utter a word. She began to cry and ran to the bathroom.

Taylor followed her and waited as she washed her face. "What's wrong?" he asked.

"Yesterday was a very bad day," she replied in a frail voice.

"What happened?"

"Well, for starters, the man I love pulled a gun on me."

He lowered his head. "I'm very sorry about that, but I thought I explained..."

"I now have a stalker, plus my boss tried to grope me."

"What?"

Wendy finally lost control and tears streamed down her face.

"Calm down and tell me about it," Taylor said in a comforting tone. "You're safe here. You have nothing to worry about."

After a few moments, Wendy was breathing a bit easier. "It was after we ate lunch yesterday, when I got back to the bank. Because of the bad weather, no one was there. It was just me, for a long time. That's when I started getting the phone calls."

"Wait a minute. The bank was closed?"

"Yes."

"Then why were you there?" Taylor asked, puzzled.

"Gayland told me that he'd pay me overtime if I worked all day and entered some records for him. I need the money, so I stayed."

"You were alone with Gayland?"

She nodded. "But before he got there, I started getting these phone calls. The first few times, the caller just hung up without saying anything. Then, he asked for me by name."

"What did he say?"

"He had a Yankee accent and said that he knew my name was Wendy and that he saw me in the Italian restaurant. He wanted to know if I was seeing either of the men I was seated with."

"What did you tell him?"

"I told him that you were my boyfriend and the other man was my boss. He said that he didn't care if I had a boyfriend or not, that he was from back east and he'd show me how to have a good time."

"Did he give you a name?"

"He said his name was Joe, but that's all. He wouldn't give me a last name."

"Hang on a minute," Taylor said and thought for a moment. "Do you remember at the restaurant when Gayland was staring at that man seated across from us? Remember how nervous Gayland started acting?"

"Yeah. Do you think Gayland knows him?"

"I don't know. What else did he say?"

"He started talking dirty, then he said that a beautiful country girl like me needed a city boy who knows how to satisfy a woman, not a country boy who screws goats."

"Is that right?" replied Taylor.

"I told him to not call me anymore—that I wasn't interested and I was busy."

"Was that the end of it?"

"No. He called back again to ask if I'd be interested if my country bumpkin boyfriend were to disappear."

"And?"

"I told him not to call me anymore, that if he did, I'd call the police. His response was, 'I'm not too worried about the police down here.'"

"Was that all that was said?"

"Yeah. Someone, I don't know who, called several times right after that, but I didn't pick up the phone. I just ignored it and continued to enter records."

"Does Gayland know about this?" asked Taylor.

"Yeah. After a couple of hours, Gayland came in. He was very drunk and agitated," Wendy said.

"What time did he arrive at the bank?"

"Around 4:30."

"Did he say where he'd been?"

"No. He started flirting heavily with me, then I told him about the phone calls. I asked him if he knew anyone named Joe. He turned very red and stormed back to his office. He made a call, then started talking. After a few minutes, he closed the door to his office."

"Could you hear anything that was said?"

"Not at first, but after a while I crept over to his door and listened."

"What did he say?"

"He was screaming. He said that he tried to get the money from Peat, but Peat didn't have it yet. He said he'd have it very soon."

Taylor's heart raced. "Go on."

"Then there was a bunch of talk about investing or something like that. I couldn't really make out what they were talking about."

"Is there anything specific that you remember? Any names or dates?"

Wendy thought for a moment. "No dates, but toward the end, Gayland got extremely irate; he was furious. He kept saying first Peat, then Hempshaw, first Peat, then Hempshaw. He repeated it several times. I don't know what that means, though."

"Anything else?"

"He ended the call by saying that he would get it from Peat as fast as he could. Then I heard him slam down the phone."

Taylor shook his head.

"Do you know what any of that means?" asked Wendy.

"What happened between you and Gayland?" Taylor asked.

Sniffling, she replied, "As soon as he hung up, I moved quietly back to my desk. After a while, he came to me."

"What did he do?"

"He told me that he was sorry for what had happened and that it was probably just a high school kid making obscene calls."

"Then what?" asked Taylor.

"He walked to the front door and locked it. He pulled down all the window shades and turned most of the lights off," Wendy said while her eyes watered over.

"What did you do?"

Wendy started to cry. "I got scared. I didn't know what to do, so I pretended that I didn't notice any of it. I just kept entering data on the computer and tried not to look up. The next thing I know, he's behind me. He reached down and started rubbing my breasts and then tried to unbutton my shirt."

Taylor clinched his fists and tried with all his might to remain calm.

"I turned and pushed him away, so hard in fact, that it knocked him to the floor. At that time, my mind was racing and I didn't know what I should do. He gave me this look like he couldn't comprehend that I would reject him, then he walked back to his office and closed the door."

"Did you grab the mace I gave you?"

"Yeah, I did," Wendy said, then wiped her face with a tissue. "I turned off my computer and was about to leave when he came out of his office."

"What happened?"

"He told me that he was very sorry—that he had too many things going on and was drinking too much. He claimed it was the alcohol, not him, and asked me to forgive him."

Taylor worked desperately to hide his anger. "What did you tell him?"

Wendy wiped her face. "My only concern was to make it out of the place, so I told him that I understood. I quickly grabbed my things and rushed toward the door."

"Did he follow you?"

"Yes. He asked if I needed a ride home. I told him no and left the bank."

"But you didn't have a car. How did you get home?"

"I walked to the restaurant next door. I was planning to call you, but I ran into a friend of mine, Joni, and she took me home. As soon as I got there, I called you, but you didn't answer."

Taylor's face turned red. "I'm sorry that I wasn't there for you."

"Don't worry," Wendy said in a soft voice. "You had no idea that Gayland would try something like that."

Taylor's guilt suddenly turned to controlled rage.

"Have you heard anything else from Gayland?"

"No," Wendy said. "I'm not scheduled to work today. I doubt that I'll hear anything. He was so drunk he probably doesn't even remember."

"Don't underestimate him. He's a wicked man who thinks he's above the law and..."

"Taylor, there's something else."

Taylor looked into Wendy's eyes. "What?"

"When Joni and I left the restaurant, someone followed us."

"What!"

"Normally I wouldn't notice such a thing, but when we walked outside the restaurant, I saw that there were hardly any cars in the parking lot, except for a man in a car with its engine running. I didn't pay much attention, but it was obvious that he was watching us. As we got in Joni's car and drove away, he followed us all the way to my apartment."

"Did you see his face?" asked Taylor.

"Yeah," Wendy said. "It looked like that guy in the Italian restaurant. And I'll bet he's the same guy who called me at the bank and told me his name was Joe."

Taylor softly shook his head.

"I know that you've told me never to drive home if someone's following me, but with the bad road conditions I was just grateful to get there safely."

"What did he do when you got to your apartment?"

"He drove by very slowly, staring at me the whole time. He had a sort of evil grin on his face—it was very creepy."

"Did you get his tag number?"

"No. I went inside, locked the doors and tried to call you. I was up most of the night, worrying that something might happen. I kept the lights on and held onto the mace."

"I'm very sorry," said Taylor. "I had no idea."

"It's all right," replied Wendy. "I'm fine, but I'm still worried."

"As well you should be."

Wendy washed her face again. She seemed much better, but was still very shaken. After drying with a towel, she looked up to find Taylor was no longer at her side. "Taylor? Where'd you go?" she called, searching the hallway. When he suddenly reappeared fully clothed, she exclaimed, "Damn! You scared me."

"Sorry."

"Where're you going?"

"I've got some business to take care of. Did anyone follow you here?"

"No. I constantly checked my rear-view mirror. I never saw anyone."

Taylor reached into his jacket and withdrew a .38 caliber pistol. Handing it to her, he said, "Take this, just in case someone did."

Wendy's eyes widened. "What is it?"

"It's a .38. Have you ever shot one before?"

"Heavens no. I don't plan to, either."

"I really doubt you'll need this, but if someone breaks in while I'm gone, switch off the safety, aim it at his chest, and pull the trigger six times. It's already loaded."

She shook her head. "I can't do that! I might kill someone."

"If it's either you or him, you'll have to."

"My God, Taylor. What's going on?"

Taylor shook his head. "I don't know, but you've got to trust me and do what I say. Okay?"

Wendy looked at the pistol in disbelief. "I can't believe that I once revered that son-of-a-bitch. He's the reason all this is happening."

"I think you're going to find that Gayland's not at all the man you think he is."

"Do you know something that I don't know?"

"In time I'll tell you everything, but right now, you just need to be concerned for yourself."

Wendy looked into Taylor's eyes. "You're not going to kill him or Joe, are you?"

"No, I have other plans for Gayland and I don't know where Joe is."

"Where are you going?"

"To Ducotey. I need to talk to Elijah and Keith."

"What am I going to do about my job?" Wendy asked as Taylor walked to the door.

"I don't know, I need to do some thinking." He stepped outside. "Lock up, then get some rest. I'll be back soon."

Chapter 25

Exercising little caution on the patches of ice, Taylor sped the old Plymouth through Ducotey to his former neighborhood. He hastily wheeled the car into the driveway, barely sliding to a stop just short of the garage doors. Jumping out, he slammed the door and quickly rushed to the porch. With his keys, he unlocked the front door and stepped into the darkness. "We've got a problem!" he shouted.

Hearing no response, he walked down the dark hall to look for signs of life. Just as he rounded the corner, he heard the distinctive sound of a gun's hammer being pulled back. Alarmed, he reached inside his jacket to retrieve his .45 pistol. Raising it, he slowly walked toward the sound.

As he crept down the hall, he quietly flicked a light switch, but to his dismay, the hallway remained dark. Since the hall deadended in a T, he had to choose between his old room on the right and the master bedroom on the left. On the hunch that the sound originated from his room, he took a deep breath and turned to the right.

The bedroom was empty, so he turned toward the master bedroom. Cold steel pressing against his back made him stop in his tracks. In the darkness, Taylor didn't recognize the person holding the gun.

"Bang, bang, you're dead," he said.

His heart jumped. Afraid that any sudden movement might evoke a violent response, he froze. "Who are you? And what do you want?"

"Just your soul, nothing more."

Taylor frowned in disgust. "You son-of-a-bitch," he said, whirling to face the man. "Are you trying to give me a heart attack?"

"No," Elijah said. "I didn't know it was you."

"Do you treat all your guests with this type of hospitality?"

"Depends on what kind of mood I'm in."

"You scared the hell out of me. That's a great way to get yourself shot."

"I have my reasons. I've been finding footprints in the backyard and hearing strange things at night. We're on a heightened alert status."

Taylor shot him an aggravated look, then headed for the living room. "Why's it so dark in here? Didn't you pay the electric bill?" he asked as he sat on the living room couch.

"The snowstorm knocked out all the electricity," replied Elijah, sitting next to Taylor. "But I don't mind. I like it dark."

"That's easy to see," Taylor replied, while lighting a candle.

Dressed in underwear and a tee shirt, Keith entered the room. "To what do we owe this visit?"

"We've got problems," Taylor said.

"Do tell," Keith responded. He sat in a chair across from the couch.

"For starters, Gayland tried to have his way with Wendy yesterday."

Elijah jumped in his seat. "I knew it!" he shouted. "I knew he would try something. When are you two going to listen to me? He's got to be stopped!"

Keith remained calm. "Was she harmed?"

"No. She knocked him on his ass and then got out of there."

"Where did it happen? Was it at the bank?" asked Keith.

"Yeah. They were the only two there."

"Now's the time," flared Elijah. "We must take him. We can't wait any longer."

"There's more. I think I know who this Joe Escartes is."

"Joe Escartes? Is that the name you saw in Gayland's safe?" said Keith.

He nodded. "It was listed with the investors, but next to his name it said that he'd been paid $15,000."

"So?" he asked.

"He's stalking Wendy," said Taylor. "He followed her home from the bank last night."

"Dear God," Keith gasped. "Is she all right?"

"Yes, but he knows where she lives now, which is obviously a problem. She didn't sleep much last night and she's still pretty rattled."

"So we'll take care of him, too," Elijah said. "Problem solved."

"Wendy overheard Gayland talking to him on the phone. Gayland told him over and over that it was Peat first, then Hempshaw, in that order."

"But they're the only investors still alive," said Keith with wide eyes. "You don't suppose?"

"Suppose what?" asked Elijah.

"Yes," replied Taylor. "I think Gayland hired Joe to kill off the investors. He called Wendy several times at the bank. She said his accent wasn't from around here, that he sounded like an Easterner."

"Could be Mafia."

"My thoughts exactly," replied Taylor.

"Wait a minute," said Elijah. "You mean to tell me that we've been doing Gayland's dirty work for him?"

"It appears so," Taylor said.

"Then there's only one thing left to do," said Elijah. "We've got to kill 'em all."

"I agree. With both of them coming after Wendy, it's personal now."

"When do you want to do it?" asked Elijah. "Let me get my coat. We can do it now."

"Hold on, men," interrupted Keith. "Let's not make emotional decisions."

"See," an agitated Elijah said to Taylor. "This is what I was telling you about the other day. He always stands in the way. No matter how righteous our cause, he's always..."

"I always supply the voice of reason," quipped Keith.

"You're being a coward!" Taylor replied.

Keith was shocked. In all the years they'd known each other, he had never seen Taylor so hostile toward him.

"For the sake of our friendship, I'll consider your emotional state before I pass judgment on that statement."

"You're just like a robot," Elijah said. "A robot that always does the right thing."

"Taylor, I agree with you, in part," Keith said. "If Gayland and this Joe person are threatening Wendy, then let's take action, but not now, at this moment."

"Then what do you propose we do?" asked Taylor.

"For starters, do you even know where to find him?"

"No. But that can be arranged."

"The most logical solution would be to remove Wendy from the area where she's the most vulnerable."

"How?" asked Taylor.

"Ask her to move in with you and quit her job."

"This is bullshit," cried Elijah. "Don't listen to him, Taylor. We need action here, not words. Wendy shouldn't have to rearrange her life because of these jackasses."

"Heed my words, Taylor. If you act in haste, you'll jeopardize the mission," said Keith.

"Things have changed. They're threatening Wendy's safety. I can't idly stand by."

"If you're in jail, you can't look after Wendy at all," Keith reasoned. "And that's where you're headed if you jump into this without thinking it through. Remember, the police are already on the lookout. We've been fortunate so far. We can't walk right into the hornet's nest."

"It's no different than what we've been doing all along, you coward," said an enraged Elijah.

"Oh, but it is," Keith calmly responded. "So far, our hits have been in places with little threat from the law. Carson has a decent police department."

Taylor wanted immediate action, but Keith's argument made sense. "So what do we do?" he asked.

"As I see it, we have two options."

"Yeah," barked Elijah. "First kill half of them, then kill the other half."

"That's not what I had in mind," said Keith. "The first option is to continue to hunt them down one-by-one and murder them in cold blood, saving Gayland last on the list so as to make him live in absolute fear and torture while he waits. This is, incidentally, the same plan we've been using and, not surprisingly, a plan which I still strongly oppose."

"Why don't you get out, then?" said Elijah. "You're not doing us any good anyway."

"I made a commitment with the two of you when this started. Unfortunately, that same commitment binds me to this project."

"You're not doing me any favors," replied Elijah. "You're welcome to leave anytime you wish."

"Piss off," said Keith.

"Do you two fight like this all the time?" asked Taylor.

Keith sneered. "Living with this wanker is just blissful, it is."

"What's your second option?" asked Taylor.

Keith smiled. "What we should have done in the beginning. Turn the whole thing over to the officials."

Elijah fell back in his seat. "Oh, that's brilliant. Turn ourselves in. Yeah, that's the answer. What's next? Testify against ourselves at the trial?"

"Discovering Joe Escartes was an incredible break," said Keith. "For all the police know, Joe Escartes did the killings, not us. They have little evidence."

"That's the most ridiculous thing I've ever heard. They have evidence that can link things back to us. Ever heard of ballistics?" said Elijah.

"All they have are shell casings. As long as they never find our guns, we're in the clear," replied Keith.

"What do you propose, then? Walk right down to the police station and have a chat with the chief?"

"No. We'll send them an anonymous letter. We'll never be considered suspects," Keith said. "All we need to do is find out where Joe Escartes is staying, then tip off the police to his whereabouts."

"You're forgetting one important item, which is the fundamental reason why we're doing this," said Taylor.

Knowing his plan was falling on deaf ears, Keith gave Taylor a solemn look. "And that is?" he asked.

"The police won't prosecute Gayland," replied Taylor. "He's too slick. Only we can represent the voices of the fallen."

"And represent them, we shall," bellowed Elijah.

"Remember, Keith, the blood's on their hands, not ours."

Keith lowered his head in disappointment. "I guess the majority rules," said Keith. "What more can I say?"

"You've said enough," responded Elijah. "Now, go bake us a cake or something."

"You truly are a miserable bloke," said Keith.

Taylor stood and paced the floor. "Our priorities have changed, but our mission is the same," he said. "We must now deal with Joe Escartes, as soon as possible."

"Do you think you can locate him?" asked Keith.

"I'll find a way," Taylor replied. "He's obviously driven by his hormones. It shouldn't be too hard."

"You might have to use Wendy as bait," said Keith. "Are you prepared to do that?"

"As long as this problem goes away, I'm prepared to do anything," Taylor said as he left the house.

He quickly jumped in his car and drove through the streets of Ducotey en route to the highway that would lead him home. Along the way, he spotted several lighted houses and yard lights. Taylor sighed and shook his head as the Plymouth roared though the night.

Chapter 26

Carol's heart jumped when she looked up from the mixing bowl and noticed Jennings walking into the kitchen. Judging by the frustrated look on his face and his slouched posture, she assumed his mood was sour, which wasn't a welcome sight. Over the last few days she was mired, almost obsessed, with doubts about their romance. Tonight, she decided, it was time to confront the problem.

"How did it go?" she asked.

Jennings tossed his briefcase on the floor beside the stove and took off his coat. "It was lovely," he replied sarcastically, "just lovely."

"From the tone of your voice, I take that to mean it didn't go well."

"You guessed right."

"Why don't you get a beer? Might make you feel better."

"Since when did you start keeping beer in the house?"

"There was a special on imported beer today, so I thought you might like a treat."

"Thanks." Jennings removed a beer from the refrigerator, then walked into the living room. "What are you making?"

"Brownies," she replied. "Would you like something sweet?"

"There's not enough sugar in the world to remove the bitter taste in my mouth." Jennings sat on the couch, grabbed the television remote, and surfed the channels.

Carol poured the batter into a baking pan, placed it in the oven, then joined Jennings on the couch. "Tell me about the trial."

Jennings looked at her briefly, then shook his head. "It was a circus. I'm almost ashamed that I was a part of it."

"What happened?"

"Everything. Outside the courtroom, the media and spectators were there in full force. People were running around in circles taking pictures. Everyone was trying to get a glimpse. It was pure madness."

"Did it impact the trial?"

"Oh yeah. The atmosphere inside the courtroom was electric, sort of like a movie premier. People were smiling and laughing. You never would have dreamed that it was a murder trial."

"I'm a little confused. Finken is rich and powerful, but he's never really been that much of a celebrity."

"He's just a small part of this. His attorneys are the big draw."

"I bet you're right," Carol said. "It's not often that rural America gets a glimpse of celebrity attorneys—especially attorneys with the notoriety of Pinkus and Newman."

"There's a special room in hell reserved for those two bastards."

"Are you still confident that we'll get a conviction?"

"I don't feel as good about it as I did, but yeah, I still feel like we've got what we need to put him away. He was very sloppy when he committed this crime. We've got the ballistics, shell casing, and the murder weapon. He has no alibi and he has a motive."

"It's the latter that worries me," said Carol.

"The motive?"

"Yes. You're banking on Finken's drug dealing to tie everything together."

"Not solely, but yeah, that's an element."

"But he's never been convicted of dealing drugs. Matter of fact, you have no physical evidence that he's ever dealt drugs."

"No, but we've cut deals with criminals who will testify that he has."

"Do you think that will sway a jury?"

Jennings hit the mute button on the television. "It shouldn't matter. But in case it doesn't, we have hard evidence, too."

"There have been lots of cases lost in spite of hard evidence. You just never know."

"True. But I have faith. We conducted a good investigation. I don't think we'll have any problems."

"Let's hope that the jury doesn't get too caught up in the hullabaloo."

He raised his beer. "Cheers to that," he said and downed the rest of the bottle. "When will those brownies be ready?"

"I just put them in, so it'll be awhile."

Jennings smiled. "I'd better have another beer, then."

As Carol watched Jennings walk to the refrigerator, she felt her heart race. Now's the time, she thought. It's better to get it out in the open than to let it sit and stew. "Sorry the brownies aren't ready. I didn't expect you to swing by so early."

"I came here straight from the courthouse," Jennings said with a fresh beer in hand. "I didn't see the need to go back to the office."

"Did you go by your house?"

"No. Why?"

Carol blushed. "Oh, I don't know. You seem to spend a lot of time over here."

Jennings sat beside Carol, then grabbed the remote and turned up the volume. "Are you getting tired of me?" he asked nonchalantly.

"Oh no. Not at all. I was just, well you know, thinking aloud."

Jennings surfed the channels and nursed his beer. "Thinking about what?"

Carol's nerves were wound so tight, she felt like screaming. "Like I said, you spend a lot of time here. More than at your own house."

"And you say you're not getting tired of me, right?"

"Right," replied Carol.

"So what's the problem?"

"There is no problem."

Jennings finally found a classic western. He didn't recognize the movie, but that didn't matter. Tossing aside the remote, he settled in for a relaxing evening. "Then what are you thinking about?" he asked, without looking away from the television.

As soon as she noticed that Jennings' focus had shifted to the television, Carol sighed. "It's nothing," she said, then jumped off the couch to check the brownies.

Realizing something was bothering her, he turned the volume down and followed her to the kitchen. "What is it?" he asked.

"I've just been wondering about us, that's all," she said, opening the oven door.

"Oh, I get it," he said with a smile. "Imported beer. Brownies. Now it makes sense."

"I don't know what you're talking about."

"We're about to have the 'relationship' talk, aren't we?"

Carol silently stared at the brownies.

Jennings laughed. "You can't fool a detective. I know when I'm being bribed."

Carol knew she was caught.

"So, out with it. Lay it on the table."

With a stoic face, Carol stared at Jennings. "We've been dating for a long time and we get along great."

"I agree. So what's the problem?"

"There's no problem. I just need to know. I like to plan ahead." She closed the door to the oven, slowly walked to the refrigerator and grabbed a beer.

"I think things are going fine. I think more of you than any other woman I've ever known. I love everything about you. These three years with you have been blissful."

"How could you love everything about me? You don't even know everything about me."

"I know the important things about you," Jennings said.

"Oh, really? What are my parent's names?"

"Okay. You got me on that one."

"You've never even met them."

"Let's not ruin it," Jennings laughed.

"But they're a part of me and you're a part of me."

Jennings placed his arm on Carol's shoulder. "When I meet them, I'm sure I'll love them, too."

"Then maybe we should go see them. Maybe we should just let things happen, go to the courthouse and get married, then run away and live happy ever after."

"We could find a hundred acres with some horses and cows, get married, and live off the land. Does that tickle your fancy?" he asked.

Carol sipped her beer. "Maybe."

"Well, maybe I've thought about that, too."

Although she tried to fight it, a smile started to break. "And?"

"My other girlfriends don't think it's a good idea," Jennings laughed. "They're mighty stingy."

She lightly punched his arm. "Be serious."

"I'm not afraid of commitment. Don't think it's about that."

"So it's a good idea?"

He cocked his head to look into her eyes. "Maybe it is. Does that make you feel better?"

"Yes, but you're really not answering the question."

"Well," Jennings said, then took a drink from his beer, "set the date and I'll be there."

"That's so romantic," Carol said with sarcasm. "My ex-husband did a better job of proposing, and he's in jail."

"I was talking about meeting your parents. Set the date and we'll go meet them."

"Oh," Carol said, with surprise. "I thought you meant…"

"Trust me, I'll sweep you off your feet when it's time for that."

With a long look and a sexy smile, Carol walked to Jennings and kissed him on the cheek. Not to be outdone, Jennings grabbed her by the waist, pulled her close to his body and kissed her savagely. The blare of the oven timer interrupted the intensifying passion.

"I guess you'd better get that. We don't want to burn the house down."

"Yeah. We don't need that."

Carol carefully removed the brownies and turned off the oven. "Oh, I almost forgot, Daddy called today."

"Did you ask about riding the horses?" asked Jennings.

"No, I forgot," Carol replied as she set the brownies on a hot plate.

"You know that's a big incentive for me to see them. I haven't been on a horse in a long time and…"

"I know, I know," said Carol. "You want to go riding, I realize that. I'll ask him, I promise."

"Thanks," Jennings said, settling back on the couch. He smiled as the Duke shot the men in black. "This stuff never gets old."

"Daddy did bring something of interest to my attention," said Carol. "How well do you know Kyle Gayland?"

"Enough to stay away from him."

Carol's interest piqued. "Oh, really?"

"Yeah. Word on the street is that he's involved in shady deals. He's got the cash to keep himself out of trouble."

"Has he ever been in any trouble with the law?"

"Not that I know of. He's slippery."

"What sorts of things has he been involved in?"

"Well, he's a banker, so that tells you a lot."

"Yeah, but what kinds of crimes have you heard about?" asked Carol.

"Laundering money from people, bribery, that sort of thing. We've been tipped off several times, but we've never found enough to prosecute him."

"That's interesting."

"Why was your dad asking you about Gayland?"

"He didn't say. He said that he was just curious."

"I see," replied Jennings.

"He also asked about us."

Jennings eyes widened. "He did?"

"He sure did."

"What did he say? Is he upset about something?"

"He was wondering when you're going to make an honest woman out of me."

"Holy shit," said Jennings. "That's all I need right now."

Carol laughed. "Don't worry about it. He's an old man. He hasn't fought anyone in...well...weeks."

"Very funny."

"Don't worry about him. He's just concerned, that's all."

"I guess I'll have to meet him," said Jennings.

"He said he's going to try to come up when he can. You'll get your chance soon enough."

"Wonderful." Jennings said, sarcastically. "Do you have any other news you need to tell me?"

"No. Nothing that can't wait."

"Good," Jennings said and looked directly into Carol's eyes. "Now where were we?"

Carol smiled. "You mean before the timer went off?"

"No, I mean with the western. When I turned the volume down I lost track."

Carol snatched a pillow from the couch and threw it at him.

Chapter 27

As Taylor pulled the Plymouth into the driveway of his apartment, sleet fell from the dark clouds blanketing the evening sky. With the temperature well below freezing, it was highly likely the next day's classes would be cancelled again.

The moment he reached his apartment, Wendy opened the door. "Where've you been?" she asked. "I didn't expect you to stay gone for so long."

"It's slick again, so I had to drive slow. Sorry."

"I was worried."

Stepping inside, he took off his shoes, grabbed a bag of potato chips and sat at the kitchen table.

"Dinner will be ready soon," Wendy said. "Don't spoil your appetite."

"It takes more than chips to spoil this appetite," Taylor replied, munching away. "What did you make?"

"Your favorite."

"Beer and cheese dip?"

"No, silly. I made voodoo chili, just the way you like it."

"With *habaneros*?" he asked hungrily.

"*Sí.*"

Taylor walked to the stove and removed the lid from the chili pot. Scooping a load onto a chip, he scarfed it down. "*I yee yi.* That's pretty hot. It's got some bang to it."

Wendy smiled. "I held nothing back. Did you talk to your friends?"

"Pardon?" he asked, after gulping a glass of water.

"You know, Elijah and Keith. Did you talk to them about what's going on?"

"Oh, yeah."

"What did you come up with?"

"A couple of things. I'd like for you to move in here and quit your job." Wendy's sour expression instantly told Taylor that she wasn't receptive to his idea. "Is that going to be a problem?" he asked.

"Yes and no. I'd love to move in, but my parents aren't going to be very cool about us living together."

"Why not? I get along fine with them."

"I know you do, but in case you haven't heard, that's called living in sin."

"I understand that," Taylor rebutted, "but you staying alone is called living in stupidity and it's out of the question. God only knows what this guy's capable of."

Wendy was silent for a moment while she thought. "This could be an isolated incident. Maybe he was just some drunk away from his wife for the week and out chasing skirts."

Taylor sighed and felt the rumblings of anger. "Don't pretend for a minute that you understand men. You don't."

"I know more about them than you give me credit," snapped Wendy.

"Bullshit," scoffed Taylor. "You're naïve. You don't realize what some people are capable of. This man's a killer and I'm not going to give him the opportunity to have his way with you."

"Killer? What do you mean? You're afraid that he'll kill me?"

Taylor instantly regretted his words. He knew Wendy's questions would be relentless. "He's dangerous. Trust me."

"What makes you think he's a killer? I have the right to know."

Taylor's first impulse was to tell her everything, but that would endanger her if he were apprehended. He feared, however, that Wendy would fail to recognize the danger if she wasn't presented with the truth. "This guy, Joe Escartes, he's a..."

"He's what?"

"A bad man," said Taylor. "A very bad man."

"But you don't even know him. What makes you so sure? And how do you know his last name?"

Taylor was out of options. He decided to use his only safety net. Looking into her eyes, he softly said, "You know I care for you a great deal, don't you?"

"Of course."

"Then believe my words. The man is dangerous and you're not safe alone."

Wendy grabbed Taylor's hand. "All right. I'll move in. I don't know what I'm going to tell my father, though."

"We won't tell them anything. We'll keep your apartment, you just won't stay there anymore. They'll never know the difference."

"Then it's done."

"What about Gayland? Have you heard anything from him today?"

Wendy released Taylor's hand and walked to the kitchen sink. "Yeah, you could say that."

"What happened?"

"I called my mom and told her what happened."

"What did she say?"

"She didn't say much of anything. Then Dad got on the phone and I repeated it all to him."

"I'll bet he was pretty mad, huh?" said Taylor.

"Yeah, he became angry, but I'm not sure to whom his anger was directed."

"I don't understand."

"Everything went fine until I told them that I was going to quit my job. They didn't take it very well."

"Did they get mad?"

"Sort of. Dad told me that it wasn't possible," she said in a weak voice.

"But why?"

"My dad and Gayland grew up together and they've been friends ever since. When my dad started farming, it was Gayland who set him up financially at the bank. Since that time, farming has become less than profitable and my father has continued to borrow money each year to make ends meet."

"I don't see how that has anything to do with you quitting your job," Taylor said.

"My dad's afraid that if I quit, word will get out and it will make Gayland look bad."

"And he'll call the notes on your mom and dad's farm?"

"Exactly," replied Wendy.

"So, basically, you're telling me that your father values money more than your own well-being."

Wendy walked to Taylor. "You don't understand. They've known each other since they were kids. If it gets out what he did to me, it will severely damage Gayland's reputation in his hometown, where my mother and father still live."

"So what? Your mother and father had nothing to do with any of it."

"It doesn't matter. Gayland is a powerful and vindictive man. He'll get even. You don't know him like I do."

"Oh, I know a thing or two about him," said Taylor, placing his hands over his face. He let out a sigh of aggravation. "So what are you going to do?"

"I don't know. I guess I'll stay there."

"Wendy, there comes a time when you have to take charge of your life."

"But I am in charge."

"No, you're not. You're letting your parents beat the drum for you."

"But I'm not independent like you. It's not easy for me to break that bond."

"You don't have to break it," Taylor said. "Just stretch it—give yourself room to breathe."

"It's not easy. My dad could lose everything that he's worked for his whole life," Wendy said with tears brimming.

Taylor placed his arms around her. "There's a time in your life when you come of age and really begin to understand the complexities of the world," he said. "Do you know when that happens?"

Wendy turned and looked him in the eyes. "No," she said. "When?"

"It's when you realize that your parents are people, just like you. They're not Mom and Dad, they're just people, the same as everyone else. They make bad decisions; they sing in the shower; sometimes the world gets too heavy and they get really piss drunk. They're still your mother and father, but they're just people."

Wendy grabbed a tissue and wiped her face. "So what are you telling me, that I shouldn't listen to them anymore?"

"No. You should always listen to them, but you must make decisions for yourself."

"I don't know. I need to think about it some more."

"It seems to me that there's not much to think about. We're talking about your safety."

"And also turning my back on my parents. I just don't know if I can do it, Taylor."

"You sound as if your mind is already made up."

Wendy shook her head, then grabbed two bowls from the cupboard. "The chili's ready. Let's forget about this and eat."

"Okay," Taylor replied, then paused. "But you were right. I don't have much of an appetite."

Chapter 28

Taylor looked at his cards and puffed on the giant cigar hanging from his lips. Wearing the stone face of a mobster, his eyes burned in the smoky air as he analyzed each opponent. Sensing their fear, he chuckled as their eyes twitched. He had all but destroyed them; the nerd poker game would soon be over.

All seven cards had been dealt—three on the table, four in each hand. Since Taylor had already taken most of their money, only the decisive final blow remained.

"I'll raise you fifty cents," Taylor said with confidence.

"What?" exclaimed Wally, who sat directly across from Taylor. "That's all I have left. You're trying to run me out."

Taylor smiled. "You catch on real fast."

To his left, Taylor saw Ralf nod. "I must agree with my colleague. The primary purpose of our gathering is recreational. Your lust and greed have mutated that paradigm."

"Money talks and bullshit walks, Ralfie Boy," Taylor said and slid his coins across the table.

"Well, sir, then walk my money shall. I fold."

Taylor laughed. "Just as well. You'll need bus money for your trip back home."

Ralf tilted his head like a confused dog. "But I don't understand. I didn't come here on a bus. I walked. I live up the street," he pointed.

"It's a figure of speech," Wally said, trying to concentrate on his cards. After stroking his chin several times, he grabbed his last five dimes and threw them in the pot.

"I'm in," he said.

Ruben was the only one left. He spent several minutes sporadically ogling his cards, then the pot. "Would you loan me a dime?" he asked Taylor.

Taylor slid a dime across the table. Ruben then scooted his last forty cents into the pot. "I call," he said.

With a smile, Taylor turned over each card. "I've got a pair of sixes," he laughed.

Ruben, Wally, and Frank moaned collectively and threw their cards on the table.

"You can't bullshit a bull-shiter," said Taylor.

"He knew we were bluffing," Ruben said in disgust.

"But how?" asked Wally, "How could you possibly have known?"

"I could see it in your eyes."

"For the sake of argument," said Ralf, "I contest. I think it brash and pretentious for you to assert that you can read our minds."

"I didn't read your minds. I read your body language."

"Hardly," Ralf sneered.

Taylor walked to the refrigerator to grab a beer. Before he took his seat again, someone knocked on the door.

"Who could that be?" asked Wally. "It's almost eleven o'clock."

Taylor looked through the peephole. He smiled and opened the door.

"It took you long enough," Wendy said. "It's freakin' cold out there."

"Sorry."

She took off her coat and walked into the kitchen. "Playing cards?"

"We were," Frank moaned, "until your boyfriend cleaned us out."

Wendy smiled as she sat at the table. "You've got to watch him. He's a card shark. He'll take your money."

"Actually," said Ralf, "tonight he relied on his ability to read our thoughts, or so he claims. I find the notion grossly absurd."

Ralf slammed the rest of his beer, then let out a rumbling belch.

"It isn't absurd," said Taylor. "But your table manners, now that's another story."

"Amen," Wendy said.

"I had a terrible hand but I knew that you did, too. You were just trying too hard to make me think that you were holding something."

"How did you know?" asked Wally, his speech slightly slurred from the alcohol.

Wendy got a cold beer and twisted off the cap. "Yes," she said, "I'd love to hear this, too."

"You tried to be brave but your anal-retentive nature was too strong," Taylor said as he puffed on his cigar.

Ralf rolled his eyes and shook his head. "Oh no, not more Freudian psychology," he said.

"It was as clear as an azure sky."

"What?" asked Wendy.

"Your boyfriend is a Freudian freak," said Wally.

"It's the truth; it controls our lives," Taylor said.

"What controls our lives?" asked Wendy.

Ralf rolled his eyes. "Taylor thinks that everyone is dominated by the id, ego, or superego," he said.

"Which means?" asked Wendy, with a blank look.

Taylor replied, "To put it in laymen's terms, in the unconscious mind, the id is driven by immediate wants, the superego questions everything, and the ego is our conscious reality."

"So? What does that mean?"

"Our conscious state of mind, the ego, is controlled by either the id or superego."

"Okay," Wendy said with a raised eyebrow. "How do you tell what you are controlled by?"

"You've seen people that act as if they can do whatever they want, whenever they want?"

"So those people are controlled by the id?" asked Wendy.

"Right. And those people, like you for example, who are afraid to do anything unless they're sure it's absolutely the right thing to do, are controlled by the superego."

"I see," replied Wendy.

"Don't be so sure," snapped Ralf. "What Professor Boy-Wonder isn't telling you is that the id and superego are always in conflict with one another. They're always present, gnawing away at our psyches."

"All three are a real component of our conscious thought, but I believe that people are most generally dominated by either the id or the superego," said Taylor.

Wendy was enthralled by the concept. "What determines the domination? Why are some people controlled by one and not the other?"

Before Taylor could answer, Ralf was quick to jump in. "When you're born," he said, "the id is the only component present. As you progress through childhood, the ego develops and then the superego."

"That makes sense," said Wendy. "A child is only concerned about his immediate wants and needs. He doesn't really understand the difference between right and wrong until he becomes older."

"Exactly," replied Taylor.

"Fascinating. You might be onto something."

"Well, I didn't come up with it," he said. "Thank Dr. Freud."

"Yeah, right," Ralf said after finishing off his beer, "that's going to do a lot of good."

"And by the way," said Wally, "as evident with Ralfie boy, alcohol tends to bring out the id in all of us."

"I think the whole Freudian thing is a bunch of bunk," said Ralf. "If you ask me, it's just plain stupid. The next thing that you're going to tell me is that I want to have sex with my mom."

Everyone in the room expected Ralf to laugh, but instead he left to get another beer.

"I see that you've drank more than your two-beer limit," said Taylor. "Maybe you should call it a night."

"Maybe he should call his mom," Wally said as everyone at the table laughed.

"Naw," Ralf said with a slurred voice. "I'm going to set a new record. A new Ralfie record. Tonight, it's three beers or pass out trying."

"You're a maverick," said Taylor, still laughing.

"So, Taylor, is that what your experiment is about?"

"Yeah," Taylor replied. "My aim is to prove that we're dominated by one or the other, even in extreme circumstances."

"Extreme circumstances? Like what?"

"Like when the subject's life is threatened."

"Oh, you mean like in war?"

"Sort of. Anytime a person's life in danger."

"So what's your thesis?"

"That in times of danger, survival is the psyche's sole function and, no matter how irrational it may seem to others, the id or superego governs the individual's actions."

"So basically, it's their instinct that reigns, not their intellect," said Wendy.

"Exactly. A person's instinct always rules; it sometimes supersedes logic."

"I think it's old school," said Ralf. "Get with the times, man."

Wally looked at Ralf. "Your mom just called. She needs you at home," he said.

"Shut up," Ralf seethed.

"But it's not always what you'd think," Taylor said. "Some people show a false sense of bravado when they know they're safe. That's why bullies always pick on the weakest kids, because they know that they won't be challenged. My experiment is finding these bullies and then challenging them."

"But how are you doing this? Are you finding bullies and then kicking their asses?" Wally asked.

"Well, sort of. That and a lot of research."

"This sounds like the sort of thing that Dr. Heinrich loves. I bet you'll do well with it. You know how he's always saying that it's our job to make the world a better place."

"I think lots of people will be better off because of it," Taylor said with a wicked grin.

"It sounds interesting. I'd love to read your dissertation," Wendy replied. "When will you be finished?"

"Soon. Very soon."

Chapter 29

*T*he id-dominated psyche sometimes uses passivity as a mask in the natural response to danger. Used by only the most cunning of creatures, the individual's emotional instincts are disguised by submissiveness until opportunity can be exploited and the danger controlled. After the aggressor subscribes to the deception, survival instincts are employed by the individual and true id instincts surface, resulting in a very dangerous animal.

Ratcliff looked up to see the morning sun cresting the nearby red hill. They'll be here soon, he thought. After scouting the area for several weeks, he knew the deer usually moved just after daybreak. On his frequent reconnaissance missions, he'd scattered ample portions of feed in specific areas, increasing the likelihood that the deer would return frequently during archery season. In fact, he couldn't wait to try his new compound bow.

Leaning on a massive branch high in an old hickory tree, he gauged the direction of the cold wind. Fortunately, it was blowing from the north—the same direction the herd typically traveled.

With daybreak came visibility, so he searched the ground below and smiled when he noticed fresh deer tracks in the snow. He was certain that he'd bag one. The conditions were perfect. The deer wouldn't suspect a thing.

Fifteen minutes passed before Ratcliff noticed movement directly ahead of him. It was a nice buck—at least a ten pointer. He was walking alone with his head held high, snorting as he neared the old hickory tree. Ratcliff's heart quickened as he watched the deer approach. If it followed its current path, it would walk just below his tree stand. Easing the bow and arrow into position, he prepared for the easy shot.

When the deer was less than thirty yards away, drawing closer by the moment, Ratcliff realized it was even larger than he first thought. His hands began to shake. The mighty deer's antlers were perfectly symmetrical—a trophy rack of at least twelve points.

The buck abruptly stopped. Startled, his ears twitched as he looked to the east. Ratcliff wasn't sure what the deer had heard, but he knew that it had sensed danger and was about to bolt. Certain that in a split second the deer would be gone, Ratcliff pulled back the string on the compound bow and lined up the shot.

While the deer stared into the distance, Ratcliff found his mark on the deer's chest and pulled back the string one last inch. In an instant, it would all be over. His excitement grew as he realized he'd soon be the talk of the town when he showed off this monster at the check-in station. Who knows, he might even have a state record on his hands. He slowly exhaled and prepared to release the string.

In a flash, Ratcliff's world went black. When he finally opened his eyes again, he realized that he was regaining consciousness, but he wasn't sure how long he'd been out or what had happened. Somehow, he was lying on his back in the snow. A searing pain burned in his right thigh. His first thought was that the branch had broken, but a glance confirmed that the massive branch was still intact. He had no idea why he'd fallen. Confused, he tried to stand. It was at that moment that the revered attorney grasped what had happened.

Ratcliff's right leg buckled from intense pain when he tried to put weight on it. Dropping to his knees, he was taken aback by the amount of blood in the snow. Feeling the wound, he realized that he'd been shot. Ratcliff wondered if a stray bullet, an infrequent yet possible hazard of hunting wildlife on public land, had hit him.

Grabbing his leg with both hands, he tried to suppress the bleeding. Although he didn't think it was life threatening, he knew if he didn't stop the bleeding, it could be. While he searched for something to use as a tourniquet, he grew angry. The asshole who did this would soon learn the power of his might!

"Looks like you've got a nasty wound there," someone said.

"And you've got yourself a nasty lawsuit," Ratcliff replied as he removed the shoelaces from his boot to wrap his leg. As he worked, he carefully watched the man standing about thirty yards away holding a rifle.

"Do you know who I am?" Ratcliff asked with a smirk.

Taylor smiled. "Oh, I'm pretty sure I know who you are. You're Zachariah Ratcliff."

"Then you must also know that you just accidentally shot the most powerful trail lawyer in this state. Soon I'll take everything you have, plus everything you'll ever make in your lifetime."

Taylor laughed. "Well, counselor, I'm sorry, but you are mistaken."

"Mistaken? About what?"

"The shooting," Taylor said, still laughing. "It wasn't accidental."

Ratcliff gasped. He'd made thousands of enemies over the years. There were housewives whom he'd demonized in divorce hearings while defending their cheating spouses; family members of murder victims who saw the killer walk free through Ratcliff's exploitation of insignificant technicalities; even frivolous lawsuits that he spearheaded that took millions from shareholders. The list was endless. He never thought anyone would try to harm him, though. He just assumed they respected and admired his courtroom skills.

"I don't recognize your face," Ratcliff said as he looked for his bow and arrows in the snow. "Are you from one of my trials?"

Taylor shook his head as he moved closer. "I'm shocked that you don't know your enemies better." Sweeping the bow and arrows out of the snow, he threw them toward the snow-covered hillside. Reaching into his jacket, he removed some paperwork. "Perhaps this will help you regain your memory," he said, handing the contracts to Ratcliff.

Ratcliff instantly recognized the papers. "My God! Where did you get these?"

"My associates and I took these from your partner after we took care of him in your office at Strong City."

"And why did you do that?" Ratcliff asked as Taylor snatched the contracts from his hands.

"In case we ever get caught."

"We?" Ratcliff said.

"My associates and me. We're systematically rubbing out all those responsible for the attempted deaths at Redtree. And guess what?"

"What's that?"

"You're next."

"Who are you with? Who are your associates? Is it Gayland?"

Taylor laughed. "No, it's not Gayland. We're saving him for last. He's just starting to feel the heat. We want him to suffer for as long as possible."

"Then who are your associates? Damn it, I demand to know."

Taylor pointed, "They're back behind that hill making sure that no hunter has the misfortune of stumbling onto us. And counselor..."

"Yes."

"You're not in the position to demand anything."

Ratcliff knew he was beat. His only hope was to distract Taylor and reach for the hidden backup pistol in the holster around his chest.

"You're right," Ratcliff said. "You're right and I'm very sorry about Redtree. The people there didn't deserve what happened to them. I only went along with it because Gayland threatened me."

"He's good at that," Taylor said with a smile.

"And remember, I never actually harmed anyone. Gayland's the one who did it. He's the monster you want, not me. I was a peacenik in the sixties, man, I've never hurt anyone."

"No, but you've raped the legal system and prevented thugs like Gayland from getting rightful justice."

Ratcliff looked into Taylor's eyes with sincerity. "You know, son, you're right. I have no excuses. I'm a complete failure in every sense of the word."

"Your sudden insight doesn't have anything to do with the hole in your leg and the 30-06 rifle in my hands, does it?"

Ratcliff smiled. "Maybe a little, but if that's what it takes for me to wake up, then so be it. By the way, would you like a cigarette?"

"No thanks," said Taylor. "We don't know each other well enough."

"Do you mind if I have one?"

Taylor thought for a moment. "Not at all," he said.

Ratcliff slowly unzipped his coveralls and reached inside his goose-down coat. Taylor watched him so closely that Ratcliff was sure he couldn't pull the pistol fast enough to fire it without Taylor blasting him again. He thought for a moment, then pulled out his cigarettes.

"So you've been systematically killing the investors?" Ratcliff asked while placing the cigarette in his mouth.

"Yes."

"I figured that Gayland was behind it."

"I'm fairly certain that he's hired a goon to do it, but we beat him to the punch."

Ratcliff reached back inside his vest jacket.

"Where you takin' those hands?" Taylor asked as he raised the rifle.

"My lighter. I need my lighter."

Taylor nodded his approval. Ratcliff reached to grab the gun. He quickly decided that his only option was to fire the weapon from inside the jacket. It was a long shot, but it was all he had.

"Are you having problems finding it?" Taylor asked.

"Yeah, yeah. My right arm isn't working very well."

"It doesn't really matter anyway," Taylor said and aimed the rifle at the attorney.

"Wait, wait," said Ratcliff. "I'm a man of peace. Can't you at least grant me a cigarette."

"Hurry it up, then," Taylor barked.

"I'm having problems with my arm. I think I'm going into shock. If you could help me, I'd really appreciate it."

Taylor walked toward Ratcliff. As he neared, Ratcliff cocked the hammer on the pistol and turned his body so that the gun was pointing at Taylor. When he was barely five feet away, he squeezed the trigger.

The bullet whizzed by Taylor's head. He immediately aimed the rifle and blasted Ratcliff's left thigh. As Ratcliff moaned in agony, Taylor reached inside Ratcliff's vest to remove the pistol.

"That's an attorney for you," Taylor said, then pressed the contracts against Ratcliff's bleeding thigh, smearing blood all over the first page.

"Why in the hell are you doing that?" asked Ratcliff.

"Just in case Gayland doesn't take us seriously. I don't think that we'll have any problems, but just in case we do, your blood on these contracts should provide the proper horror-show graphics to scare the hell out of him."

Taylor turned and walked back toward the hill.

"Where are you going?" Ratcliff said.

"To my nice warm house," Taylor responded while he continued to walk.

"But I'll bleed to death."

"That or freeze. Either way, it makes no difference to me."

"You can't leave me like this!" Ratcliff howled.

Taylor ignored his screams and continued to walk to the hill. Along the way, he gathered Ratcliff's bow and arrows.

When Taylor finally reached the hill, Elijah and Keith joined him.

"I see you didn't finish him off," Elijah said.

"I thought I'd let him suffer," Taylor said. "Did you see anyone?"

"No," Elijah and Keith said in unison.

"You realize that it's very barbaric of you to leave a wounded man," said Keith. "He's suffering and I think it's appalling."

Elijah was quick to grab the bow and arrow from Taylor's hands. "For once, the woman's right," he said. "Besides, I need some practice." Loading the bow with an arrow, he aimed it at Ratcliff, who was still screaming some seventy yards away.

"That's not what I intended," spoke Keith.

"Not to worry," Elijah said, as he skillfully released the arrow. A breath later, the screaming stopped.

"He's not suffering any more," said Elijah.

Chapter 30

T aylor, Keith, and Elijah were furiously running toward
Running Bear Cliff, just a few hundred yards ahead. As
they advanced, Taylor heard the bullets from the lawmen's guns
shattering rocks behind him as they struck the canyon walls. He
swore he could feel the warmth of bullets ricocheting in every
direction around him.

There was no time to think. His instincts were guiding him. The
persistent lawmen were closing fast. Their only hope was to reach
the ravine that ran through the canyon near Running Bear Cliff—
only there could they find refuge.

After sprinting for several minutes, Taylor passed Running Bear
Cliff and turned the corner around a huge boulder. Since he'd finally
reached the bottom of the shallow ravine, he paused for a moment
to catch his breath. He quickly studied the deep gorge curving up
the side the mountain. Since he'd hiked the landscape many times
as a child he knew it well.

"We should be safe up there," he said, pointing. "It will be rough
to get through the big rocks, but if we can make it around the bend,
they'll never find us. There are a thousand places to hide after we
pass the turn."

As Taylor further studied the ravine, he noticed that he couldn't
hear either Keith or Elijah behind him. Alarmed, he spun around.
They were nowhere to be seen. He slowly walked out of the ravine
and carefully slid past the huge boulder. He looked across the rocky
terrain where he'd just been. The lawmen continued their advance,
but Keith and Elijah had disappeared.

Without a weapon, Taylor had few options. His only hope was

to calm himself and devise a solution. Walking to Running Bear Cliff, he studied the water some two hundred feet below. The world suddenly turned surreal.

The water was no longer clear and slow moving. Instead, the blood-red river churned and streamed rapidly down eroding banks. Shocked, Taylor realized the sky was neon-green, the once white canyon walls and floor were blue, and even his own skin had changed to orange.

A high-pitched shriek pierced the air. The sound was so intense that Taylor had to cover his ears. He turned toward the ravine to find its source, but saw nothing but rock. The shriek blasted again. This time Taylor knew the sound was coming from behind him. He turned, taking two steps toward the edge of the cliff. A young injured eagle stared at him from a perch on the rocks of the opposite bank of the river. The wounded eagle opened its beak and once again, the air was filled with a shrill screech. Taylor was awestruck.

"That can't be," he said. "That simply can't be."

In the distance behind him, Taylor heard his name. He quickly turned to walk back to the large boulder. He quietly peeked around the massive rock and spotted Keith and Elijah casually walking in front of the approaching lawmen barely two hundred yards away.

"Go over!" Keith yelled while he continued toward Taylor. "Go over the edge!"

Keith and Elijah were a mere seventy-five yards away. They now walked briskly forward, waving their arms as if they were motioning him to jump off Running Bear Cliff.

Taylor stepped backward, toward the cliff. Keith nodded. "Go over!" he cried.

Dumbfounded, he couldn't make sense of the world. The armed lawmen walked steadily behind Keith and Elijah, but seemed to be in no hurry whatsoever to apprehend Taylor, who was now out in the open. The lawmen easily could have shot Taylor, Elijah, and Keith, but they didn't seem to care.

"Jump!" Elijah screamed.

Taylor turned and looked at the cliff. There's no way, he thought. He'd have to jump over one hundred feet horizontally to reach the opposite bank. It was impossible. He'd surely fall the two hundred plus feet into the river.

"Damn it Taylor, jump!" Elijah screamed.

Taylor was confused but realized that it was time to cut his losses and find safety. He would be of no help to Elijah and Keith if he was apprehended with them. Taylor ran back to the ravine and began scurrying up the rocks.

"Taylor!" a voice bellowed from the heavens. As Taylor looked up, he began shaking violently. He tried with all his might to stabilize himself but was helpless. Angered, he looked to the sky and shouted: "What do you want from me?"

"I just want you to wake up," Wendy said. "It's almost time for dinner."

Disoriented, Taylor jumped from the couch. "Where the hell have I been?" he barked.

"You've been asleep on the couch."

Taylor walked in circles, trying to acclimate himself.

"Did you have a bad dream?"

Taylor rubbed his eyes and let out a deep breath. "Yeah, you could say that."

"Are you all right?" She asked.

"Yeah, yeah, I'm all right. It just seemed so real."

"What were you dreaming about?"

"I think it was a vision."

"Why do you say that?"

"Because....It all seemed so real."

"What happened?"

"I was back on Running Bear Cliff with Elijah and Keith. We were running from someone. Elijah and Keith were about to be apprehended. They told me to jump over the cliff."

"You couldn't survive that fall. It's too far to the water."

"I know. I couldn't understand any of it."

"You sure you weren't smoking some peyote?" Wendy joked.

"And then I saw this eagle," said Taylor.

"Like the one we saw when we were there and I took pictures?"

"Yeah, but it was younger, much younger, and it looked sick or hurt. It just sat there, squawking on the rocks."

"I wonder what that means."

"It let out these shrieks that were incredibly loud. It was so intense I had to cover my ears."

Wendy thought for a moment. "Maybe your subconscious mind is trying to tell you something."

"Maybe so," Taylor said. "It got weirder. The river was rapidly flowing with what appeared to be blood. And the colors... Everything looked different—the sky was green, the walls of the canyon were blue."

"You say that Elijah and Keith were there?"

"Yeah."

"Could you tell who you were running from?"

"No, why?"

"One of the famous chiefs, I can't remember which one, had a vision before Custer came to Little Big Horn," said Wendy. "He saw the white soldiers coming. They were upside down."

"That was Sitting Bull."

"Well, maybe you're right. Maybe you had a vision."

"Yeah. Maybe so."

"Now tell me this," said Wendy.

"What?"

"Why the hell would anyone be tracking you down?"

Taylor laughed gently so as not to arouse suspicion. "It must have just been a crazy dream."

"Must have. How long have you been asleep?"

"All afternoon, I guess."

Wendy walked to the kitchen and looked through the refrigerator. "I guess you know the weather broke and the snow's finally melting. We'll be back in school tomorrow."

"I figured so. I knew it was too good to last forever."

"You can say that again."

"Why are you all made up?" Taylor asked after noticing Wendy's high-heel shoes and dress. "Have you been interviewing for jobs?"

Wendy looked to Taylor without replying. Taylor sensed that she was about to tell him something he didn't want to hear.

"I went back to work at the bank," Wendy said in a soft voice.

Taylor felt a familiar anger rumbling within. He walked to the kitchen table and sat. "And what prompted this?"

"My dad's putting a lot of pressure on me. That, and well, Gayland called the answering machine at my apartment and said that he really missed me and wanted me to come to work."

"He really missed you, eh? He said that?" Taylor's blood pressure soared.

"I've known him my whole life, Taylor. He's almost like a dad to me."

"So what was the other night? Almost like incest?"

Wendy shook her head, then closed the door to the refrigerator. "He told me today that he doesn't remember any of what happened the other night. He said that sometimes he blacks out and does stupid things."

Taylor let out a cynical laugh. "And you believe that?"

"I don't know what to believe! None of this makes much sense." Wendy sat at the table across from Taylor. "I just want to graduate and move out of here. I'm tired of dealing with all this!"

Realizing that she was about to break, Taylor thought it was time to change the mood. "Look, I know that you're in a difficult situation. I'm just very concerned for your safety," he said in a calm voice.

"I know you are and I appreciate that. But you've got to understand that this is not my choice. I'm not doing this for me—it's for my parents."

"Then I guess we don't have many options."

"No, we don't."

Taylor thought for a moment. "I'll agree to this, but only under one condition. If he so much as lays a finger on you, you promise to call me immediately and I'll be there in a flash. And it won't be pretty, either."

"Understood."

"Then it's settled," Taylor said in an upbeat tone.

Wendy stood and walked to the kitchen sink. She leaned against the counter and placed her hands on her face.

"Is something wrong?" Taylor asked.

Wendy stared at the floor in silence.

"Wendy, is something wrong?"

"Yes, Taylor," Wendy said in a weak voice. "Something is very wrong."

"What?"

Wendy moved her hands down to her side and nervously tapped her fingers on the counter. "After work, I went by my apartment to pick up a textbook."

"So?"

"I uh…I think someone's been inside my apartment," she said as her hands began to shake.

Taylor had never seen Wendy so frightened. He placed his arm around her and held her tight. "Are you sure?" he asked.

Wendy nodded. "Yeah. Do you remember the picture I have of you from the psychology banquet last year?"

"Yeah."

"It was in the toilet. Somebody defecated on it."

Taylor smiled. "That's flattering. Must be a fan of mine. What else did you find?"

"All my panties are missing from my drawers," Wendy said, then completely broke into tears. "My God, Taylor, I'm really scared."

Taylor held her even tighter. "Don't be. Fear is the enemy. It restricts our ability to conquer our problems. If you give into the fear, you're defeated."

"Well it's not so easy for me to be brave."

"But you must. Don't worry about him. I'll take care of it."

Wendy wiped her eyes with a tissue. "How?" she asked.

"Fight fire with fire. This man must be dealt with. You do understand that, don't you?"

"Shouldn't we go to the police?"

Taylor walked to the table and looked Wendy straight in the eyes. "He's a very evil man who's doing business with other evil men. This group is above the law. The only justice that will be imposed will be by our own hands."

"What are you talking about? What evil men?"

Taylor shook his head. "Just believe what I say."

Intrigued, Wendy wasn't about to stop asking questions. "Does this have anything to do with you pulling a pistol on me when I drove up behind you on campus the other day?"

"Let me ask you a question."

"Shoot."

"Do you trust me?"

"That's a stupid question," Wendy replied. "Of course I trust you."

"I don't mean boyfriend-girlfriend trust. Do you trust me with absolute faith?"

"You mean with my life?" asked Wendy.

"Yes."

Wendy thought for a moment. "Yes, yes I do."

"Then you must also believe that I place your best interests in front of mine. Correct?"

"Yes. But I don't understand why you can't just tell me what the hell's going on."

"That's why you have to trust me. I don't want you involved in any of it, not even the slightest knowledge."

"But maybe I can help. Maybe I can be of use somehow."

"I'm sorry, but no. There's too much at stake here. Your involvement will only complicate matters."

"Is this why you've been out 'till the wee hours with Elijah and Keith?"

Taylor sighed. "I can't tell you."

"So all you'll tell me is that some terrible man, who's involved with other terrible men doing terrible things, is stalking me. And we can't go to the police because these terrible men are above the law?"

"That's right," replied Taylor.

"In order for me to defend myself, if need be, would you answer just one question?"

Taylor thought for a moment. "Okay."

"Is Kyle Gayland involved with these terrible men?"

"Yes," Taylor responded. "He sure is."

Chapter 31

S mith is on the stand tomorrow," Lewis said while he paced. "I believe his testimony will significantly sway the jury."

"I wouldn't bank on Smith. After all, he is a convict. He'll get torn to pieces on cross examination."

The young district attorney smiled as he crossed back and forth in front of Jennings' desk. "Yes, there certainly is a credibility issue, but I think the jury will buy it. He seems to be a nice kid, clean cut and educated. He just got caught running with the wrong crowd."

Jennings rolled his eyes. "He got caught running three kilos of blow across state lines. He is the wrong crowd."

"That doesn't matter." Lewis shook his head and gazed at Jennings. "He's our only link and he's willing to testify that he ran drugs for Finken in the past."

Jennings softly lowered his head onto the desk. He'd seen it before—a relatively young lawyer looking to make a name with a massive media exposure case. The taste of power was so intoxicating that it distracted the focus of the trail.

"Look, Lewis," Jennings said calmly. "This is the first time you've ever gone up against attorneys of this caliber. Don't take them lightly. They fight dirty."

"I beg your pardon," snorted Lewis. "I've successfully tried many cases during my career. I'm not intimidated by them one bit."

"And you shouldn't be, but the bottom line is that they're going to pull out all the stops. Let's face it, these are unusual circumstances. We normally don't try cases of this caliber around here."

"We've got the shell casing and the murder weapon. Finken has no plausible alibi and he has a motive."

"Our motive is weak. We haven't found any drugs," said Jennings.

"That's why we have Smith."

Jennings shook his head. "I'm just not so sure. Finken has a lot of money and a lot of stroke. This isn't going to be easy."

"Trust me," said Lewis. "We conducted a strong investigation and have solid proof. I'm not scared of Pinkus and Newman. These Hollywood types intimidate and throw their weight around in courtrooms in California, but not here. Not in my backyard. Everything is going according to plan. Is there anything else we need to talk about?"

Jennings felt a glimmer of hope that the boring meeting would soon be over. "No, I don't think so. That pretty much covers everything," he replied.

"Good. Now, pertaining to your concerns about these high-profile lawyers that we're up against, I'd like to tell you about an event that occurred early in my career," Lewis said. He smiled and suddenly became animated like a grandfather telling fishing stories. "You see, I was fresh out of law school and had just passed the boards. I was working for a district attorney down in Mississippi."

Jennings didn't hear a word, he merely nodded randomly as Lewis retold the story he'd heard a hundred times in the past. Each time, the story would get a little better, a little more self-glorifying. Disgusted, he rubbed his eyes, then fell into his usual escape. He visualized living his childhood dream—riding a sorrel horse through lush green pastures, driving a herd of cattle across the open range. As he swatted a horsefly from the young gelding's neck, he laughed because he was far away from the district attorney, the drug dealers, and all the other day-to-day agonies of police work.

Sensing that he was losing his audience, Lewis slammed his hand down on the desk to emphasize a point. The sound snapped Jennings from his trance, but his mind still wandered. He remembered himself as a young man entering the police academy, promising that he would retire on the day his twenty years was served. He'd buy a little farm outside of town and raise cattle and horses. The simple life awaited.

Jennings' twenty-year anniversary had come and gone several years ago, yet he remained. Since that time, he constantly told himself that he'd stay until his passion to serve was overshadowed by the stress of the job. Over the past several months, that stress had started to strangle him.

He still reported to the office before seven and most always stayed until after five, but his heart was elsewhere. Each time he witnessed an attorney twist the law and win freedom for the puke they represented, he felt a little more of his passion escape.

Lewis slammed his hand on the desk again. Jennings decided that his mind had roamed enough for now and his most important concern was the matter at hand. His dream was a demon in need of reckoning someday, but not that day. Although he wanted to go home, he continued to politely nod and pretend to listen.

"Have I got some news for you," someone called from the hallway outside his office. He looked up from his desk as Quana stepped through the door. Eager to end the meeting with Lewis, Jennings stood and smiled. "Hello, Quana. What brings you out this way?"

Quana looked at Lewis, who was still rambling about his days in Mississippi. After completing his long-winded sentence, Lewis finally stopped and glanced at Quana.

"Can I help you?" asked the district attorney.

"I'm sorry," Quana replied. "I didn't realize you were in a meeting. I'll wait outside until you're...."

"Oh no, no. There's no meeting here. We were just shootin' the shit, right counselor?" replied Jennings.

Lewis was obviously disappointed. "Well, I guess we could talk about it some other time, but..."

"Right, right," Jennings interrupted as he walked around the desk and gently grabbed Lewis' arm. "We'll talk later," he said, then politely led him out of his office.

Jennings shut the door and returned to his seat. "You don't know how thankful I am that you came by. I was considering shooting myself so I could have an excuse to leave."

"Glad I could help," replied Quana.

"So what's happening? What brings you to Carson?"

"There's been another hit."

Jennings' eyes widened. "Really? Where?"

"Durham. It's a little town about twenty-five miles northwest of Ducotey."

"Who was the victim?"

"A big-shot lawyer named Ratcliff. Some hunters found him

earlier today."

Jennings stroked his chin. "Ratcliff. I think I've heard of him. I believe he represented some drug dealers in Carson once. As I recall, he got them off. I remember him as cunning and very shrewd. A real son-of-a-bitch."

"That'd be him. A complete scumbag. He was high on many people's shit lists."

"Where did it happen?"

"In a wooded area, a few miles outside of town. Apparently, he was out hunting. He was shot by a high powered rifle in both legs and then shot through the heart with an arrow."

"Damn," said Jennings.

"I'll say," replied Quana. "Someone knew what they were doing. The arrow went all the way through and stuck to the tree he was leaning against."

While Quana spoke, Jennings grabbed a pencil and began jotting notes. "Did they find any shell casings or footprints?" he asked.

"That's where it gets difficult," Quana said as he sat back in his chair and crossed his legs. "Much of the snow has melted, so the tracks aren't very distinct. Besides that, there have been countless hunters in and out of the area. There's too many footprints to gather any hard evidence."

"What about casings?"

"They've found shells from several different weapons, but remember, it's a high traffic public hunting area," replied Quana. "There's various shells scattered all over the place."

Jennings continued to write down details. When finished, he briefly reviewed the notes, then looked at Quana. "Do you think it's related to the others?"

"The sheriff isn't sure, but I have my suspicions."

"Why's that?"

"I think it fits their style. They try to leave a message."

"What's the message here?" asked Jennings.

As Quana collected his thoughts, he sat up in his chair. "They wanted to leave no doubt that it wasn't an accident. It was murder. We're not dealing with locals here, Jennings. These guys are professionals."

"I agree. They leave little evidence; it's always very clean. But what makes you so sure that this case is related to the others?"

"We can rule it out as being an accident, right?"

"I'd think. The odds of accidentally being shot with both an arrow and a rifle are astronomical."

"So we both agree that it's probably murder?"

"I would think."

"Then why did they use the arrow?" asked Quana. "They could've shot him with a rifle from a hundred yards and left hardly any signs. Instead, they were bold and daring enough to use an arrow, too."

"That makes sense," added Jennings. "They were letting the police know that they could have made it look like an accident if they wanted, but instead, they made a statement."

"Since hunting season's open, they knew that there would be a great deal of traffic in that area. Lots of footprints."

Jennings stroked his chin. "They may not be just sending a message to the police. It might be that they enjoy terrorizing their victims before they hit them."

"And there are probably others out there who know they're next," said Quana.

"Could be. Look at the profile of the victim—another small-town-wealthy man who's despised by many. It adds up."

"I'm almost sure now that these are professional jobs carried out by two to three people," said Quana. "Probably three, judging by the amount of casings that have been found. It's all beginning to make sense."

"I agree."

"I'm surprised you haven't been called to Durham yet."

"They'll probably sit on it for a while before they call us in. That or they're turning it over to the feds."

"Naw, it's too soon for that. It will take awhile for the locals in Durham to put all this together. When they do, they'll call in you guys first."

"I hope," Jennings said. "I just wish we had more to go on. We're not exactly blazing the path with new leads."

"It will come," replied Quana. "Remember, patience is a virtue."

Jennings pushed his chair backward, then placed his feet on the desk. "Yeah, that's what I tell myself," he said.

"I heard Finken brought in Pinkus and Newman for his trial."

"I guess you've been watching the news, huh?"

"Yep. It's all they've been talking about. Will you get a

conviction?"

Jennings stared at the glass wall above his door for a few moments, then let out a deep sigh. "If there's any justice in the world, then yeah. Having said that, we probably won't."

"You're not letting this get to you, are you?"

"A little, I suppose." He pushed his chair closer to the desk, then leaned close to Quana.

"Everyday I go into that courtroom, I wait for a bomb to go off," Jennings said in a low voice. "We conducted our investigation by the book. We made no mistakes that I can see, yet I know that those vultures will search and search until they find a small insignificant technicality to exploit."

"I hope they don't find anything, but you're right, they'll use every trick in the book, you can bet your ass on that."

"I've seen it all before. Rich scumbags like Finken hire the best lawyers money can buy, then boom, they walk. It's such a shame."

"Don't give up the faith. You're due for break."

"I'll try to remember that," Jennings said.

Quana stood and walked to the door. "I've got to be getting on back to the house."

"Me, too."

"Have you and Carol made plans to come to Ducotey?"

"Nothing definite, but I'm sure we'll be heading that way soon."

"We'll be looking forward to it," Quana said while walking out of the office.

Jennings grabbed his coat and briefcase, then turned off the lights to his office. As he closed his office door, he suddenly remembered something. He looked down the hall to see if Quana was still in the building.

"Quana."

"Yeah," replied Quana from down the hall.

"Do you have any horses?"

"Of course. Everyone in Ducotey has at least one. Why?"

"Does he buck?"

Quana laughed. "They all buck."

"Think he'd go easy on an old white detective?"

"Probably not, but we can try anyway."

"Then it's a date," Jennings said with a smile.

Chapter 32

Wendy's temper flared when she realized it was already past 6:30 p.m. As she filed the last record into the massive metal drawers near the safe, her anger became so intense that she could actually feel the heat throbbing in her forehead.

Gathering her things, she couldn't help but notice that Gayland was in his office, a rarity at that hour. Ignoring him, she put on her winter coat and headed for the front doors. Half way across the parking lot, she suddenly stopped to open her backpack. A quick look confirmed that she'd forgotten her sociology textbook, which she needed for a study session later in the evening. Turning back, she went back into the bank.

When she passed Gayland's office, she heard him speaking on the phone.

"Yes, give me room number thirteen," he said into the handset.

Wendy quickly retrieved the book from her desk and began walking back to the front doors. As she passed Gayland's office, she glanced inside. The moment he saw her, his face turned white and he quickly hung up the phone.

"Wendy?" said Gayland, who appeared mortified.

"Yeah."

"I thought you'd already left."

"I did. I had to come back because I forgot one of my textbooks," Wendy said and held the book for Gayland to see.

"Oh."

"I've got to go," she said and continued walking.

"Goodnight," he called.

"Yeah," Wendy said in disgust. Her toes curled when the cold water from the parking lot's melted snow soaked through her dress shoes and touched her skin. The unpleasant sensation sent chills up her spine, aggravating her already foul mood. She squinted and walked hurriedly toward her car, which sat in the darkness on the far end of the bank's empty parking lot.

Neither the homework that she had to do, nor the hours of studying for the next day's exam had peaked Wendy's ire. She was upset because she'd told Gayland that morning that she needed to leave early to study and wrap up a class project. Gayland gladly agreed, then just as she was about to leave, handed her an enormous stack of paperwork to file and told her it had to be done before she left for the evening. The moment she saw the stack of papers she knew the job would take hours, which proved to be true. Maybe Taylor was right, she thought as she made her way to her car. Maybe it's time to move on, regardless of the fallout that her parents might suffer.

After the long trek through the puddles of water that were turning to ice on the pavement, Wendy finally reached her car. With her thumb on the discharge button of a mace canister, she walked a circle around the vehicle to check for anything suspicious. As she walked past the passenger's side front door, her heart quickened when she saw a shadow near the front bumper. She stood still, frozen.

Every muscle in Wendy's body tightened and seemed unresponsive. Her muscles were so tense that she wasn't even sure she could push the mace trigger. The world stopped moving. Time stood still. Her worst fear was at hand. That terrible man on the phone had found her.

After a few moments, the numbness in her body began to fade. With her thumb poised on the trigger of the mace, her confidence started to return. To her relief, Wendy found nothing unusual near the front bumper. She let out a long sigh then quickly walked to the driver's door and peered through the window. After inspecting both the front and back seats, she unlocked the door, jumped in and started the engine. As she pulled the car out of the parking lot, she turned and noticed a yellow-colored vehicle parked at the opposite end of the parking lot turn on its lights and drive toward her.

As Wendy drove through the salt-covered streets toward her apartment, she kept a constant eye on her surroundings. She steered the car onto a side street and, after driving a few blocks, noticed that the yellow car appeared to be following her.

After Wendy reached the apartment complex, she parked her car and cautiously left the vehicle. As she crossed the lot, she realized that the light by her front door wasn't on, leaving the area near her door completely dark. Again, fear gripped her. She was certain that something was wrong. She distinctly remembered leaving the light on when she left. Had the man who made the crude phone calls returned again?

Wendy jumped back in the driver's seat and started the engine. As the car crept forward, she remembered Taylor telling her to be strong and not to be consumed with fear. After a few moments of contemplation, she put the car in park, closed her eyes and breathed deeply. She soon felt the fear drifting away. She opened her eyes and looked at her apartment. Everything seemed normal, except the lack of light around the door. She was less troubled when she realized that it could have burnt out on its own. After all, since she'd lived in the apartment, she'd never actually replaced the light bulb.

She took a deep breath, grabbed her mace and slowly walked to her apartment. Along the way, she noticed a yellow car slowly enter the apartment complex's parking lot. Was it the same car that followed her? She wasn't sure. She quickly made her way to her apartment door. In complete darkness, she reached into her pocket, retrieved her keys, and placed the can of mace on the window sill. As she struggled to find the key to the deadbolt, she heard something moving in the darkness, around the corner of the building.

"Is somebody there?" she asked in a weak voice.

No one replied. She held her key ring close to her face, trying in vain to locate the correct key.

"You've been avoiding me," a man whispered from around the corner.

Wendy dropped her keys. Her arms felt as heavy as lead pipes as she struggled to wrap her fingers around the canister of mace. A hand suddenly grasped her throat. As she tried to scream, the assailant quickly pulled her close and placed his hand over her mouth. Grabbing her by the shoulders, he dragged her around the dark corner of the building.

Knowing that her screams were muted, Wendy bit the assailant's hand with all her might. As he recoiled in pain, Wendy wheeled to face him. By the light of the moon, she saw the silhouette of his face. Instinctively, she pushed the can of mace close to his eyes and pressed as hard as she could. He moaned in agony, letting go of her so that he could rub his eyes with both hands. Recognizing her opportunity, she kicked him squarely in the testicles. He dropped to his knees in pain.

Running, she grabbed her car keys and bolted to her car. After locking the door, she sped out of the parking lot, sliding into the street. A glance in her rear-view mirror confirmed that the yellow car was still sitting in the parking lot with its engine running.

Pushing up to his knees, Joe Escartes used one hand to wipe the mace from his eyes and the other to soothe his testicles. He was in so much pain he wasn't sure that he could stand upright, but knew that his intended victim was probably on her way to the police. He had to leave the premises quickly, so he stumbled to his car in agony. As soon as he was behind the wheel, he grabbed a towel to wipe the mace from his eyes. Starting the car, he drove into the night with the yellow car following at a distance.

"Are you all right?"

Wendy shrugged. "I'm not sure."

Taylor had never seen her so shaken. She'd cried most of the makeup off her face, but more importantly, in the hour since he returned home, she had been uncharacteristically quiet. With one of his mother's soft hand towels, he dried her tears. "You're safe now."

Wendy gulped a glass of water. "Did you find out where he lives?" she asked.

"Yeah. He's staying at a motel on the other side of town. I followed him all the way. I even know his room number."

Still holding the glass in her hand, she stared at the floor. Suddenly, she began crying uncontrollably.

Taylor wrapped her in his arms.

"I can't believe he touched me," Wendy cried. "Thank God I had the mace."

"I'm sorry I wasn't there," said Taylor. "By the time I realized that something was wrong, you were running to your car. Don't worry though, I wouldn't have let him get very far."

"I was so scared."

"It's over now. And what's more, he'll never attack you again. I promise."

"How can you be so sure?"

"Trust me, he'll never bother your again."

"What makes you so sure? Did you go to the police?"

"The police are of no use to us."

"Why?"

"For starters, it was dark. Could you make a positive identification?"

Wendy shook her head. "No, I couldn't see much at all, except when I kicked him in the nuts. But even then, I couldn't tell if it was the same guy we saw in the restaurant."

"Then how are we going to give a description? We have nothing to offer the police. Besides, he's affiliated with Gayland. He's above the law..."

"Wait a minute," Wendy interrupted. "I just realized how he knew when I was leaving."

Taylor was puzzled. "What?"

"That son-of-a-bitch!" seethed Wendy.

"What are you talking about?"

"I asked Gayland if I could leave early today. I told him I had a test and some projects due."

"So?"

"He said that would be fine, but just as I was about to leave this afternoon, he gave me a bunch of paperwork to file. It took me a long time. When I finally finished, it was after dark."

"Are you sure he just wasn't being a shithead?"

"Oh no, it was more than that," Wendy said while she paced the kitchen floor. "Those files were tax records for clients. They've been sitting on his desk for months. There was no hurry."

"That is strange."

"And another thing," said Wendy, now fuming. "In the four years that I've worked for him, tonight's the first time he's stayed past three o'clock."

"It does look odd. And I wouldn't put it past him."

"There's something else," Wendy said in a softer voice. "After I left the bank, I realized that I had forgotten one of my textbooks, so I had to go back to my desk. As I walked by his office, I heard him talking."

Wendy's face suddenly turned pale.

"What did he say?" asked Taylor.

"You said that you followed that bastard back to his hotel room, right?"

"Yes."

"Did you get a look at the room number where he's staying?"

"Yes."

"Was it room number thirteen?"

"How did you know that?"

"Dear God," Wendy said in disbelief.

"What is it?"

"As I walked by his office, I heard Gayland make a call. He was asking for room thirteen."

"Holy shit!" said Taylor. "What else did he say?"

"Nothing. When he saw me, he turned as white as a ghost. He acted guilty and said that he thought I had already left. He was beside himself. I didn't think much of it. I was pissed off and just wanted to get out of there."

Taylor sat beside Wendy, who, once again, began to cry.

"That son-of-a-bitch," said Taylor.

"That's why he stayed so late and gave me those papers to file," she sobbed. "He was keeping me there until after dark. And then he called that thug to tell him that I was leaving. That's how that man knew when I would be there."

"He's an evil man, Wendy."

"He's everything you've been telling me. God only knows what that man would have done to me," she said and wiped her nose. "I'll never set foot inside that bank again."

"What about your parents? They won't be very happy to hear that you've quit."

"When I tell them what he did tonight, they'll understand. That and my dad will kill him."

Taylor grabbed Wendy's shoulders and turned her to face him. "That's why you're not going to tell anyone about this. Not the police, not your parents, not even your friends."

"I don't understand. We've got to tell the police. They're the only ones who can stop him."

"Remember, it was dark. You can't positively ID the guy. We have no physical evidence that anything happened."

"But what about the phone call that Gayland made to the hotel?"

"You know he'll deny that."

Wendy thought for a moment. "But there's got to be something we can do."

"Not with Gayland. He's too big, too powerful. If we tell the police about Joe Escartes, it won't do any good. If they were to arrest him, Gayland would have lawyers swarming all over this. Besides that, Escartes is an experienced hitman and knows how to play the cops."

Wendy was aghast. "A hitman?"

"Yeah, a hitman."

"What do you mean?"

"I mean he kills people for money. He's a hired gun."

"Does he work for Gayland?"

"He does, but that's all you need to know right now."

"I can't believe this. I just can't believe this."

"You must."

Wendy thrust her fists on the table. "What am I supposed to do? Wait for it to happen again so we can get some evidence?"

Taylor walked to the phone. "Of course not. Go take a shower then hit the books."

"Who are you calling?"

"Some friends."

"Who?"

"Elijah and Keith," replied Taylor.

Wendy looked at Taylor suspiciously. "Why are you calling them?"

"I need their help."

"Taylor, please don't go and get yourself hurt. This man sounds dangerous."

"So are my friends."

Chapter 33

Gayland slowly bumped the green Suburban over the rusted cattle guard that marked the entrance to his farm. With a disturbed, distant look on his face, he traveled down the gravel road leading to the old white farmhouse and barnyard. At the end of the road, he never pressed the brakes. The vehicle slowly drove through the beautiful white picket fence surrounding the house, stopping only when it crashed into the cement porch.

Unfazed by the incident, Gayland eased the Suburban into Park and stumbled out of the SUV. After practically crawling up the concrete porch steps, he sat on the ancient wooden rocking chair and lowered his head into his hands. The chipped paint on the floor held his attention until he drifted off to sleep.

"Gayland!" thundered a voice from above. "Wake up, damn it!"

Startled, Gayland jumped to his feet. "What? What is it?" he said in an effort to gain his bearings.

Peat looked at Gayland warily. "Have you been drinking?"

Gayland pulled out a handkerchief and wiped his brow. "Yeah, I had a long night."

"Does that have anything to do with why you called my secretary this morning and arranged this emergency meeting?"

"Uh, yeah, it sure does," Gayland said as he reached into his pocket to retrieve a set of keys. He unlocked the door to the farmhouse and stepped inside.

"I was afraid you were going to say that," Peat said, following Gayland through the house into the kitchen. Peat watched as he filled an old jelly jar with water and slumped into a chair at the kitchen table. He seemed fascinated with the bits of debris floating in his glass. "What's the matter?" Peat asked, gingerly sitting in a brittle wooden chair at his side.

"You know, when I foreclosed on this place ten years ago, I promised myself that I'd hook it up to the rural water system and plug that damned gypsum-infested water well."

"Well?"

"I'm still drinking gyp water. I've done a lot to improve the place, huh?"

Peat knew Gayland was deliberately making meaningless conversation in order to postpone facing the issue at hand, since he had witnessed the maneuver several times over the years. As always, he decided to play along. "Who was the poor bastard that you took this place from?"

"A farmer by the name of Flockett," Gayland said with a somber face. "Cattle prices fell something terrible that year. He missed a couple of payments. I'd always wanted this place so I moved in swiftly with the foreclosure."

Peat smiled. "Yeah, I've done that a few times in my day, too. The look on their faces when you serve the papers is just priceless."

Gayland's eyes turned misty and he stared at the wooden table as he talked. "He and his family had no place to go. All they had left after the auction was an old beat-up pickup truck and half a tank of gas," Gayland said and took a sip of water. "His family had been on this property since before the land run. Close to one hundred years. They had one bad year and I took it from them. One bad year."

Peat was surprised. He'd never seen Gayland in such an emotional state.

"Don't you go growing yourself a sense of decency on me," Peat said, brashly. "It would have been a very foolish business decision for you not to do what you did. Besides, you don't control the price of commodities. It's not your fault they went under."

Gayland pulled a flask of whiskey from his coat pocket. He unscrewed the top and took a pull. "Maybe I should have had some compassion. Hell, it was Christmas."

"You foreclosed on that poor bastard at Christmas?"

Gayland nodded and had another drink from the flask.

"You're a legend," Peat said with admiration. With a smile, he patted Gayland's leg. "In fact, you're an inspiration to bankers everywhere…"

"I'm a damned robot," Gayland said, then wiped his eyes. "A goddamned robot."

"What's gotten into you? You stop feeling sorry for yourself this second," Peat barked. "That family got what was coming to them."

Gayland poured another shot directly into his mouth. "Peaty, old boy, we're about to get what's coming to us."

Peat was overcome by a sense of impending doom. He felt like a great monster had reached inside him and violently squeezed out every drop of courage in his body. "What are you talking about?" he weakly asked.

"Ratcliff is dead," Gayland replied.

"No shit?"

"No shit."

Distraught, Peat reached across the table for the flask of whiskey. As he drew it back, he realized that his hand was trembling. "Did Escartes do it?"

"I'm not sure," Gayland said. "Make no mistake, though. He was murdered."

Peat took a long shot from the flask. "How do you know?"

The blissful burn of alcohol had apparently revived Gayland's spirits. Seeming more himself, he cleared his throat and explained, "He was out hunting. When they found him, he'd been shot twice with a rifle and once through the heart with an arrow. I seriously doubt it was a hunting accident."

"When did you find out?"

"Late last night. As soon as I got wind of it, I went to Escartes' hotel room. I knocked on the door for a good twenty minutes. He never answered. There was a Do Not Disturb sign on the doorknob. I guess he didn't want to be bothered."

"Oh my God. I thought you told him to back off."

"I did. Evidently he doesn't listen very well."

Peat's hands were shaking violently. "Do you think he'll come after us next?" he asked in a shaky voice. "Hell, aside from Hempshaw, we're the only ones left."

"I don't put anything past him. But I do know one thing. If he doesn't get your cut of the money very soon, the odds of us being hit next will greatly increase."

"I'll get it, I'll get it. Don't worry, I'll find a way. Do you think he's still upset?"

Gayland grabbed the flask from Peat's hand and took another shot. "I'm doing my best to subdue him. He's been hot on the trail of my part-time secretary so last night, I kept her at the bank until after dark, then I called him and told him she was headed home."

"Did that appease him?"

"I don't know. I went by his room again this morning and knocked until my knuckles bled. He never answered."

"Maybe he shacked up at your secretary's apartment. Maybe that's where he was all night," Peat said with forced optimism.

Gayland stroked his chin. "Could be. She didn't show up for work this morning. Maybe they hit it off."

"I'll bet they did. He's probably in a much better mood now."

"We have another concern," Gayland said.

Peat was aghast. "You mean there's more?"

"I don't think it's anything to worry about too much, but our friend in Ducotey is becoming a problem."

"What friend?" Peat asked, still shaking.

"Hempshaw."

"Holy shit again."

"Stop worrying so much," Gayland said with reassurance.

"Stop worrying? All we need now is to have that crazy sumbitch after us, too. I've heard about him. They say he's nuttier than squirrel shit."

Gayland padded Peat on the back. "Everything will be all right."

Peat wasn't convinced. "What else did he say? Did he mention my name?"

"No, he didn't mention your name. He was just upset about some things."

Gripped in fear, Peat's mind was racing. "When did he call? What's he so upset about?"

"He called this morning. Normally I don't talk to him when he rings me, but like I said, my secretary didn't show up for work this morning and her replacement didn't screen the call."

"What did he want?"

"As usual, he wanted to know why in the hell his contract hadn't been returned to him."

"Why's he got a contract? I don't have a contract!"

"You trust me, don't you?"

"Well, uh, yeah, I guess," Peat said, reluctantly.

"Then don't worry about it."

"But where is Hempshaw's contract?"

"I'm not real sure. Ratcliff lost it."

Peat placed the flask on his lips and turned the container upside down to finish off its contents. He slammed the flask on the table. "You got any more of that?" he asked.

"Yeah," said Gayland. "In the cabinet below the sink."

"What did you tell him, then?"

"I told him that I had the contract in my office."

"Did he believe you?"

"Yeah, I told him I'd bring it to him the next time I was in Ducotey."

"How will you do that if Ratcliff lost it?"

"It's no problem, really. I have some old contracts in my office. I'll make one look official and send it to Hempshaw. That ought to satisfy him. Then I'll send Escartes to Ducotey to take care of him."

Peat wiped his brow in relief. "That ought to satisfy the problem." Crossing to the sink, he opened the cabinet and pulled out a bottle of Crown Royal. Returning to the table, he unscrewed the cap.

"Hempshaw is concerned about Ratcliff," said Gayland.

"Oh?"

"Yeah, he heard about it on the news. As a matter of fact, he's heard about all the investors on the news."

"That's not good," Peat said as he hands started shaking once again. "That's not good at all."

"Relax. He doesn't know that there are any other investors involved in our deal. He thinks that just he and I are the only ones in on this."

"So we're in the clear with him, then?"

"I wouldn't say that. Not only is Hempshaw mean, but he's pretty smart, too. He was asking some very suspicious questions," Gayland said. "He kept saying that all these unusual murders told him something was wrong. He insisted there must be something I needed to tell him."

"Do you think he knows what's going on?"

"I don't see how he possibly could."

"God help us if he figures it out. We're doomed if he does."

"Not if Escartes gets to him in time."

"You've got to find Escartes," Peat said. "You've got to tell him to hurry things up."

"Don't worry. I'll get on it as soon as possible."

Peat checked his wristwatch. "I see that it's past noon and I'm completely drunk."

"As am I."

"Mind if I pass out on your couch? I don't really feel like dealing with the bank's problems while I'm in this state."

Gayland smiled. "Make yourself at home. When are you dropping off the money?"

"I'll bring it by your house this evening."

"Good. That'll give me a good reason to visit Escartes."

"Are you going back into town?"

"I'd rather not," replied Gayland. "However, I better go check and see what calamities that substitute secretary has created. You know how difficult it is to find good help."

Chapter 34

Jennings rocked back in the recliner, propped his feet on the footrest, and closed his eyes. With a soft sigh, he nestled in for a post-dinner nap.

"Would you like a beer?" Carol asked as she cleaned off the kitchen counter.

"Well, I was going to take a nap, but that sounds good," Jennings replied without opening his eyes. "I'll bet that would hit the spot."

"Then get off your ass and get one," she said with a laugh as she started to scrub the dirty dishes.

Jennings jumped out of his chair and strolled to the refrigerator. "You're such a tease," he said with a smile.

Just as he reached for a beer, the doorbell rang. "Are you expecting anyone?" Jennings asked, twisting off the cap.

Carol shook her head. She quickly dried her hands, scurried to the door, then smiled as she peered through the peephole.

"Who is it?" Jennings asked.

She quickly unlocked and opened the door. "What a surprise!"

Her father, Fred Parker, rushed inside with a blast of winter air.

"What brings you to town?" asked Carol while giving him a hug.

"One of the mares cut her leg this morning. I needed some Vetwrap and salve. That stuff's too expensive in Ducotey."

Not knowing Fred's views on alcohol, Jennings was quick to hide his beer behind the aquarium.

Jennings extended his hand and said, "I'm Stan Jennings."

"Fred Parker. It's about time we finally met. Carol has told me a great many things about you."

Jennings laughed. "Don't believe any of it."

"Don't worry," Fred responded as he took off his coat and hung it on the rack, "it's all been good."

"Can I get you a beer, Daddy?"

"Sure."

Carol left to get the beer as Jennings and Fred took seats in the living room.

"Is your horse badly hurt?" asked Jennings.

"No, not really," said Fred. "Not any worse than she's been before."

"What happened?"

"Not sure. She came in from the pasture this morning with some cuts on her back legs."

"Probably got caught in a fence."

"With horses, there's no tellin'. Do you own any?"

"I wish. I grew up on a ranch and rode horses every day when I was young. I haven't been on one since I left for college."

"That's a damned shame."

"Yes, it is."

Carol handed Fred a beer. "We're planning to visit Ducotey in the next few days," she said. "I promised Jennings that you'd take him riding."

"I'd love to," Fred said and took a drink. "Of course, your safety is in your own hands. Those horses have been turned out all year and are liable to buck a little."

"I'll be fine, rest assured."

"What's a matter, don't you like beer?" Fred asked.

Jennings blushed. "Uh, well, actually I do as a matter of fact."

"There's a beer behind the aquarium that's goin' to waste," Fred replied with a smile.

He laughed. "Yeah, I stashed it there. I wasn't sure how you'd feel…"

"How I'd feel about a beer drinker courting my daughter?"

"Well…Yeah."

"Don't give it a second thought."

"Glad to hear you say that," Jennings said, crossing to the fish tank.

"How are they treatin' you two at work?"

"Too many demands and not enough money," Jennings laughed.

"Yeah," Carol responded. "We've been very busy. Jennings has been helping the district attorney with the Finken case and we've both been working on these damned bizarre murders that have been plaguing the area."

"Do you have any solid leads?"

"No," Jennings said. "Other than the murders look like they're being committed by professionals. But that's just between us."

Fred nodded.

"Are you hungry?" asked Carol. "I wish I would have known you were coming. We just ate."

"Thanks, but I've got to be gettin' home soon. Besides, I grabbed something on the road."

"Oh, you'll never guess who I saw the other day," Carol said with bright eyes.

"Who might that be?"

"Quana Smith. He's been helping us with the case."

Fred rolled his eyes. "That's nice," he replied in a sarcastic tone.

Carol immediately sensed his resentment. "You two need to get over this little rift you have with one another," she said with fire in her voice. "He's been a friend of the family for as long as I can remember."

"He painted the door to my house that disgusting orange and black!"

"You painted his car!"

"Yeah, but he started it!"

"What color did you paint his car?" Jennings asked, trying to ease the tension.

"It was a lovely shade of crimson and cream," Fred proudly announced.

Laughter overcame Jennings. "This doesn't have anything to do with a certain football rivalry, now does it?"

Fred noticed Carol's face was glowing with anger.

"Mom and I think that you're both acting like children," she said. "It's time to make amends."

He gulped a few swigs of the beer. "I'll think about it," he said. He turned to Jennings and laughed. "You should have seen his face when he first saw his car. I've got a picture of it at home."

"I'll bet it was priceless."

Feeling guilty for coming down on her father so hard, Carol

finally managed a smile. "Yeah, it was worth a thousand words."

After the laughter subsided, Fred's pulse quickened. For the past couple of days, he'd been rehearsing a speech for the two detectives. As he sat with the empty beer bottle in his hand, he felt his arms shake slightly. He removed his handkerchief and wiped his sweaty brow.

"Is something wrong?" Carol said. "Why are you shaking?"

"There's something we need to talk about."

"How 'bout I get you another beer first?" Jennings asked.

"Sure, that'd be great."

On the way to the refrigerator, Jennings' stomach began to turn. This is it, he thought. The old man is upset that I've been dating his daughter too long without popping the question. He's probably some fundamentalist that thinks that premarital sex is the work of the devil. In his day, if a boy kissed a girl then he was obligated to take her hand in marriage. I've been through this before—the outcome is never pretty.

Ready for the bombshell, he took a deep breath and returned to the living room. With a somber look on his face, he handed a fresh beer to Fred and sat beside Carol on the couch.

Fred paced nervously for a few moments, then began. "Before I tell you this, you've got to promise that it never goes beyond these walls."

Both Carol and Jennings nodded their agreement.

"How well do you know Kyle Gayland?" Fred asked.

Jennings let out a breath of relief as he realized that the old man's angst wasn't directed at him. "Whew," he silently muttered.

"I don't know him hardly at all," Jennings said. "All I know is that he's a very powerful man."

Fred was relieved. "That takes a load off, then."

"Why?" asked a puzzled Jennings.

"I was afraid that you might be close to him."

"No. I hardly know him. Wouldn't care to, either."

"Why do you say that?" Fred asked.

"I've just heard things, that's all. He's well known as being a dirty player. We've investigated him several times in the past on various complaints, but each time we got close to pinning something on him, our efforts have been thwarted by outside forces."

A suspicious expression arose on Carol's face. "Why are you

asking, Dad? What do you know?"

Fred took another drink, then sat in the recliner.

"Not long ago, some people down at the Redtree got pretty sick."

"What's the Redtree?" asked Jennings.

"It's a Native American housing unit near Ducotey," Carol answered. "It's basically a neighborhood of government houses where some of the Indians live."

"Oh, I know what you're talking about. It's right off the highway, near the reservation," said Jennings.

Fred nodded.

"So, some folks got sick?" Jennings asked.

"Yeah, some of them got pretty bad sick."

"How are they doing now? Mom's told me that some of them were in critical condition for a while."

"I think they're all going to be okay."

"What does this have to do with Gayland?" asked Jennings.

"The same thing happened a few years ago, at the Kickingbird Housing Unit."

"Quana mentioned something about that the other day. He said some Indians got sick."

"Yes. Many became sick. Some died."

"What caused it?"

"No one knows. A few county officials came out to Kickingbird, but they didn't find anything."

"Maybe something was tainted at Redtree, like the water," Jennings said. "Some waste from a natural gas well might have seeped into the underground water supply. It might be that the incident that occurred recently at Redtree is related to the one that occurred a few years ago at Kickingbird."

"I'm almost sure that they're related, but it wasn't due to bad water."

"That is strange," Carol said. "I haven't even thought about all this until now, but you're right, something could be very wrong."

"Would someone mind filling me in," said Jennings.

"When the people became sick years ago, Redtree didn't exist," she said. "That incident occurred at the Kickingbird Housing Unit which is miles away."

"You mean the same thing happened but at two different

locations?"

"That's right," responded Fred. "Not long after the sickness, Kickingbird was condemned. The government bought more land and built new houses at what is now Redtree."

Jennings looked at Carol. "That's very odd."

"I agree, but what does this have to do with Gayland?" asked Carol.

"Many of my people think that he was behind the sickness at Kickingbird."

"That's a pretty serious assertion. Do they have any proof?" asked Jennings.

"It was long ago. The law overlooked it then and it will be overlooked now."

"Daddy, do you know something that you're not telling us?"

Fred looked at his beer and paused.

"Is something the matter?" asked Jennings.

"I saw him at Redtree a few days before the sickness came."

Jennings' eyes widened. "You saw Gayland?"

"Yes."

Her curiosity piqued, Carol moved to the edge of her seat. "What was he doing?"

"Nothing. He was in his car with another white man. They were watching the exterminator."

"Exterminator?" said Jennings. "You mean bug exterminator?"

"That's what it looked like."

"It's too cold to spray for bugs this time of year," said Jennings.

"I thought the same thing. That's why I asked around."

"And what did you find?"

Fred stared at his beer. After a few moments, he raised his head to look Carol straight in the eye. "None of the residents called an exterminator."

The words echoed in Jennings' mind. "Holy shit," he said.

"My thoughts exactly," Fred announced, then raised his beer and chugged a few times on the bottle.

"Are you sure?" asked Carol.

"Yes," answered Fred. "I've talked to everyone who lives there. No one called the exterminator. Matter of fact, no one has even seen any bugs."

Jennings' mind was reeling. "Why in the hell would Kyle Gayland want to poison some Indians? What could he possibly gain from sick Indians?"

"Don't know," Fred replied. "Doesn't make much sense to me, either. The only thing that I can figure is that he must not like Indians very much."

"No," Carol said. "If he's involved, there's more to it than that."

"When you were asking everyone about the exterminator, did you tell them anything about seeing Gayland there that day?"

"Oh no. I'm smarter than that. If I were to place Gayland with the sickness, why there's no tellin' what they'd do. I'm sure a few of the younger men would even things out, if you know what I mean. Everyone's mad enough already that nothing's being done by the authorities."

"Indeed," Jennings replied. "We certainly don't need any of that. We've got to let the rule of law run its course."

"Look," Carol interjected, "let's not jump the gun here. We don't have any proof. There could be a thousand reasons why Gayland was at Redtree that day. Although I'll admit, it does look suspicious."

"We can at least start asking questions. Fred, did you recognize the exterminator's van or the guy who was spraying?"

"Naw, I don't remember much about the van. Just that it was white with no logos on it. I did get a look at the guy spraying, though. He had dark hair; I'd never seen him before."

Jennings rose to his feet and walked to the kitchen counter. He opened a drawer and pulled out a notebook and pen. As he wrote down some notes, Fred walked over to the door and retrieved his coat from the rack.

"Leaving so soon?" asked Carol.

"Yeah, I'd better get on back to the house. Your mom will start worrying."

"I'll call her and tell her you're on your way."

"That sounds fine."

Jennings followed Fred to the door and extended his hand.

Fred looked at him and smiled. "It's too bad I had to drive all this way just to meet you. We do allow city folk in Ducotey, you know."

Jennings laughed as they shook hands. "I guess I had that coming. I apologize that we haven't made it your way. I promise we'll get there soon."

"I'm gonna hold you to it."

"Don't worry, Daddy, we're planning a trip," Carol said as she hugged her father. "I'll call in a couple of days and let you know when."

"You folks take care," Fred said as he opened the front door.

"Will do," replied Carol. "You be careful driving."

As soon as Fred's pickup disappeared into the night, Carol closed the front door. Smiling, she asked, "That wasn't so bad, now was it?"

"No," Jennings replied. "He seems like a nice guy."

"Were you expecting anything less?"

"Of course not," Jennings said as he went back to his notepad on the kitchen counter.

"What are you writing?"

"Everything your father said. I'm very curious about him spotting Gayland. It's pretty strange."

"Agreed. It will be hard to do anything about it, though. You'd have to find some hard evidence first."

"Even then I'm not sure we could get a search warrant. Hell, Gayland owns most of the judges."

"It's worth a look, though."

"That it is. I think I might swing by the bank tomorrow and just have a chat with him."

"Won't that arouse his suspicion?"

"Yeah, probably so. I'll figure something out, though."

"Do be careful what you say. Pissing that man off could end your career."

Jennings bowed his head. "Sometimes I wonder..."

"Is something bothering you?" asked Carol.

"Just everything."

"Did something happen today at the Finken trial?"

"His attorneys are contesting every little minutia of our case. They're grasping for anything. It pisses me off because they know, I'm sure, that the son-of-a-bitch is guilty, too. Everyone knows."

"Stop worrying about it so much. The truth will come out, one way or another."

"Man, I hope so."

"Did you hear about Ratcliff?" asked Carol.

"Yeah, that was yet another piece of wonderful news."

"I heard that some hunters found him. I didn't get the details."

"He was found with an arrow through his heart and both legs shot."

"Any solid evidence this time?"

"There's actually too much evidence. He was found in a heavily hunted area, so we've recovered tons of shell casings. It will be a chore sorting through it all."

"Did they find anything else?"

"Lots of footprints, but again, scores of hunters have been through there. It's a mess, so I hear."

"Any eyewitnesses?"

Jennings shook his head. "None. However, there was a car spotted about four miles away on some government land. Some hunters wrote down the tag and called it in."

"Why would they do that? A bit unusual, don't you think? There's tons of vehicles on government land during hunting season," replied Carol.

"Well, they thought it was unusual because it was a car. Most hunters drives pickups or SUVs. It was abandoned and they just thought it was strange, so they contacted the county sheriff."

"Who does the car belong to?" asked Carol.

"Some kid. He's going to school here in Carson. I'm planning to ask him some questions tomorrow."

"What about the site where they found Ratcliff? Are you going up to look at it?"

He nodded. "Then I'll probably swing by and see Gayland on the way back."

"You know...I've seen Ratcliff with Gayland around town at expensive restaurants, and places like that."

Jennings nodded. "Ratcliff was a very popular attorney. He had hundreds of clients."

"Right," Carol said. "Just something to think about."

"I'll keep it in mind. As if I didn't have enough up there already."

Chapter 35

"Hatred splintered the tribes from one another," Campanow said as he stoked the fire. "Had all Indians stood together as one, the white man would never have made it farther west than the great river."

Sitting with his legs crossed on the floor, Taylor was positioned directly across from Campanow. "You mean the Mississippi River?"

Campanow nodded. "A united front among all the tribes would have stopped them cold. Custer and the other murderers would have never made it to Cheyenne."

"But the end result would have been the same," Taylor countered. "The white man would have just regrouped and fortified their efforts. A unified Indian nation might have held them off longer, but ultimately the white man would have conquered. They had the weapons and their diseases were devastating."

Campanow's face twitched. Taylor sensed that anger was rapidly growing within him. "You underestimate our people," Campanow said with thunder in his voice. "We would have stood strong and fought with honor."

"I have no doubt of that," Taylor quickly responded. "But the peaceful Native American society was no match for the white man's war machine."

"Silence!" Elijah flared with rage. "Had we stood as one, we would have beaten the white savages back to Europe. The ocean would have turned red with their blood."

"Let's not allow emotions to rule our analysis of history," snapped Keith. "Remember, the white man has a tendency to win the wars in which he fights."

Elijah jumped to his feet. "You are a traitor," he roared. "You are no different than the trash which we are disposing."

After a long pause, Campanow looked directly into Taylor's eyes. "You speak the truth," he muttered. "The white man would have won regardless. But we could have staged a better front. We could have held them off longer. History might be different."

Still sitting, Taylor turned and spotted Elijah. Incensed by Campanow's admission that the war was truly hopeless, Elijah's expression was all too easy to read. Taylor quickly focused his attention back on Campanow.

"Our people had no ownership; we had no wants other than our needs. The new way of life introduced by the white man was just as lethal as the sickness and the butchery he imposed on our people," Campanow softly replied. He reached into his medicine bag and removed an opaque powder. With the powder in his fingertips, he chanted in his native tongue.

Taylor glanced at Keith, who was sitting on the floor right beside him. Mesmerized by the event, Keith whispered, "This is very interesting. I feel like I'm witnessing a piece of history."

As Taylor smiled and nodded, the old Indian became silent, closed his eyes, then extended his hands over the fire, above the flames.

"It's time to go," Elijah said. "It's getting dark outside. We have things to do."

"No," Keith said with authority. "I'm intrigued by this ritual. I'm not going anywhere. You'll have to wait."

"I'm tired of waiting. While we wait, the banker grows stronger."

Still seated, Keith turned and looked up at Elijah. "Are you out of your mind? The banker is all but destroyed. We've almost completely disbanded his entourage."

"What's this we, white man? You've done nothing but sit in the car like a coward while the real men take care of the business."

"Not this again," said Keith. "We've been through this so many bloody times."

Taylor was initially inclined to jump in and stop the argument, but then had second thoughts. They've been fighting for so long, he thought. Perhaps it would be best to just let them physically settle their differences.

Elijah walked to Keith, who was still seated. "Yes, we have been through this many times, and you still refuse to answer the call."

"Why don't you go outside and cool off," snapped Keith. "I'm trying to broaden my horizons."

Taylor looked at Campanow who continued to silently chant. He seemed unfazed by the bickering.

"Why don't you go with me and we'll settle this once and for all?" said Elijah.

"I've got a better idea," said Keith.

"What's that?"

"Why don't you go wank yourself?"

Campanow released the powder into the fire. As the green flames shot high into the air, Elijah grabbed Keith by the shoulders and began dragging him outside. Keith was quick to strike with evasive action by firmly grasping Elijah's testicles and pulling on them with all his might. Elijah moaned in agony, but continued dragging Keith out the door. As the two tumbled into the cold night air, Taylor's attention turned back to the fire, which had receded to a yellow and red glow.

While the flames entranced Campanow, Taylor noticed a neon-blue light illuminating the floor. He quickly looked around to locate the source of the light, but found nothing. This mystery didn't faze Taylor at all. It seemed that each time he visited the old Indian, light did strange yet magnificent things.

Campanow stared deep into Taylor's eyes. "I sense tension in you," he said. "Has remorse found its way into your soul?"

Taylor lowered his head and took a deep breath. "As usual, your intuition is accurate. But there is little room for remorse in my mind, not after what those men have done."

"If not guilt, then what plagues you?"

Unsure that he wanted to speak, Taylor tried to stall the answer by looking up and watching the smoke rise through the smoke hood. He waited for a moment of enlightenment to inspire him. As he watched the smoke dance away from the fire and through the pipe into the cold world above the roof, he searched for words in silence.

"Perhaps you are not ready to speak," Campanow said while slowly waving his hands over the fire as if casting a spell. He lowered his head and closed his eyes.

Taylor stroked his chin and spit into the fire, which was emitting a purple glow. "I had a strange dream," he said.

"Dreams are sometimes used by the spirits to send us messages," said Campanow. "Tell me about your dream."

"I saw an eagle, a young eagle, at the bottom of an abyss. He was shrieking as if he were trying to communicate with me. The eagle appeared to be in pain and wanted my help. I don't know what he was trying to say."

"Some elders have said that the eagle represents our spirit. Perhaps your spirit is clouded by turmoil and is beckoning for its freedom."

"I've had my share of turmoil lately."

"And why do you suffer such anguish?" asked Campanow.

"It doesn't seem to bother me much anymore," he said in a soft voice.

Campanow's eyes remained closed. "The killing?" he asked.

"Yes. I feel like I've turned into a machine, unable to feel compassion for these pigs. I'm afraid that on a subconscious level, I'm enjoying the killing and the torment."

"Oh?" Campanow said with a raised eyebrow.

"For example, do you remember when I told you about the contracts we took from the lawyer's office when our mission started?"

Campanow stared at Taylor with a blank look on his face.

"They were the contracts that Gayland and his attorney drew up at the insistence of the investors," said Taylor.

Campanow's eyes widened. "Yes," he said. "I believe you showed those to me."

"I did."

"Do the contracts trouble you?"

"No. It's what I did with the contracts that bothers me," Taylor said and lowered his head. "I have copies that bear Ratcliff's blood. I'll soon be mailing them to Gayland."

Campanow quickly moved his attention to the fire. After a few moments, he looked to Taylor.

"Why do such a thing?"

"Because I want to make Gayland suffer," Taylor said in a cold voice. "I want him to know that he's being hunted."

"I see," Campanow said.

"It scares the hell out of me," Taylor said and looked up to find Campanow's chiseled jaw twitching. "I'm also concerned about

Gayland. We've been lucky with the other investors because we've been able to easily track them down. Gayland won't be so easy. We're going to have to take the hit to him and innocent blood could spill as a result."

"Ease your mind," Campanow said.

"He's never alone. He always surrounds himself with innocent people. It will not be easy."

"Your anguish is unfounded. Our plan is working very well. The banker will come to us and all will be taken care of."

"Gayland is smart. He won't come to us."

Campanow nodded. "Oh, but he will."

"How?"

"Do you remember when you met Gayland and you told him that you had an Indian friend named Kacey who wanted to sell some minerals?"

"Yeah," Taylor said. "It was at that Italian restaurant. Joe Escartes was there, too."

"Kacey called Gayland. They're going to meet."

"Oh," Taylor said, relieved. "I guess that's good news, then."

"Kacey will lure him right to us."

Taylor lowered his head.

"Are you upset by this news?" asked Campanow.

With his head still lowered, Taylor briefly contemplated his answer. "No," he replied and raised his head. "I'm just not sure I can kill this instinct that's alive in me now."

"I do not understand," Campanow said, then closed his eyes.

"When our project is over, I fear that I will not be able to turn off my instinct to kill."

As if shaken by Taylor's words, Campanow opened his eyes abruptly. He looked into Taylor's eyes, then shifted his focus to the fire.

"Ease your mind, young warrior. By destroying this sickness, you are saving the innocent lives of our people. These men are evil and will bring much wickedness if they are not destroyed."

"But when this is over, what if I can't stop the killing?"

His eyes glowing from the reflection of the fire, Campanow turned his head and stared at Taylor. Smoke from the fire grew thicker and thicker in the room. Taylor wondered if the old man was using his magic.

"The mind cannot be controlled by two masters," Campanow said. "Only one."

The smoke was growing so thick that Taylor had to use his shirtsleeve to rub the haze from his eyes. When he reopened them, he gasped when he noticed Campanow sitting very close, deeply peering at him with piercing eyes. Taylor felt intimidated as he sat helplessly while Campanow peered into his soul.

"History now stands before us once again," Campanow said, sternly, "and your mission will soon be complete."

The smoke grew heavier with each passing second. Taylor looked down and noticed that the fire was burning savagely with green flames.

"But I'm growing numb," Taylor said as he stared at the emerald flames. "I fear that I won't be able to rid myself of this instinct. What if I can't stop killing?"

Taylor looked for Campanow but he had disappeared into the smoke. He frantically searched the room but could not locate him.

"Then I will destroy you," Campanow's voice thundered through the haze.

Never had Taylor before heard so much might in the old man's voice, nor had he ever known Campanow to threaten violence. Somewhat shaken by Campanow's words, Taylor quickly decided to make an escape. As he stood, he noticed that the fire had returned to its amber color and was now burning quietly. The smoke in the room was dissipating rapidly.

As Taylor walked to the door, he scanned the room. Campanow was nowhere to be found as Taylor quietly slipped outside into the cold night air.

"Taylor!" a voice echoed in the darkness outside Campanow's cabin.

His car keys in hand, Taylor turned and noticed Keith walking briskly toward him and the car.

"Where's Elijah?" Taylor asked.

"We had a bit of a disagreement."

"And?"

"Things turned rather violent, you could say."

"And he didn't kill you?" Taylor asked, jokingly.

"Oh, I think the thought crossed his mind," Keith quickly replied, "but I did a number on his yarbles. I dare say he won't be walking upright for a while."

Taylor rolled his eyes. "You didn't hurt him did you?"

"Not permanently, but he won't be visiting the ladies anytime soon."

"Where did he go?"

"I suspect he's wandering back to the house."

Taylor opened the door to the car and stepped inside. "It's awful cold out here. We should try to find him."

"If you insist."

After Keith entered the vehicle, Taylor drove the car into the night.

"He's growing worse, you know," Keith said while shivering in the passenger seat. He placed his hands over the defrost vents to feel the warm air. "He'll soon be out of control."

"We've all changed," Taylor said. "Even you."

"Not to Elijah's extent. I'm afraid the poor bastard has drifted deeper into the netherworld of delusion."

Taylor frowned. "Don't mention it to Campanow," he said while he turned the wheel and steered the car onto the highway.

"Why's that?" asked Keith.

"He just told me that..." Taylor stopped.

"What? What did he tell you?"

Taylor contemplated his words. "Let's just say that he'll take extreme measures in the event that our vigilante campaign extends beyond our known targets."

Keith thought for a moment. "I see. Perhaps we should stop it now, before it proceeds any farther."

"I don't think that's an option, either. We can't stop now, even if we wanted to. Campanow won't allow that. Besides, we can't let Gayland get away. We're too close."

"I'm ready for it to be over," Keith said. "I'd like to return to the land of normalcy."

As the car sped down the highway toward the city lights of Ducotey, Taylor sighed. "I'm not sure we'll ever return there. The belt of insanity that we wear will be a permanent fixture in our lives. I'm afraid there's no going back."

"To sanity?" Keith asked with a perplexed look on his face.

"Yeah," Taylor said as the car entered the city limits. "I don't know that we'll ever be the same. This is not what I envisioned."

"How so?"

"I'm not angry any more. Before we decided to do this, I allowed the hatred of those bastards to swell inside me. While we were tracking them down and slaughtering them one by one, I used that angst in the place of courage to help me carry out the mission."

"I certainly can relate to that."

"But it's different now. I'm not so angry any more. Now, I don't feel anything."

"Really?"

"Really."

Keith paused for a moment to compose his thoughts. "Are you telling me that you're sensing remorse down deep in that shiny melon of yours?"

"I don't know what I feel," Taylor said while he turned up the heater. "At first, anger fueled the killings. Now, killing those bastards is like a second nature to me. I'm not mad anymore, yet I can still hunt them down."

Keith stroked his chin. "Perhaps you've been touched by intuition. Maybe we should give this more thought. You never know, perhaps those mystical forces in the universe are trying to tell you something."

Taylor slowed the car and turned onto the street that led to his old house. "Maybe so, but it doesn't matter," he said. "The law won't put Gayland away. It's up to us."

"But is it worth spending the rest of our lives in jail?"

Taylor steered the car into the driveway of his former home. "The bottom line is simple. If we don't stop Gayland, he'll regroup, find more cronies, and will ultimately kill again. It will be easy for him to find more scumbags to join his cause. He's a banker. He has the connections."

"You never know," Keith replied. "This whole ordeal might have frightened the hell out of him. Perhaps even scared him straight."

"Men like him don't change. The task before us is difficult, but it must be finished."

"And what if we lose our grip on sanity? You know, many wise men have said that sanity is a fleeting thing."

"These feelings will pass," Taylor said. "They must."

Judging by the tone of Taylor's voice, Keith sensed that Taylor was ready to call it a day. "I'm getting tired," Keith said and opened the door. "I think it's time to turn in."

Taylor looked up to the house for signs of life stirring inside. "Do you think Elijah's made it back yet? It doesn't look as if anyone's inside."

Keith glanced at the house. "He's here," Keith said. "The front door is cracked. No matter how cold it gets, he can never close the door behind him."

"Should I stay for a while? Do you think he might try to retaliate?"

"No worries, mate," Keith replied. "He's much calmer when you're not around."

"Are you sure? I don't mind talking to him."

"Forget it. If he wanted to harm me, he would have done it already."

"If you say so," replied Taylor.

Keith stepped out of the car, then turned to face Taylor. "I know I complain about Elijah often, but I really do sense that he'll soon be out of control, if not already. I'm afraid there'll come a day when we won't be able to turn him off."

Taylor smiled. "Maybe when his yarbles heal he'll feel better."

"I'm glad to hear that you find humor in this mess. You do realize, however, that he'll be no different once the swelling goes down in his testicles."

"I'll do some thinking."

"Some hard thinking," Keith said. "Remember, sanity is a fleeting thing."

Taylor grabbed the shifter and shoved it in reverse. "I'll try to remember that."

Chapter 36

The bells atop the old alarm clock shattered the peaceful aura of the bedroom. As soon as Taylor recognized the sound, he rolled over and noticed that the clock read 8:30 a.m. Since his first class wasn't until ten that morning, he reckoned that his late-night plan to get up early and jog would have to wait for another day. He reached to reset the alarm for 9:30, then collapsed on the bed and quickly returned to sleep.

Just as Taylor drifted into a peaceful state of slumber, he felt something tugging at his legs. In the far distance, he was almost sure he heard bells again. He struggled, but finally managed to open his eyes. He saw someone over him, uttering words he didn't understand.

"Damn it, Taylor, get up!" shouted Wendy. "Taylor! Get your ass out of bed."

"What, what is it?" Taylor asked as he regained consciousness.

"Someone's at the door," Wendy said.

"No. That's the alarm clock and I already turned it off."

"It's not the alarm clock! It's the doorbell. Someone's at the door."

Taylor sprang out of bed and ran to his old oak dresser where he quickly retrieved a pair of jeans and a tee shirt. He put on the cloths as he briskly walked down the hallway toward the door.

The doorbell rang again as Taylor looked through the peephole to see a man standing outside, dressed in slacks and a heavy coat. He cautiously opened the door.

"Taylor Hayes?" asked the stranger.

"Yeah."

"My name is Detective Jennings. I'm with the State Bureau," Jennings said while flashing a badge. "Mind if I come in and ask you a few questions?"

Taylor's heart raced. They must have made a mistake, he thought. With all the planning and all the cautionary measures, they must have made a mistake. They left a fingerprint, a tire mark, something.

Even though he felt like his chest was on fire, Taylor knew he had to remain calm. "Sure. Come on in."

The detective walked inside and politely wiped his shoes on the mat. His eyes darted about the room as if he were searching for something.

Taylor pointed at the living room couch. "Have a seat. Can I get you something to drink?"

Jennings shook his head. "No, but thank you."

Surprised by the detective's reluctance to initiate the conversation, Taylor decided to counter his silence with small talk. "Is it any warmer outside this morning?" he asked as he sat on the rocking chair directly across from the couch.

The words prompted Jennings to make eye contact. "No," he said and shook his head. "In fact, it's quite a bit colder. I don't know if we're ever gonna thaw out."

"There could be some relief coming. I heard on the news last night that it's supposed to warm up. Of course, that only applies if you believe the weather man."

"I sure hope he's right," Jennings said with a smile.

When Jennings smiled, Taylor felt a great relief fall over his body. He immediately recognized the good ol' boy persona that Jennings was projecting. He wasn't hostile or authoritative. In fact, he was coming off as quite friendly.

"I'll say."

"I see a lot of books lying around," Jennings said. "Are you a student?"

"I am. I'm working on my masters in psychology."

"That sounds interesting."

"It is. Especially in your line of work."

"My line of work?" asked Jennings.

"Yeah, you know - establishing motive and profiles, that sort of thing."

"So what do you know about my line of work?" asked Jennings

with a stone face.

The subtle warmness that Taylor detected in Detective Jennings when he entered the room had instantly faded. His heart jumped with fear that he'd unknowingly said something incriminating.

"You said you were a detective and I've seen you on television talking about some bizarre case."

"And?"

"I think a psychological profile of this killer could possibly help you."

"Is that right?" Jennings said in a slightly condescending tone.

"Absolutely. I'm sure you're familiar with the work that the FBI does with psychological profiles."

"Very familiar," Jennings said and rolled his eyes. "In fact, our department does an awful lot of that, also. It's very tiring."

"But it's sound police work. In most cases, criminals' behavior can be predicted based on how and where they commit the crimes."

"What about you?" asked Jennings.

Fear shot up Taylor's spine.

"What about me?" he asked.

"You say you're a psych major…Have you sketched a profile of this killer?"

Taylor knew he was skating on thin ice. He could dazzle the detective with his brilliant psychoanalytical skills but in the process, he could say too much and indict himself. Treading carefully, he said, "Based on what I know, which is limited, I'd say that these are outside jobs, committed by professionals, probably hit men."

Jennings' eyes widened. "Professionals, eh? More than one?"

"I've been following the story in the newspapers. It seems that you haven't been able to collect much evidence. This tells me that these people know what they're doing. That or you're not releasing much information to the public."

"We have a tendency to do just that," Jennings said, flashing a quick smile.

"I've always thought it was more than one person because I heard somewhere that you found multiple shell casings at one of the hits. Of course that doesn't mean anything. The killer could have used more than one gun, I suppose."

"That's certainly possible."

"The other reason I think it's an outside job is the nature of the crime itself."

Jennings nodded. "Go on."

"This is rural America, a place where crimes like these typically don't occur. This crime is one of passion. It's either about big money, sex, or revenge. Since the victims have all been middle-aged fat white men, I doubt sex has anything to do with it, so it's either money or revenge."

Jennings thought for a moment. "That's an interesting take, although I've heard that before. It does sound like you've put some thought into this, though."

Taylor smelled a trap. "No," he quickly responded. "I'm fascinated with it, but that's all. I haven't had a chance to do much research – just what I've read in the papers or seen on TV. But I've thought about pursuing that line of work, so I guess that's why it holds my interest."

"You've thought about doing work as a criminal psychologist?"

"I've considered it. I tend to do well in that sort of thing, in class that is."

"I see," replied Jennings.

A long silence filled the room. Jennings sat on the couch pretending to be occupied with the textbook covers that lay on the table. Taylor saw through his tactics, however. He knew that Jennings was playing him, trying to see how nervous he would become after a long awkward pause.

"Surely you didn't come here today to talk to me about criminal profiles," Taylor said, politely.

"No, I didn't," Jennings said while laughing briefly. He shifted his eyes back to Taylor. "A few days ago, your car was spotted near a little town out west, Durham. Do you mind telling me why you were there?"

He knew something, Taylor was sure of that. The trick now was to feel him out, to make sure that he didn't know too much.

"I was in that area to take pictures of the massacre site," Taylor replied calmly.

"Massacre site?" asked Jennings.

"Yeah, a Native American massacre site."

Jennings tilted his head in confusion. "A recent massacre?"

"No, it happened in 1868."

"Oh. Was this for a class project?"

"No, I'm a sort of an Indian buff. A long time ago, a group of peaceful Indians were slaughtered on the Washita River near Cheyenne, a small town which is not too far from Durham. I just wanted some pictures of the site and the surrounding area."

"Some hunters spotted your tag and thought it odd that someone was that far out in the boon docks in a car and not a pickup."

"I don't doubt that. But I wasn't there to hunt. I was only taking pictures."

Jennings nodded. "Would you mind if I took a look at those pictures?"

"Sure," Taylor said, then pointed to the coffee table by the couch. "They're on the table, underneath one of the psych books."

Detective Jennings picked up a textbook and found the pictures in an envelope. He slowly thumbed through the pictures. Jennings held up a photo. "This is interesting. Where exactly did the battle take place?" he asked.

"It wasn't really a battle—like I said, it was a massacre. The government calls it the Battle of the Washita because it happened on the Washita River, but it was no battle."

"Why do you say that?"

Taylor was surprised by Jennings' ignorance of the event and assumed that he wasn't a native of the area.

"Because the Indians were slaughtered."

"You're telling me that the Indians didn't put up a fight at all?"

"Not much of one. The government made peace with a Cheyenne chief, Black Kettle, and promised him refuge if he moved his people to the Washita River," said Taylor. "Black Kettle's camp was housed with mainly elders, women and children."

"And then what?" Jennings asked.

"Like I said, Black Kettle was a peaceful Native American. He even had the American flag flying at the camp. Early one cold morning in November, Custer and his men raided the camp and the slaughter was on."

Jennings moved his eyes back to the pictures. "You're right," he said. "That's not much of a battle."

"It's a dark day in the history of this country," Taylor responded.

"I can't deny that."

"I have more pictures around here somewhere, if you'd like to see them."

Jennings didn't respond. Instead, he continued to thumb through the pictures. "If memory serves me correctly," he said, "The Battle of the Washita occurred at Cheyenne which is about thirty miles south of Durham."

"That is correct. I went to Durham before I went to the massacre site in Cheyenne. I've found a lot of arrow heads in the area around Durham and I know of a few Indian campsites. Again, I was there to take some pictures."

From Jennings' remarks, Taylor knew he had known all along about the massacre site. He was just trying to find holes in his story.

"These are very interesting photos," Jennings said. "This part of the country is rich in wild west history. I'd love to buy a big ranch and live off the land, just like the Indians. Maybe buy a few hundred acres with some horses and some cows."

"As would I. I'd be careful, though."

"Why's that?" asked Jennings.

"Some white men don't seem to like the Indians or their way of life too much."

Jennings tilted his head in confusion. "The massacres were over long ago, Taylor."

"I wouldn't be so sure. History has a way of repeating itself."

Slightly perplexed, Jennings quietly set the pictures down on the table and looked at his wristwatch. "Goodness, I'm already late for a meeting," he said and stood. "Thank you for your time," he replied.

"Happy to give it. If I can do anything to help, please don't hesitate to let me know."

"Thanks again," Jennings said on his way out the door.

"No problem." Still seated, Taylor immediately exhaled a large breath and bent over, placing his head and upper body on his legs.

"Son-of-a-bitch, that was close," he muttered to himself.

"What's wrong?" asked Wendy.

Still analyzing Jennings's visit, Taylor didn't feel much like moving.

"Taylor, what's the matter?"

"Nothing," Taylor said, his head still stationed between his knees.

"Who came by?"

Taylor looked up to see Wendy standing over him. She was wearing nothing but string panties and a tee shirt.

"That was Detective Jennings."

"Detective Jennings!" cried Wendy. "What the hell did he want?"

"There was another murder out west."

"Where?"

"On some hunting land near Durham," Taylor answered with a distant look in his eye.

"And?"

"Some hunters saw my car in the vicinity. He wanted to know what I was doing there."

"What did you tell him?" Wendy asked.

"I told him I was in the area taking pictures of Indian sites."

"Oh my God! Does he think that you murdered someone?"

Taylor stood and walked to Wendy. He wrapped his arms around her warm body and held her tight.

"No, he was just asking questions," Taylor replied. "We got along fabulously."

"Oh, dear, that's all we need," Wendy mumbled.

"Don't worry. I'm sure they'll catch the real killers soon. They have no evidence on us."

"I should hope not."

"Don't worry about it," Taylor said as he released Wendy and walked to the kitchen.

"I'm sorry, but with all I've been through lately, I'm just a little jumpy."

"I haven't felt like myself, either. I'm getting behind on my studies, too. Things need to slow down."

"Speaking of your studies, I was in your office last night and saw something unusual."

Taylor's heart instantly jumped into triple time. In his office, there was plenty of evidence to link him to the murders: Notes, plans, even maps of the investor's homes and places of business.

"Something unusual, huh?" Taylor said in a weak voice.

"Yeah, I was using your computer to type in some notes for an upcoming test and I came across some contracts on top of your desk. What are they?"

The hair stood on Taylor's neck. "They're just copies of some contracts I found. Why?"

"Just curious," Wendy said. "It looked like blood on the cover page. How'd that get there?"

Taylor struggled to think of a quick lie. "I'm not sure. Like a said, I just found them. It's probably ketchup or something."

"Where did you find them?"

"In an alley down by the school," Taylor said as his heart jumped furiously in his chest. "Did you read them?"

"No," Wendy replied. "The blood sort of grossed me out. I almost threw them away, but I thought they might be important. Do you need them for something?"

Relieved, Taylor shook his head. "No. Don't worry about it. I'll throw them away myself."

Wendy walked to the couch to sit at his side. Taylor sensed that she was growing nervous.

"Is something wrong?" he asked.

"Uhm, Taylor, there's something that we need to talk about."

Taylor immediately sensed that Wendy was bearing heavy news. She was either pregnant or trouble had arisen with Gayland. He poured a glass of tea and asked, "What is it?"

"While you were gone last night, I had a long talk with my parents on the phone."

"Don't tell me you talked to them about Gayland," Taylor said.

Wendy looked at the floor. "Yeah, his name came up several times."

"So what did they say?"

"They said lots of things, but the result of the conversation is that I'm going back to work at the bank."

Taylor was shell-shocked. "You're kidding me."

Wendy's eyes were covered in a light mist of tears. "No," she said. "Gayland brought the hammer down on Dad and told him that he was getting too far behind on the farm's payments. Gayland said that he was going to be forced to foreclose."

Taylor was caught between emotions, but definitely felt at least a little relief. "Well, I hate to hear that, but there's nothing we can do about it. Your dad will find something. He and your mom will get by. You don't have to go back to work for Gayland."

"But that's just the thing. Dad asked me to talk to him."

Taylor shook his head. "Your dad has some nerve—he must not understand how dangerous he is. What did you tell him?"

Wendy walked to the kitchen table and sat. "I told him that I wasn't talking to Gayland anymore, that one of his goons tried to jump me and I was pretty sure Gayland was behind it."

"What did your father say to that?"

"Of course he was concerned. He wanted to know if I was all right. After I assured him that I was, he wanted to know why I was so sure the man who grabbed me worked for Gayland. I told him that we knew that the guy was staying at some hotel in room thirteen and that I'd overheard Gayland calling a hotel, asking for room thirteen."

"Let me guess. Your dad said that wasn't enough proof."

"Exactly. He said that there are many hotels in Carson and that I shouldn't go jumping to conclusions without real evidence."

Disgusted, he sighed. "This is unbelievable. I'm really beginning to dislike your father. So did you call Gayland?"

"Yes." Wendy answered.

"And?"

"I asked him if he was going to foreclose on Daddy. He said that he was, but if I came back to work, he might reconsider."

"That dirty, rotten, piece of shit!" roared Taylor. "He'll stop at nothing."

"I'm going back to the bank tomorrow."

"Please don't do this! You're making a huge mistake."

"I don't have a choice! My daddy needs me. I'm his only hope."

"But Wendy," Taylor's voice thundered, "Gayland's already proven that he can't be trusted. He's made his moves on you once. He'll try again."

"I'm not happy about this either, Taylor, but I have no choice. I've got to help."

"No you don't. You can tell your dad to piss off, that his farm is not worth risking your safety."

"He doesn't see it that way. To him, Gayland's the same good-old-boy from his childhood. He refuses to believe that Gayland has grown into a monster."

Taylor rubbed his face with his hands. After several moments of contemplation, he exhaled deeply and looked directly into Wendy's eyes. "Under one condition," he said.

"All right. What would that be?"

"That you learn to shoot the .38 I gave you. You must keep it loaded in your purse and you must promise me that you'll shoot that bastard between the eyes if he ever tries to harm you."

"I promise," Wendy said with conviction.

"Good, then get dressed."

"Where are we going?"

"To Running Bear Cliff. It's time you learned the art of shooting a firearm."

Chapter 37

"A gentleman by the name of Kacey is here to see you," the young attractive secretary spoke into the phone. While she talked, she flashed a quick seductive smiled to Kacey, who in turn, blushed and smiled back.

"It will be just a few moments," the secretary said as she hung up the phone. "Mr. Gayland has to make a few notes then he'll be right with you."

"Thanks," Kacey replied. He sat in the leather chair in front of the secretary's desk.

"My name's Veronica," said the secretary.

"Nice to meet you, Veronica."

"You're not from Carson, I presume."

"Now what makes you say something like that?" Kacey asked.

"I don't know," she said. "You're dressed in blue jeans and you act pretty carefree, like you're from the country. Most people who come in to visit Mr. Gayland are either from Carson or from some metropolis. They all wear five hundred dollar suits and are very uptight and serious. They make me sick."

"Is that right?"

"It sure is."

"I'm from a little town out west, Ducotey."

"I know where that is. My boyfriend is from Ducotey."

"Well, I'll be," Kacey said. "Small world. How long have you been working here at the bank?"

"Just a couple of days. I'm going to college here in Carson. I didn't want this job, but my daddy knows Gayland and sort of forced me into it."

"You shouldn't be forced into anything," Kacey said, then smiled. "Unless you're willing."

Veronica laughed. "Maybe I like being forced into doing some things," she said.

"Maybe I do, too."

"My daddy owes Gayland a lot of money," Veronica said in a whisper. "And besides, I kind of like the way he flirts with me."

The phone rang and Veronica answered. "I'll send him right in," she said into the receiver. "He'll see you now."

"It was very nice to meet you," Kacey said. "If you're ever in Ducotey, look me up."

"You can count on that," she answered with a smile.

Kacey walked through the office doors and found Gayland seated behind his desk, smoking a cigar.

"Hello," he said with a forced smile. "How does this day find you?"

"Fine," Kacey replied as they shook hands. After Gayland shut the office door, they took their seats.

"I'm sorry you had to wait."

"No problem. I enjoyed talking to your secretary. She's a very personable young lady."

"She's more airhead than anything else," Gayland said. "She's just here while my regular secretary is out. Wendy should be back this week."

"I see."

Gayland gave Kacey a hard look. "Have we met before?" he asked.

"I believe we've run into each other on the street once," Kacey said.

"Yes, I remember. So, have you found a buyer for those minerals yet?"

"No, sir. I sure haven't. I'm not sure what I'm going to do with them."

"Might I offer you a cigar?"

"You bet. I gave up smoking years ago, but I do enjoy a fine cigar."

"You, sir, are in for a treat, a treat indeed," replied Gayland. "These are the world's finest from Cuba. I have an attorney friend who often travels abroad and he picked them up for me." He reached into his desk drawer and removed a cigar. After clipping the end of the stogie, he handed it to Kacey and offered him a light.

"Thank you," Kacey said after he sporadically sucked on the cigar until it lit. "This has a very mild taste. Where can I get more of these?"

"Of course, you know they're illegal," Gayland said. "I tell you what—let's talk business first. I might be able to throw in a few if we can reach an agreement."

"That'd be great."

"I'm just afraid those minerals aren't worth much," said Gayland. "I have a friend who's a land man. I asked him to check into your minerals for me. He went up to the courthouse in Ducotey and ran the records. I hate to tell you this, but he said that your minerals are practically worthless."

Kacey knew he was being played, but at the same time, amazed that Gayland actually thought that he was so stupid. The land was rich in oil and natural gas. On several occasions, he'd been offered thousands of dollars per acre just for the mineral rights. For Gayland to tell him they were worthless was almost humorous.

"I don't doubt that they're worthless," Kacey said, playing along. "I inherited the land and the minerals along with it, so I don't have anything invested. I'd just like to liquidate them."

"Well, I really don't need them. My hands are full with all sorts of things right now," Gayland said while puffing on his cigar. He looked outside the window, then expelled a deep breath. "I tell you what. I know they're not worth it and I know I'm going to regret it, but I'll give you fifty dollars an acre. How's that sound?"

Kacey bit his tongue to hide his reaction to Gayland's insulting offer. "Wow," Kacey said after a few moments of contemplation. "That's a lot of money."

"I know, I know, but I like to give things back to the community. I'll just write the deal off as a loss on my taxes."

"You sure know how to take care of people."

"It's just a way of life for me."

"I'll need to think about it a little, but I'm sure we can come to an agreement," Kacey said. "Is there a chance we can do this in Ducotey?"

Gayland was quick to go in for the kill. "Why not just do it here, today? I can call and get us a deed drawn up immediately."

"I would, but my wife would skin me alive if I did something like this without talking to her."

"So, you're gonna let your wife tell you what to do with minerals that you inherited?"

"Absolutely. No worries, though. Just come to Ducotey. That'll give me enough time to talk her into it."

"Well," Gayland said, "I don't like to wait until tomorrow to do things that can be done today."

"It would be better if we waited and did this in Ducotey. Trust me, it will work out for the best this way."

"All right, all right," Gayland said. "I do have some business to do up there anyway."

"Oh? With whom?"

"A fellow named John Hempshaw. Do you know him?"

"Yeah," Kacey said. "He has a convenience store there, just outside of town."

"I have some paperwork I need to get to him. Just typical loan type information."

"See? That works out great. Tell you what, we can just meet there at his store."

"That sounds fine," Gayland replied and looked at his wristwatch. "I hate to break up our meeting, but I have other business to attend to."

"I understand." Kacey continued to sit in his chair and puff on his cigar.

Since Kacey didn't immediately take the hint and leave the office, Gayland opened his briefcase and pretended to look busy by searching through its contents.

"Some news this morning, huh?"

"What news?" Gayland asked, looking down at his briefcase.

"You mean you haven't heard?" Kacey said while pulling a deep draw of smoke from the cigar.

Gayland was growing angry. "What news?" he asked without looking up.

"Joe Escartes. They found his body this morning," Kacey said as he slowly exhaled the smoke.

Gayland froze. After a few moments, he looked at Kacey, whose face was hidden in the smoke that eerily blanketed the office. "Joe Escartes, huh?" he weakly muttered. "Who's that, a Mexican worker?"

"Oh no," Kacey replied. "He was a Mafia hitman."

Gayland paled. "Dear God!"

"Hard to believe, isn't it?"

"Where? Where did they find him?"

"In some hotel." Kacey replied as he watched Gayland's hands begin to shake. Going for the throat, he added, "The worst part of it was that his killers gutted and hung him in the bathroom like a deer. Certainly looks like a professional job. Imagine that, a Mafia hitman getting snuffed in a small Midwest city. Truth is stranger than fiction, huh?"

Gayland stumbled to the window and struggled to open it. While the smoke billowed out, he stuck his head in the cold air and breathed deeply.

"Mr. Gayland?" Veronica's voice crackled on the intercom speaker.

"He's uh, busy, at the moment," Kacey replied, watching Gayland gasp for air.

"Please tell him that a Detective Jennings called a few minutes ago from the police station. He'll be here directly."

"Holy shit," Kacey muttered.

"What?" she asked.

"Uh, nothing. I'll tell him."

After several minutes of slow breathing, Gayland finally began to feel better. He wiped his brow, then closed the window.

"What did she want?" he asked as he turned toward his desk. To his dismay, Kacey was nowhere to be found. "Kacey?" he said and walked around the room. "Kacey?"

"I'm sending Detective Jennings in," Veronica announced on the intercom.

"What?" Gayland said. He ran to the intercom and pressed the button. "Don't let him. . ."

Gayland stopped cold when he heard the doorknob turning.

Jennings confidently approached the desk. "Hello, Mr. Gayland."

"Hello," he replied in a weak voice.

"I'm Detective Jennings. I have a few questions, if you don't mind."

"Have a seat."

"Thank you." Jennings chose a wingback chair as Gayland slumped in his leather seat.

"Are you feeling all right? You look pale."

"I'm uh, a little under the weather," Gayland replied.

"The cold air will do it to you, that's for sure."

"It happens to me every year. I guess I should be happy to get it over with so early in the season."

"That's one way to look at it," Jennings responded.

"Say, I just heard that they found someone in a motel."

"That's right. Joe Escartes."

"I heard that he was a hitman or something like that."

"That's the rumor."

"I also heard they found him hanging in the shower like a side of beef."

"I don't know many details, just what I've heard on the news," said Jennings. "The hotel maid found him."

"How long had he been dead?"

Jennings gave Gayland a hard stare. "Apparently he'd been dead for a couple of days. Whoever killed him turned the air conditioner on full blast and placed a Do Not Disturb sign on the door."

Gayland felt himself getting weak again. "What a horrible way to die."

"Evidently the television stations got to the maid before we did," Jennings said. "The details of the crime should never have been released. She'll be getting a call from the department."

"Do you have any leads? Any idea who did it?"

"Like I said, I heard about it on the news. Are you sure you feel all right? You look like you're about to pass out."

Gayland wiped his brow with a handkerchief. "I must have a fever," he said. Noticing that his hands were shaking again, he quickly moved them under the desk. "What can I help you with today?"

"Have you recently been to Ducotey?"

Gayland felt like all the blood in his body had suddenly been drained.

"Ducotey?" he muttered.

"Yeah, it's a little town out west of here. Have you been there recently?"

Gayland froze, trying to think of what to say. He knew he had to be very careful.

"Mr. Gayland, have you recently been to Ducotey?"

"Uh, yes," Gayland said. "I have."

"Was it for business?"

Gayland's mind was running in circles. His plan was crumbling before his very eyes.

"Mr. Gayland, why were you in Ducotey?"

"Yes, yes, it was for business. The bank has farm loans to people in that area."

Jennings hesitated, then asked, "Have you ever been to the Redtree Indian Housing Unit?"

"The what?" he croaked.

"The Redtree Indian Housing Unit."

"Uh, yeah, I think I have."

"Could you please tell me what you were doing there?"

"I uh, a couple of weeks ago I was there because I..." Gayland's voice trailed off.

Jennings inched forward in his seat. "You what?"

"I met a uh, a business associate there."

"And who was that?"

"A banker. Jonathan Peat." Gayland said and wiped his brow again.

"Does he live in Ducotey?"

"Uh, no. He lives here in Carson."

"Was it just the two of you?" asked Jennings.

"Yes."

"What were you two doing at the Redtree Housing Unit?"

"I'm about to foreclose on a farming family in that area and was showing the farm to Mr. Peat, who's interested in buying it after the eviction. He was unfamiliar with the area and I was just showing him all the sites of Ducotey.

"I see," Jennings said.

"Why? Is something the matter?"

"There was an incident."

"Oh," said Gayland. "What kind of incident?"

Jennings paused for a moment, trying to analyze Gayland's behavior. He wondered what he knew. "Some of the Native

Americans living in the complex were poisoned around the time you were there."

"Poisoned? Dear God, that's terrible."

"That it is. It's very sad. Fortunately, no one has died. At least not yet."

"Good news, indeed. I'll bet it was something in the environment. The heathens from those damned oil and gas companies drill a lot of wells in that area. I'll bet some chemicals seeped into those poor Indians' water."

"That's what I'm trying to find out," Jennings replied.

"What will those poor Indians do?" Gayland asked.

"What do you mean?"

"Well, surely they can't stay there. Those houses will probably be condemned."

"I'm not sure. I know very little about the case."

Gayland's facial expression turned aggressive. "Oh," he said. "But your department has sanctioned an investigation, right?"

"No, they haven't."

"They haven't?" he replied.

"No, I'm just trying to find out a few things."

Gayland's eyes turned cold and his voice firm. "Then sir, we have nothing further to discuss. I'll not have some maverick harass me for a crime I didn't commit."

"I'm not harassing you," Jennings said, puzzled. "I'm only asking questions."

"I happen to know the police chief very well and you, Detective Jennings, will be reported."

"I encourage you to do just that," he said.

"Good day, sir."

Jennings stood and walked to the door. "Good day."

Chapter 38

"That looked good, very good," Taylor said as the loud blasts subsided. "You're staying steady as the gun recoils. Earlier, you were jumping like crazy."

"It does feel like I have more control over it now," Wendy said. She lowered the .38 to her side and followed Taylor to the target about forty yards ahead on the canyon wall.

"You've improved tremendously."

"That's a good thing. We've been doing this practically all day. I'm getting tired of it."

Taylor picked up the cardboard silhouette of a man's head and torso. After analyzing the bullet holes, he grinned and proudly declared, "You're turning into a regular Belle Star."

Wendy placed the gun on a rock, removed the camera from around her neck, and started taking pictures of the terrain. "Remember those pictures I took of this place for my photography class?"

"The last time we were here?"

"Yeah."

He nodded. "How'd everyone like them?"

"All my friends love them. They want me to bring them up here."

"I hope you told them no," said Taylor.

"I did. I remember our talk."

"Good. Has your professor graded them yet?" Taylor asked.

"Not yet. I should get them back soon."

Wendy snapped pictures of the two horses tied to a tree several feet away. "I'm surprised the horses aren't bothered by the gunshots. I've heard that horses scare easily and aren't very fond of loud noises."

"I've ridden hundreds of miles and fired thousands of rounds of ammunition from their backs. Believe me, nothing fazes those guys."

"Speaking of bothering people, are you sure we won't get into trouble for shooting guns out here?"

"I'm sure. Ducotey is the nearest town and nobody there cares what we do out this way."

"What do you guys call this place again?" asked Wendy.

"Running Bear Cliff."

"And no one knows about it?"

"Just me, Keith, Elijah, and an old friend of mine in Ducotey."

Wendy put on a seductive smile and rubbed Taylor's thigh as he studied the pattern of bullet holes on the poster. "Do you think they could hear screams of passion?"

Taylor laughed. "I know they wouldn't, but it's a little cold here on the rocks, don't you think?"

"I don't know. We've done things in stranger places than this. In colder weather, too."

Still focused on the shooting pattern of the target poster, Taylor pointed to the various bullet holes in the silhouette.

"You realize that not all of these shots are kills, don't you?"

"No." Wendy replied.

"Well, some of them aren't. Remember, you've got to make every shot count."

"Would you mind if I told you something?" she asked.

"Of course not."

"All this talk about kill shots is freaking me out and like I said, I'm getting tired of shooting this damned gun. My ears are starting to ring."

"I'm sorry," Taylor said, then pointed at the poster. "But this is important."

"I hardly think that it will ever be of use," Wendy replied nonchalantly.

"Look, if Gayland, or anyone else, comes after you aggressively and you fear for your life, you've got to react. It's important you understand this."

She frowned. "I understand, but Taylor, he's not going to do that. If he gets fresh with me, I'll kick him in the nuts."

"No!" he shouted, "you don't kick him in the nuts, you disable the son-of-a-bitch. Go for the head, the heart, or the lungs."

Wendy was a little shocked by the anger in Taylor's voice. "Okay, okay, I just don't think..."

"Listen to me, Wendy," he said in a calmer voice, "you've got to take this seriously. If he tries anything, you've got to destroy him before he destroys you."

"I am taking this seriously, but it's a little crazy. You're asking me to kill someone for coming on to me?" Wendy asked. "Isn't that taking this to an insane extreme?"

"Groping your breasts is a little more than coming on to you, don't you think?"

"Yes, but is it reason to kill someone?" she asked. Wendy saw the veins in Taylor's neck bulge.

"Not for groping your breasts. But what if he doesn't stop there? What if he hits you, throws you to the floor and rapes you? Would you then feel compelled to stop him?"

"Of course I'd try to stop him."

"Good. I'm glad we see eye to eye. Now, how's the best way to do that?"

Wendy pointed to the silhouette and said in a monotone voice: "Go for the head, heart or lungs."

"That's right. Aim and pull the trigger six times."

Dismayed, Wendy moved away, stopping close to the cliff's rocky ledge. "You're acting like you're on the edge. Would you mind telling me what the hell is going on?"

"I'm just trying to help you protect yourself."

"No, it's more than that. You've been acting very strange lately. You leave for hours on end and I have no idea where you've been; you pulled a gun on me at school and now you're telling me about kill zones."

"I'm just trying to help you ready yourself in case a situation arises where your life is in danger."

"Taylor, he's just a horny banker. He's not a rapist or a murderer!"

"How do you know?" asked Taylor. "He could be a murderer. He could be responsible for several deaths for all you know. He could be a monster wearing the mask of a businessman."

"Of course I don't know, but I just think you're taking this a little too far, that's all."

Taylor shook his head and exhaled a deep breath. "Do you remember how scared you were when Escartes grabbed you at your apartment that night?"

"Of course I do."

"And will you at least admit that Gayland could have been behind it?"

"It's possible, but like my dad said, there's no proof."

"But you overheard him trying to call..."

"That's not proof, it's only a possibility," Wendy interrupted. "Gayland could have been calling anyone. We don't know for certain."

"I can't believe you're making excuses for that son-of-a-bitch!"

"Why do you hate him so much?" she asked with her back turned to Taylor.

"Because I know what he is. I see through the façade that you and many others embrace. He's a terrible human being. There are things about him that you don't know."

"Then tell me," Wendy said as she suddenly wheeled around to face Taylor. "Let me in on the secret."

"For your own good, I can't. And that's all that I can say."

"Does this have anything to do with your experiment?"

"What?" said Taylor, somewhat stunned.

"Last night, when you were gone, I logged onto your computer and read it."

"You read my dissertation?"

"Yes," Wendy said and crossed her arms. "And I want to know where in the hell you acquired your research. It seems to me that the victims of your study conveniently fit into your thesis."

An opportunity for truth presented itself to Taylor. This was his chance to tell her everything. If her love was undying, there was a possibility that she'd understand. "You had no business reading my dissertation," Taylor replied, hesitant to open Pandora's Box.

"But you're turning it in. If your professor is going to read it, why can't I?"

"I don't have a problem with you or anyone else reading it, but the project isn't finished yet, that's all."

Wendy's eyes widened. "Where did you obtain your research, Taylor? Where did those case studies come from?"

"I uh," Taylor said, trying to think quickly. "I uh, found that information in the library."

"Bullshit!"

"I did. My research came from a prison study based on death row inmates."

"You expect me to believe that the state did a whacked-out Freudian experiment on convicts?"

"No, the Freudian part is mine."

It was obvious Wendy wasn't buying it. "Look, my dissertation states that people are genuinely controlled by either the id or the superego. I'm searching to find which of these elements surfaces when they're put in extreme duress, and if that element is consistent with the element that controls their lives on a day-to-day basis. I used that research from the Department of Corrections because I wanted to know if those inmates behaved any differently when they faced the chair."

"You know I don't understand a damned thing about this id/ego business."

"It's simple," Taylor replied. "Freud thought that personalities develop in stages. First is the id which controls our immediate wants, then the ego, which is our conscious reality, then the superego, which questions everything we do. To simplify it, we live in ego. The id is like the little devil on our shoulder that tells us to do what we want and the superego is the angel on the other shoulder which tells us we'd really better think about it before we listen to the id."

Wendy shook her head. "That's mumbo jumbo to me."

"The id and the superego are our subconscious mind. The ego is our conscious mind, what we're using right now. The three components are supposed to live in harmony, but I believe that most people are either dominated by the id or the superego."

"That sounds really interesting, but I'm not buying it."

"It's just a theory. A widely held theory, I might add."

"Have you been hunting down the people who murdered your parents?"

Holy shit, thought Taylor. She's figuring this out. He looked deep into Wendy's eyes, then turned and walked to the edge of the cliff.

"I know you're very smart, Taylor, so smart that you've left virtually no evidence for the authorities to use to apprehend the killers. I've been reading about it in the papers. These aren't random murders. This is not a killing spree. This is calculated. The men who are dying are scumbags. I know this for a fact because I know these men. Ratcliff once sued my dad, so I know all about him."

"We should go now, it's getting late," Taylor replied as he stared at the water moving far below the cliff.

"What about Keith and Elijah? Are they helping you? Are they in on this with you?"

"Keith would never allow us to do this. He doesn't have the heart for such things."

"How 'bout Elijah? He's an Indian, right? Did they murder his parents, too? From what you've told me about him, he'd lead the charge to hunt them down."

"They're not like that," Taylor lied again. "They don't get along well enough to help me do something so sinister."

"Bullshit!"

"You can call it what you want, I don't care," Taylor said as he walked closer to the edge.

"Which one of you gutted the guy who attacked me? You remember, Escartes?"

Taylor stopped cold in his tracks. "What?"

"In the hotel room. I heard about it this morning on the radio."

"I uh, don't know what you're talking about."

"You know exactly what I'm talking about," Wendy said with authority. "The news said he'd been dead for a couple of days, which is about the time he attacked me and the same time you left that night after talking to Keith and Elijah on the phone. I know it was you. You told me you followed him to that hotel. You knew where he was staying."

"That's doesn't prove anything," Taylor said. "We had nothing to do..." Lying to his soul mate was more than Taylor could handle. He yearned to run to the hills, but knew Wendy would read that as an admission of guilt. His only hope was to rely on that quick wit to convince her that she'd been watching too many detective shows on TV. He hated to lie, but after all, it was for her own good. "I think you've worked yourself into a frenzy over nothing," Taylor calmly said. "All this talk makes for a great story, but unfortunately, none of it's true."

"Why haven't I ever met Keith and Elijah?" she asked.

"I just haven't had a chance to get everyone together."

"It's because you don't want to involve me in any way. You're protecting me. If I don't know them, how could I ever testify against them? That's why they've never come around."

Growing weary of Wendy's accusations, Taylor decided to end the conversation. "It'll be dark soon. I'm going to get on my horse and head back to the stalls. You can join me if you'd like, or you can stay here and continue developing this fascinating fictitious story. Maybe you ought to write a novel."

"If I'm wrong and you're telling me the truth, you'll take me to them. They live just a few miles away. You have no other excuses."

Taylor was at the end of his patience. He turned and said, "If I agree, will you get on the horse right now and stop making these ridiculous assertions?"

"You bet I will."

Darkness was just beginning to settle in the evening sky as Taylor pulled into the driveway of his old home. He looked around the outside of the house for signs of life, but regretfully found none. Under normal circumstances, he would have been pleased that Wendy would miss the opportunity to meet Elijah and Keith, but he really wanted to put her mind at ease.

"My God!" she exclaimed. "You used to live in that house?"

"Yeah."

"Aren't there zoning laws in this neighborhood? I've never seen a house so run down. Look at the cracks and rotten boards—I suppose it's okay if you're going for that haunted house look."

"I don't think anyone's home," Taylor said.

"I'm not sure I'd want to be home at this place."

"They haven't done a very good job of keeping it up, but my old house isn't so bad."

Wendy looked at the other dilapidated houses in the neighborhood. "All these houses are in terrible shape. What's the deal? Don't people around here care about their property?" she asked.

"Some do, some don't," Taylor said as he opened the car door. "Come on. Let's see if they're here."

The two approached the front door and knocked loudly. After

waiting a few moments, Taylor led the way to the back of the house. Wendy hesitantly followed.

A chilling gust of wind howled, making her shiver. "Where are you going?" she nervously asked. "This place is giving me the creeps."

"To see if they left the back door open."

"We don't need to do that," she quickly answered. "They're probably not home."

"I thought you wanted to meet them. I'll bet they're sleeping and didn't hear us knocking."

"To be honest, this whole neighborhood feels like a ghost town. I'm getting scared, Taylor."

"Well, I'm sorry, but if meeting them will clear my name, then we're staying until we find them."

Wendy's skin crawled when she saw the backyard. There was no snow on the ground, nor was there any grass. It was completely bare, just dirt. It looked like a graveyard without any graves. Wendy grabbed Taylor's hand and froze when several loud banging noises cut through the air.

"What's wrong?" he asked.

"What the hell was that?" she whispered.

"I'm not sure. It sounded like it was coming from the shed. I'll bet it's just a piece of tin on the roof banging in the wind."

"Taylor, I'm getting a bad feeling," she said. "Maybe we ought to just get the hell out of here."

"Getting a bad feeling? I'm here, don't worry. Let's go check out that noise. The shed is just ahead."

As they drew closer, Wendy heard a shrieking sound behind her, coming from the house. She turned to see a brilliant streak of blue light flash across the yard, a few feet from where they stood. For the first time in Wendy's life, she felt as though she was among ghosts. "Oh my God!" she gasped in terror. "Taylor, we're getting the hell out of here, now!"

"Why are you so freaked out?" he asked. "This is my old house. No one's going to hurt us here."

Wendy's legs were frozen with fear. She couldn't move a muscle. "I think I just saw a ghost," she said.

"Really?" said Taylor in a calm voice. "That's interesting. Other people have said that when they visit."

"Let's get out of here."

"Don't worry. You have nothing to fear from the ghosts."

"Nothing to fear, my ass!"

"Look," Taylor said. "This is where my parents passed on into the spirit world."

"What do you mean?" Wendy said, shaking.

"I mean, this is where they died."

"Here?"

"Yes, here. In this very back yard. All the houses on this side of the street lost someone. They all died within hours of each other."

"So all these ghosts are people that you once knew?"

"Right," Taylor said. "I'm not sure, though, there could be others that I'm not aware of."

"Listen to me, Taylor Hayes, if you love me you'll take me right back to the car this very instant."

"All right, all right," Taylor replied. "I'm just telling you that you have nothing to fear, that they're friendly spirits, that's all."

On the walk back to the car, Wendy's grip on Taylor's hand seemed to relax a little.

"Were there any others that died?"

"No. There were five houses, all in a row, that got hit with the poison. Our house was in the middle. All the other houses in the neighborhood were fine."

"You think they were poisoned?"

"Absolutely. I have no doubt. They all died suddenly the same way, within hours of each other."

"What about the police? What did they do?" asked Wendy.

"They did nothing. There were powerful forces involved. The police had their hands tied."

The two finally reached the parked car. Before Wendy opened the door, she checked the back seat for visitors, just to be sure.
Taylor started the car and wheeled it out of the driveway.

"I'm sorry we missed Elijah and Keith. I'd really like to prove to you that I have nothing to hide."

"I believe you," Wendy replied and grabbed Taylor's hand. "Just keep driving and promise to never take me back to that place again."

Chapter 39

"It's a little early to start drinking, don't you think?" someone called from the hallway.

Staring at the computer screen in his office, Jennings tried in vain to quickly identify the person, but couldn't place the voice. He hastily grabbed the soda can that was half filled with Jack Daniel's and slid it out of view.

"It's after five and it's only soda," Jennings said while he wheeled his chair around to face the accuser. He relaxed when he saw the familiar, beautiful face.

"You're acting awfully nervous for an innocent man," Carol said with a smile.

"I didn't recognize your voice. You scared the hell out of me. I almost spilled all my whiskey."

Carol laughed. "Sorry. I saw your soda can and figured you were partaking of the hooch, so I thought it would be funny if I imitated Director Flemming. I guess it worked."

"That's all I need—the director of the State Bureau catching me drinking. It'd be a riot," Jennings said with sarcasm.

"I just got your message. You said there was something we needed to discuss."

"There's actually several things we need to talk about," he said.

"You look stressed out," observed Carol. "Are you feeling okay?"

"It's been a bad day. The kind of day that makes you want to buy a goat ranch in the desert and never come back."

"A goat ranch?"

"I was being facetious. How 'bout a nice ranch with some horses and cows," Jennings said.

"I'll go for that. What happened today?"

"Several things, but…"

Jennings heard someone approaching, so he stopped talking.

"Who could that be? I thought everyone went home."

"I don't know," Jennings whispered.

"Hello?" someone called from just outside the door.

"Yeah," Jennings answered.

"I have a special delivery," the man added.

"We're not interested," Jennings replied.

"You should at least find out what it is before you refuse it," Quana said, then held up two one dollar bills. "I have two tickets for a weekend adventure in luxurious Ducotey, the heart of the heartland."

Jennings laughed a sigh of relief. "I'm not sure I want to spend a weekend in a place that only costs two dollars."

Carol jumped up to hug Quana. "What brings you here?" she asked.

"I don't know," he replied. "Jennings called and told me to get up here, pronto."

Glancing at Jennings, she asked, "Are we having a party?"

"Well, now that you mention it, I do have some whiskey and there are some sodas in my refrigerator." He reached into the bottom drawer of his desk and pulled out one-liter bottle of Jack Daniel's whiskey.

"Damn," replied Quana after seeing the massive bottle. "You're well prepared."

Jennings gave them each a can of soda then shut the office door. "I had an interesting meeting this morning. That's why I've called you both here."

"Oh yeah, you mentioned that you were going to talk to some kid whose car was seen at the Ratcliff site."

"That's not the meeting I'm talking about," Jennings said. He opened his desk drawer and pulled out a pack of cigarettes. "Today, I learned of the power of Kyle Gayland."

"You seem pretty worked up about this. I haven't seen you smoke in quite some time," Carol said as Jennings lit a cigarette.

Quana was quick to drink a large amount of cola. He slid the can across the desk to Jennings and said, "Fill her up."

"Me, too," Carol replied and handed the can to Jennings.

"What did you find out?" asked Quana.

"For starters, he was very unhappy to see me and he was completely rattled when I got there," Jennings said as he carefully poured whiskey in the soda cans. "He was sweating profusely and looked pale. He claimed to be sick, but I saw no signs of sickness. His nose wasn't running, his throat was clear, his voice didn't have that congested sound that most sick people have."

"So you think he was nervous?" asked Carol.

"Definitely. His hands were shaking like crazy. He couldn't control them."

"That sounds uncommon for a big powerful man of his stature," remarked Quana. "Hard to believe anything would spook him."

"Well, he was definitely shaken. Then he started asking all sorts of questions about Escartes."

"You mean Joe Escartes?" asked Quana.

"Right, the hitman. Gayland wanted to know everything about the murder."

"I heard about that on the news," Quana said. "They reported a lot of details, things that normally aren't released to the public."

"It was the maid. Once the press got wind of it, they talked to her and she sang like a canary."

"From what I heard, it sounded like the assassin got assassinated," Carol said.

"It looks that way. Gayland kept asking about it, though," Jennings remarked and took another swig. "He was asking very specific questions, things that most people wouldn't care about."

"So what do you think?" Carol asked.

"I think he knows something. The way he was acting – it was almost surreal."

"Again, that's odd. He's a big, tough guy who's had his nose in deep shit before," Quana said. "It's interesting that your visit fazed him."

"Maybe it's because I surprised him. Maybe he's guilty of something and just didn't expect to see someone from the Bureau."

"That is often the case in arrogant men such as Gayland," said Quana.

"Well, things really got interesting when I asked him about Redtree."

Quana's eyebrows raised. "Redtree?" he asked.

"Yeah."

"What do you know about Redtree?" asked Quana.

"Not much. Just that some Native Americans got sick and that Gayland was seen there during that time frame."

"Who told you he was there?" asked Quana.

"A source. I asked Gayland what he was doing there and, once again, he started acting very nervous. He said he was showing a local banker, Jonathan Peat, some property in Ducotey for an upcoming eviction."

"Maybe he was," Carol said. "It's certainly possible."

"Sure, but he asked me something that really caught my attention."

"What's that?" Quana asked.

"He wanted to know if the houses had been condemned."

"Condemned? That's odd," Carol said. "What's it matter to him?"

"Exactly. Why the hell would he care what happened to those houses?"

"'Cause this is not the first time it's happened," said Quana.

"Oh?" commented Jennings. "Where else?"

"Kickingbird, a few years ago," Quana said. "Same thing happened, except that time people died."

"That's right. Fred mentioned it the other day," Jennings stated. "He said the authorities never found out what happened."

Quana nodded. "They just moved the Indians onto the land that is now the Redtree Housing Unit and built new houses."

"Who did the government buy the land from for the houses at Redtree?" asked Jennings.

"I don't know," Quana replied.

"This is really getting interesting. What else did Gayland say?" Carol asked.

"He asked why I was asking questions and if the department had sanctioned an investigation. When I told him no, he became belligerent. He pretty much told me to get the hell out of his office."

"So what did you do?"

"I left. That's when my day turned to shit. When I got back here, I called the sheriff in Ducotey to ask about the Redtree houses. He played it off, said it was definitely something in the soil and water, probably from some industrial site or a natural gas well."

"Did they run any tests?" asked Quana.

"He said they did, but didn't find anything."

"I guess that all depends on how hard you look," Carol replied.

"As soon as I got off the phone, Director Flemming called me into his office. That was an enlightening conversation, let me tell you."

"What did he say?" Quana asked, his speech slurring slightly.

"He said the Carson Police Chief had given him a call, madder than hell. He wanted to know why I was questioning Gayland."

"Was Flemming upset with you?" Carol asked.

"Not really. But he did tell me that Gayland is a very powerful man who's in bed with most of the politicians around these parts. He said that Gayland could make all of our lives very miserable and it's best not to go snooping around him unless we've got hard evidence."

"You're not going to get that with Gayland," Quana said with confidence. "He knows exactly what he's doing."

"I figured that," Jennings said. "The whole ordeal really pissed me off. I mean, is Gayland above the law? Is he free to do what he wants, when he wants with impunity?"

Carol nodded. "I think we're getting ahead of ourselves with Gayland, but it certainly won't hurt to keep our eyes open and look into some things. We've just got to be careful that we don't get caught."

"I learned long ago that the world sometimes isn't fair, but this is blatant. Even if we find something, I don't know that we can do anything," replied Jennings.

"I know something we can do," Carol added. "We can go to the courthouse in Ducotey and research the land where the Redtree Housing Unit stands. We can find out who sold the land to the government."

"I'll do that in the next couple of days and give you a call," Quana said.

"That might be a good lead," Carol replied.

"Getting the hell out of here sounds like the most appealing lead right now," Jennings said.

"Why don't you guys just up and do it, then," Quana said. "Come this weekend. You can stay with Carol's parents. You'll enjoy it, Jennings, I promise. Carol and I can show you around. Trust me, we'll have a big time."

Jennings slammed his drink then slapped his hand on the desk. "Tell you what," he said. "I'm in. Let's do it."

"Really?" Carol said. "That's not just the alcohol talking, is it?"

"No, no, I'm serious. We both need to get out of town. The Finken trial should wrap up tomorrow or the next day, then I'm through for the week."

"Then it's a plan," Carol said with a smile. "And about freakin' time."

"The Finken trial, huh?" said Quana. "What's the real deal behind Mr. Finken? I've heard only bits and pieces about it. He supposedly murdered some kid."

"That he did. Then he brought in some high profile lawyers, Pinkus and Newman, who are absolutely pulling every string they can pull. They're building straw men, just so they can knock them down for show and I'm afraid the jurors are beginning to believe their bullshit."

Carol grabbed the cigarette from Jennings' mouth and took a drag. "He murdered a local high school kid over a drug deal," she said. "I mean, he allegedly murdered a high school kid over a drug deal."

"That's right," said Jennings. "Prosecutors are trying to prove that he had a local high school kid, Freddy Johnson, pushing cocaine and marijuana for him down here in Carson. As near as we can tell, the kid stole some of the junk and couldn't pay for it. Finken became enraged and killed the kid at home one night when his parents were gone."

"You've mentioned before that you have a strong case against him," said Quana.

"Very strong," Jennings replied. "We're got good hard evidence: Ballistics, shell casings, and the murder weapon."

Carol took another puff off the cigarette, then handed it back to Jennings. "The defense is trying to show that Finken has absolutely no ties in the drug world," she said.

"Which we all know is bullshit," interrupted Jennings. "We just can't seem to catch him in the act, but we know he's dealing."

"Right, but we have no hard evidence that he's a drug dealer. We relied on an inmate who testified that he dealt drugs for Finken. Of course the defense did everything they could do to discredit him, which wasn't difficult considering he's an inmate."

"And you say you expect the trial to be over this week?" asked Quana.

"It's possible," Jennings said. "Most of the testimony has been wrapped up. His lawyers are basically just peeing on everyone's shoes telling them that it's raining. I don't know how those bastards sleep at night."

"I'm sure they sleep well," Quana said. "To them, it's just money."

"I guess everyone's got a price."

"Well," Quana said, "I hate to spoil the party, but the wife's probably getting worried about me. Besides, if I drink much more, I doubt that I'll want to leave."

"Are you headed back to Ducotey?" asked Carol.

"Yeah."

"Speaking of Ducotey," said Jennings, "that kid I talked to this morning is from Ducotey."

"Really?" asked Carol. "What's his name?"

"Taylor...I can't remember the last name."

"Is it Taylor Hayes?" asked Quana.

"Yeah, that's it."

"Why in the world were you talking to him?"

"His car was spotted near the site where they found Ratcliff. I just asked him what he was doing there."

"He's a nice kid," Carol said. "I've known him practically his entire life. Our parents were good friends."

"Were?" Jennings asked.

"His mom and dad were victims of the poisoning at Kickingbird."

"Oh really? He's a white boy, he didn't look Native American."

"He's not. He was adopted. He pretty much grew up with the Indians, though."

"Did you find out why he was in that area?" asked Quana.

"Yeah. He said he was out taking pictures of some Indian relics. He showed me the pictures. It all seemed to check out."

"He really honors his parent's heritage," Quana said. "You don't see that much anymore with kids."

"He seemed pretty sharp. He's getting his masters in psychology. Said he might be interested in doing police work when he graduates."

"He graduated with top honors in his high school class and got a full academic ride to college. He goes by and visits my parents frequently. Speaking of my parents," Carol said, "Quana, it's time for you and dad to bury the hatchet. Mom tells me that it's eating Dad up inside."

Quana smiled. "So I'm finally getting through to that cranky old bastard, huh?"

"Yeah, you've finally broken through. I think it hits him the most now that he has to watch football games by himself."

"Well, I have to admit—we're in the heart of football season and it's not the same if I can't make fun of his team."

"Fred told me all about it."

Quana chuckled. "Yeah, it was a messy chain of events."

"World wars have been started over less," Jennings joked.

"That's about what it's become," Carol replied. "But seriously, it's gone on long enough. I know he would never admit it, but Dad really admires you, Quana. You're like a son to him."

"Well, I tell you what. If you two will get your butts up to Ducotey this weekend, I'll see if I can't make all this madness go away."

"Get that peace pipe warmed up," Jennings said. "'Cause we'll be there. That is, if I can find my way home."

Carol grabbed Jennings' car keys from his desk. "I believe I'll be taking care of that."

"Let me know if something develops with Gayland," Quana said as he walked out the door. "I'm very interested in his involvement with Redtree."

"We'll keep you advised," Jennings said.

Quana smiled and waved.

"Grab that Jack Daniel's, honey," said Jennings. "Let's call it a day."

Chapter 40

Taylor walked to the edge of Running Bear Cliff and looked down to the blood-red river, which still churned and moved rapidly along its banks. Startled by sounds behind him, he turned to gaze past the blue canyon walls to where the orange-skinned lawmen approached at a slow pace. Taylor sensed a great deal of confidence in their stride. Their glowing red eyes and painted smiles silently declared they would apprehend him in due time.

The wounded eagle's high-pitched shriek pierced the neon-green atmosphere. Taylor glanced into the canyon. He found the eagle sitting atop the rocks of the opposite bank, staring directly at him. Taylor faced the canyon to look closer. The eagle was trying to communicate something important, but he couldn't decipher the hollow shrieks.

"Go over," a voice whispered in Taylor's ear.

Startled, Taylor quickly turned to see Elijah standing directly in front of him. Elijah placed his hands around his mouth. "Go over," he called.

Standing next to Elijah, Keith nodded in approval.

"What in the hell are you guys doing?" Taylor asked. "We can't make it to the other side, it's too far."

"Go over," Elijah whispered. "It is time."

"The lawmen are coming," Taylor said. "We've got to follow the ravine up into the mountain. They'll never find us up there."

Elijah and Keith just looked at Taylor with content expressions.

"What in the hell is going on here? Aren't I getting through to you? If they catch us, we'll never get out of jail. We'll be in for life. I can't let that happen."

Taylor winced when he heard the eagle shriek once again. The sharp sound seemed to shred his ears and vibrate inside his skull.

Elijah smiled and grabbed something from the ground. Taylor didn't recognize the object.

"Go over!" Elijah's ground-shaking voice boomed through a megaphone.

The sound startled Taylor so much that he fell backward and rolled toward the cliff. As he passed over the ledge, he reached out with one arm to grasp a rock, temporarily saving him from certain death. As he clung to life, he looked up at Keith and Elijah, who were standing over him smiling.

"Help me!" he shouted. "I can't hold on much longer. Give me a hand!"

Elijah and Keith did nothing but smile.

"Keith, I've always watched out for you. Help me, damn it!"

Keith leaned down. "That wouldn't be proper, ol' boy," he said in a strong British accent. "What's done is done."

His strength waning, Taylor gave a hard look to Keith, then Elijah. "Damn you!" he shouted. "Damn you both!"

The intense pain from the cramps in his hand were more than he could endure. He sighed as he released his hold and fell into the netherworld of the abyss.

As Taylor searched for light in a world of darkness, a voice bellowed from above—*Taylor, snap out of it!*

Startled, he opened his eyes. Lying in a pool of sweat, he rubbed his eyes and sat up on the couch.

The aroma of spaghetti filled the room. He looked over his shoulder and saw Wendy stirring tomato sauce at the stove. Rushing to the sink, he poured a glass of water. "How long have I been asleep?"

"A couple of hours. I've been trying to wake you for a good ten minutes."

"How long 'till dinner?"

"It's ready right now," Wendy said as she handed him a plate. She noticed his sweat-soaked shirt. "Why are you sweating so much? Are you sick?"

"I had another weird dream," he replied.

"What was it about?"

"It's complicated," Taylor replied. "I was on the cliff again with Keith and Elijah.

"What happened?"

"It was very similar to the last dream I had."

"Was there an eagle?"

"Yeah."

"What was it doing?"

Taylor's eyes widened as he remembered the details of his conversation with Campanow. "It acted like it was trying to tell me something," he said.

"Maybe it was," Wendy said.

"I had a talk with an old friend about my dream. He told me that the eagle is a metaphor for my spirit, which is clouded by turmoil and is beckoning for its freedom."

"Is this from one of your psychology friends?"

"No. It's from an old Indian friend of mine."

"I've never known what to make of dreams," said Wendy. "Maybe your friend is right."

"Maybe so," Taylor said while he stared at the wall, lost in deep thought.

"We'd better eat before it gets cold."

Taylor built a colossal plate of spaghetti with tomato sauce, topped with bread.

Wendy was quick to fix a plate and sit down beside Taylor. "I had a message from my photography teacher today," she said.

"What did he want?" Taylor asked as he wheeled spaghetti around his fork. "He didn't ask you to pose for some compromising pictures, did he?" he added with a laugh.

"No, dear," Wendy said and rolled her eyes. "He graded those pictures of Running Bear Cliff that I turned in. He fell in love with them and wants me to take some black and white pictures for an upcoming contest. He really thinks they'd do well. He says it has a majestic aura that's perfect for still shots."

"That sounds great. Congratulations."

"The thing is, he wants to go up there with me."

"Absolutely not," Taylor said with animation. "You haven't told him where it is, have you?"

"No. I know you don't want me to share the location."

"Thank you."

"The contest deadline is in two days. I wish I would've known earlier. I could have taken the pictures when we were there. Oh well, we'll have to go pretty soon."

"I'm going to be very busy for the next couple of days, but you're welcome to go. Do you remember where it is?"

"I do. I'll see if I can get up there tomorrow."

Taylor's pulse quickened. "Uh, no!" he said. "Not tomorrow. Anytime but tomorrow."

"What's wrong with tomorrow?"

"I uh...I have..."

"Is something going on there?"

"Yes, that's right. There's a big Indian festival in Ducotey and people will be everywhere, especially on the reservation. You won't be able to get near Running Bear Cliff."

"Oh," Wendy said, disappointed. "I see. I guess I'll have to make it the next day."

"That sounds much better. I'll bet I can find some time then."

"I'll probably be very busy tomorrow anyway," Wendy said. "That's my first day back to work. I'm sure Gayland has loads of grunt work waiting for me. I have a ton of things for school to catch up on, too. I really need an afternoon by myself."

"Are you absolutely certain that you should go back to work?" Taylor asked.

"I have to. My mom and dad depend on it. It's out of my control."

"I wish you'd rethink this. It doesn't make much sense to me."

"I don't expect you to understand."

"Remember to take your gun. If nothing else, remember the gun."

"It's in my purse," Wendy replied.

"Are you ready to use it, if needed?"

She looked at her plate of spaghetti and remained silent.

"Is something the matter?"

"I just don't think I'll have to use the gun. I know Gayland's not a nice person, but I don't think he'll put me in a position to use it."

"He might not, but in case he does, you'll be prepared, right?"

"Right."

"Remember, Wendy, there are things about that man that you

don't know. He'll take advantage of you before you even realize it."

"Okay," Wendy said in a soft voice.

"Do you believe me? It's very important that you take this seriously."

"I believe you and I will take it seriously, but I just don't think that. . ."

"Then let's speak no more of it," Taylor interrupted. Sensing the growing turmoil in Wendy, Taylor quickly decided to change the subject. "By the way, this is some fine spaghetti."

Wendy continued to stare at her plate. "I'm glad you like it."

"Is something wrong?" Taylor asked. "You're hardly eating."

Wendy dropped her fork and looked directly into Taylor eyes. "I'm sorry I accused you of killing those people. I feel terrible about it. I guess all this stress from school and Gayland and everything else is finally getting to me."

"Forget about it. Stress can do funny things to a person's mind."

"I know, but I shouldn't let it get to me that much. I should be whipped for calling you a serial killer."

"It's no problem. Let's just enjoy our meal."

Wendy smiled and took a bite of spaghetti. "You do know that I love you very much, don't you?"

"Sometimes it's the only thing that keeps me going."

Chapter 41

Jennings' patience was wearing thin as he surfed the channels in search of a cowboy movie. After finding nothing of interest, he finally gave up and turned to the local PBS station. Pouring himself another drink of Jack Daniel's, he pushed back the recliner to watch a group of psychology experts debate Freud's theories. He laughed as the participants riled each other in the heated conversation:

"Freud's psychoanalysis theories have been criticized the most because their assertions cannot be tested in the laboratory! You simply cannot test a person's id and superego."

"True. But his work laid the foundations for developing a highly subjective approach to understanding individual complexions that earmark the human subliminal self."

"The truth to the matter is that his impact on psychology was indeed profound. He provided important insights into understanding the emotional lives of humans, encouraged psychologists to consider the impact on behavioral processes not immediately available to conscious inspection, and also helped to legitimize the study of human sexuality."

"I guess that's why some men dress up in women's clothing."

The last statement caught Detective Jennings' attention and he bolted upright.

"What're you watching?" Carol asked, tying her robe as she entered. Fresh from the shower, her hair was wrapped in a towel.

"Just some pinheads arguing about Freud," Jennings replied.

"Pinheads, huh?" Carol said and sat.

"They seem to be. Did you take any psychology classes in college?"

"Yeah, a few. Psychology was my major for a while, but that was a long time ago."

"Do you know anything about Freud? As I remember, he blamed everything on penis envy."

Carol laughed. "Well, yeah, but there's lots of other things he's known for," she said, gazing at the television. "The people on TV are talking about his study of the human psyche. He broke down personalities into the id, ego, and superego."

"Yeah, I remember studying his theories. Do you believe they're real?"

"Of course," Carol said. "Although Freud said the id and superego were in the subconscious mind, I think they're part of our consciousness. If you look at the way people behave, you can see that they're controlled by either an aggressive personality or a submissive personality, hence the id and superego."

"What am I?" Jennings asked.

"Id. Definitely id."

Jennings frowned and took a swig. "Sorry, I don't try to be."

"No need to apologize," Carol laughed.

"Something one of them said caught my attention," Jennings said. "He joked about men dressing up in women's clothing."

"And?"

"An eye witness noticed that one of the killers was dressed like a woman."

"That can mean a host of things," Carol said. "Maybe they're just trying to throw off the police by disguising their appearance."

"Maybe."

The ringing phone interrupted their discussion. "Wonder who in the hell is calling at this hour?"

Carol picked up the phone. "It's for you," she said and handed the receiver to Jennings. After listening and pacing for a few minutes, he slammed the phone on the table. From his pale face, she immediately knew something was wrong. "What is it?" she asked.

"That was the D.A."

"What's wrong? What did he want?"

"Things didn't go well at the Finken trial today," Jennings said, as he lit a cigarette.

"Oh? What happened?"

"The judge ruled that he's not going to admit the gun as evidence."

Carol jumped out of her seat. "He not going to admit the gun as evidence! Are you serious?"

Jennings dropped his head to his hands. "As serious as a heart attack," he muttered.

"What happened?"

"Do you remember when they did the investigation at the crime scene?"

"Yes," Carol answered.

"And they found the murder weapon?"

"Of course."

"Today, Jackson, the investigator who found the gun, was on the witness stand."

"We expected that."

"Right, but Finken's attorneys managed to discredit his testimony."

"I don't understand how they could…"

"If you'll remember, Jackson found the gun in the wood stove."

"Right."

"The fire was still burning when he found the gun, so he used a metal poker to retrieve it."

"So?"

"The investigators had been looking all day for the murder weapon. I guess in his excitement, Jackson didn't think much about it being so hot."

"I don't understand," Carol said in confusion.

"He used a towel to retrieve the gun from the end of the poker, but the towel didn't help. The gun had been in the fire for some time. Towel in hand, he grabbed the gun but it quickly burned through the towel and scorched his hand."

"I'm sorry that he got hurt, but what does that matter?"

Jennings inhaled a deep drag from the cigarette. "Jackson dropped the gun on the floor. He was in a lot of pain due to the burn on his hand so he immediately headed to the sink and ran cold water over his hand."

"Okay, but I don't see the problem with…"

"While Jackson was tending to his hand at the sink, another

investigator, Robertson, wrapped a towel around the gun and picked it up. The gun was still extremely hot, so he took it outside to cool on the porch."

"So?" Carol said. "Big deal."

"A rookie newspaper reporter was on the front lawn taking pictures and saw Robertson lay down the gun. One of the detectives inside asked Robertson a question about the gun, so he turned and talked to the investigator. When he turned back around to grab the gun, he discovered the newspaper reporter had picked it up."

Carol was aghast. "Oh my God!" she exclaimed. "The chain of evidence was broken."

"Exactly," Jennings replied while inhaling another drag from the cigarette.

"You've got to be kidding me."

"I wish I was. Finken's attorneys claimed that since Jackson and Robertson didn't bag and initial the gun before the newspaper reporter handled it, the gun is inadmissible. The judge agreed."

"This is ludicrous!"

"Of all the bullshit technicalities to get someone off, this goes down in the book of world records," Jennings replied. "And another rich and powerful criminal will soon be walking the streets again."

"You think Finken will walk?"

"I know he will. Remember Smith, the convict who testified that he dealt drugs for Finken?"

"Yes."

"Well, it turns out that he's also a child molester. Finken's attorneys were all over that today. The jury won't buy a word of his testimony. I don't know why we're so surprised. We knew those bastards would pick through the case with a fine-tooth comb until they found something."

"When do you expect the verdict?"

"Tomorrow. Closing arguments were this evening. It won't take the jury long to deliberate."

"I suppose you're right."

"Sometimes I wonder if I'm just wasting my time. I know it's a job that has to be done, but *boy oh boy* does this shit get old."

"I guess this frees up our weekend."

"I'll say."

"Do you want to go to Ducotey tomorrow?"

"We might as well. There's no point staying around here. I'm already pissed off beyond belief. Getting out of town would probably do me some good," Jennings said.

"I'll call Mom and Dad in the morning. They'll be pleasantly surprised."

"Call Quana, too. He wanted us to keep him posted."

"I expect to hear from him soon. He's going to the courthouse to check the Redtree records."

"Are you going to the office tomorrow?" asked Jennings.

"Yes," Carol answered. "I've got a few things to do."

"Have fun. I have a feeling that I'll be calling in sick and sleeping late."

Chapter 42

For the first time in days, the early morning sun filled Gayland with hope. Even so, his optimism was short-lived as he realized the irony of having Peat as an ally. In the past, he had only tolerated Peat's constant whining and bitching because he needed his money and Escartes could easily silence him once the transaction was complete. His stomach clenched as he realized the desperation of the situation.

Had the years of playing dirty finally directed the universal force of karma to strike him down? He'd been worried about such mysterious forces before, but never like this. A madman with a thirst for his blood was on the loose—it would soon be time to atone for his sins.

The sound of tires crossing the cattle guard drew his attention to the gravel road. Old Peaty was approaching with a broad smile. My, oh my, thought Gayland. Was his world about to change.

"Top of the morning" Peat said as he stepped onto the porch. "How does this day find you?" He paused as Gayland motioned for him to join him inside, then added, "Is something the matter? You look as though..."

"We're being hunted," Gayland said without looking at Peat. He poured himself a drink of straight whiskey and slammed it on the spot.

Peat instantly paled. "What? That can't be."

"I'm afraid it is. I got the contracts in the mail this morning."

"Contracts? What contracts?"

"The contracts Ratcliff drew up with the investors. When they murdered Ratcliff's partner, they took them. I thought it was Escartes the whole time. He told me he took the contracts and destroyed them, but I've got proof that he lied. It appears that the son-of-a-bitch lied about everything. He didn't kill anyone, they were the ones doing all the killing."

"You mean someone else has been killing the investors?" Peat stuttered. "Oh, dear God!"

"You can say that again."

"Are you sure? Maybe Escartes killed the investors and lost the contracts. Maybe someone found them and wants to blackmail us."

"In case you haven't heard, Escartes is dead. They butchered him like they butchered all the others."

Peat placed his hand over his mouth. "I didn't know."

"They found him in his hotel room, hanging in the shower."

"But he was a hitman. Maybe someone tracked him here and found the contracts in his room after they killed him. They saw our names and…"

"It's possible," Gayland said, "but I doubt it. Every time I talked to Escartes, he was clueless about what was going on. When I asked questions about the killings, his answers sounded made up. I'm almost certain he didn't kill any of them."

Shocked, Peat eased into on an old wooden chair and stared blankly at the table.

"There's blood all over the contracts that I received in the mail this morning. The message is clear—we're next."

"But who could it be? Who in the world knows what we're doing?"

"That's the million dollar question," Gayland remarked. "I haven't a clue. But you can bet your ass that they're toying with us, letting us know that we're next. Our only hope is to be prepared. Do you own a gun?"

"No…No, of course not," Peat said. "I've never had a need."

"Well, you do now. Here," Gayland said, placing a .9 millimeter on the table.

The weight of the gun surprised Peat. "Dear God. I knew I shouldn't have gotten myself into this," he said as tears came to his eyes. "How could you let me get myself into this!"

"Calm down, boy! It ain't over yet."

"You son-of-a-bitch! You told me that this would be like taking candy from a baby. You said you've done it before—that everything was worked out!"

Gayland took the gun, then slapped Peat hard on the face. "Get a hold of yourself! We're not finished yet, damn it!"

Peat buried his face in his hands and cried uncontrollably.

"Look Peaty, if you don't straighten up and start acting like a man, you're done for. From what I've seen and read about the murders, these people are trained killers. They'll sense your fear and use it to kill you. You've got to be strong."

Peat grabbed a paper towel from the center of the table and wiped his face.

"You only have two options—kill or be killed. It's as simple as that."

"I'm sorry, Gayland," Peat said, trying to compose himself. "I'm not strong like you."

"No worries. The important thing to remember is that there are some positives in this dilemma."

"Like what?"

"It's good that the killers mailed me copies of the contracts."

"Why?"

"Because it means that they're not going to the police. The contracts themselves are enough to get us both the death penalty. Hell, not even Pinkus and Newman could get us out of this mess and I own every judge in this town."

"But if they're not going to the police, what do they want?"

"They might be blackmailing us, I'm not sure," Gayland said. "One thing's for certain—they mean business. What's important for us to remember is that they may be coming to kill us. Be suspicious of everything. Carry that gun at all times." He paused and smiled. "Things aren't hopeless yet. I've been talking to a certain politician who's very interested in buying our land for future Indian housing. Of course, we're going to have to kick him back a little when the deal is done, but he's certainly interested and feels that he can find the proper government funding."

Peat let out a slight breath of relief. "I suppose that is better news," he said. "Who exactly will they be buying it from?"

"Through my connections, I created an identity, a Mr. Arnold Lane, who will be selling the land to the government. It's already set up."

"That is good news. Now all we have to worry about is staying alive long enough to split the check."

"And there's one more positive note," Gayland said while pouring another drink.

"Yes," Peat said, his hands shaking.

"My initial plans were to have Escartes remove Hempshaw, but since things have changed radically, I say we use this to our advantage."

"How so?"

"Hempshaw is the meanest son-of-a-bitch in this state. This man has the demeanor of a wounded mama grizzly bear and is always lookin' for a fight."

Distressed again, Peat replied, "What's to keep him from coming after us?"

"Relax, he has no idea of our prior intentions."

"I'm not so sure that I like being in bed with another madman," he said. "It sounds to me like he's just as crazy as those bastards who are hunting us!"

Gayland patted Peat on the back. "He's on our side, Peaty old boy. Don't worry about him."

"But what if he knows? What's to stop him from killing us all? What's to stop him from doing to us what we planned to do to him?"

"Peaty, relax. He's a reasonable man. I'm going to Ducotey this afternoon to show him the contracts and talk to him. I'm going to tell him that somebody's trying to kill us. Trust me, that'll piss him off good. He'll be ready when these thugs go after him. I wouldn't be surprised if he doesn't up and take 'em all out if and when they pay him a visit."

"I'm not so sure I like this. I think you've gotten us into a mound of shit."

Gayland reached for the bottle of whiskey and poured Peat a shot. He slid it across the table. "Drink it down," he said. "It'll calm your nerves."

"That won't help! For the love of God, we're not safe anymore!"

"You're safe here," Gayland said. "Now drink that whiskey."

Peat reluctantly grabbed the glass of whiskey. The blast of alcohol felt like gasoline in his throat, but he managed to force it down.

"It appears that you haven't spent much time with whiskey," Gayland laughed.

"How can you laugh at a time like this? We're being stalked!"

"Damn it, Peat, get ahold of yourself this instant. I don't have time to sit here and babysit you. It's time to start acting like a man!"

Peat contemplated his limited options and reached for the bottle. "You're right," he said, then drank another shot of mash before snatching the gun.

Gayland smiled. "I'm glad that you're finally seeing things my way. Trust me, it's your only alternative."

Peat didn't share Gayland's happiness. While he drank the whiskey, his eyes remained fixed on the gun in his hand. "Would you mind if I stay here for a little while and collect myself? I'm getting pretty lightheaded and shouldn't go back to my bank with alcohol on my breath."

"Sure, suit yourself. Take a nap and sleep it off. I promise, you'll feel better when you wake up," Gayland said while walking to the front door.

"I hope you're right."

"Trust me, we're going to be fine."

"Try not to mention my name to Hempshaw," Peat said. "I've got enough to worry about."

"I won't say a word," Gayland said as he left.

Peat sighed and poured another shot. The whiskey didn't burn his throat as much as before, so he had another. The rush was a splendid feeling.

Moving to the den, he kicked off his shoes, then tucked the pistol beneath his belt buckle. He felt wonderful—uninhibited and confident. The couch looked very inviting, so he stretched out and closed his eyes. The world seemed much less dreary as he drifted off to sleep.

Chapter 43

If the individual's personality is principally ruled by submission, the id and superego are disguised and sometimes indistinguishable in times of danger. Aggressive behavior, fueled by the id, can be mistakenly identified as superego-driven compliance. Rather than standing to fight, the id directs the victim to vigorously negotiate a non-violent outcome. The threat of hostility from the individual is minimal, but the individual's chances for survival are heightened.

"He's leaving," Taylor said with the binoculars still pressed tightly to his eyes.

"Is Peat in the car with him?" asked Keith.

"No. Gayland's alone."

"If you must do it, you might as well do it now," Keith said. "He's out here alone. This might be our best chance."

"No," Taylor said. "We'll do him in Ducotey. He called Kacey this morning and told him that he'll be at Hempshaw's store this afternoon. He thinks he's going to buy Kacey's minerals."

"I have something special planned for him there," said Elijah with a wicked grin.

Taylor stepped out of the car and focused the binoculars on Gayland's farmhouse. "Peat's car is still at the house. He must be inside."

Sitting in the backseat of the car, Elijah wheeled out a .44 magnum and loaded it with six bullets. "Very good," he said with a cold grin. "There's about to be one less piece of shit in the world."

As soon as the green Suburban crept out of sight, Taylor

jumped back in the car and sped down the gravel road to the old farmhouse.

Peat felt something crawling on his face. In a semi-conscious state on the couch, he was completely relaxed. The whiskey was working. Tranquility was finally settling in. He lazily brushed the insect away from his face and drifted back to sleep.

The insect returned. Growing annoyed, he used both hands to slap it away, but the bug persisted. It's just like Gayland to have bugs in his house, thought Peat, his eyes still closed. Even though the weather outside was very cold, Gayland should have sprayed the place for insects. Insects? Peat's mind became cognizant. There are no bugs in the winter.

As soon as Peat opened his eyes, he gasped for breath. Standing over him was the manifestation of all the fears he'd avoided his entire life. It was scary, it was surreal, and it held a large chrome-plated gun, aimed right at him.

"Oh, my God!" Peat groaned. "Who in the hell are you?"

"I'm the cleanup batter. And you're next on the list."

Sweat instantly beaded on Peat's forehead. "You don't understand! I'm not a violent man...I played no role in any of this."

Taylor smiled. "Don't lie to me, Jonathan Peat. I know you gave money to Gayland to buy the land. You knew he tried to kill the Indians at Redtree. Hell, you were spotted there with him."

"Kill him now," Elijah screamed from behind Taylor.

"Hear him out, Taylor," countered Keith.

"I'm not denying any of that," Peat said, his voice shaking. "I was there with Gayland and I gave him the money, but you've got to believe me, I didn't want anyone to die. Those Indians all pulled through. I know that for a fact because I checked on them at the hospital."

Taylor adjusted his wig as he laughed. "You're right, fortunately no one died this time, but you disrupted their lives for your own personal gain."

"Believe me, it was all Gayland's idea," Peat said as tears came to his eyes. "He's been doing this to Indians for years. He's the one you want, not me."

"Kill him!" screamed Elijah. "His hands are dirty, too."

Peat completely broke down. "Please forgive me. I'm sorry about what happened to those poor Indians. You've got to believe me, mister, I never knew anyone would get hurt. By the time Gayland told me all the details, it was too late. I couldn't say no. Gayland is a powerful man."

Keith sighed. "I believe him. Gayland would have killed him had he not gone along with his plans."

Peat sat up on the couch. "Here," he said and handed Taylor the pistol that was tucked underneath his buckle. "Take this gun. It's proof that I'm not a violent man. You've got to believe me."

Taylor grabbed the gun and stepped back to Keith and Elijah.

"I say we cut this one loose," Keith said quietly. "Look at the poor bastard, he's suffered enough."

"I can get you anything you want," Peat said. "Money, drugs, whatever. I have connections. I can even get you Gayland."

"We don't need any help with Gayland," Taylor said. "He'll soon be taken care of."

"Let's tie him up and get out of here," Keith said. "We've made our point here with…"

"You people never cease to amaze me," Elijah said and aimed his .44 Magnum at Peat. Before Taylor could react, Elijah cocked the pistol and fired several shots. Keith and Taylor stood in shock as Peat reeled from the impact.

"You son-of-a-bitch!" said Keith. "What the hell was that?"

"He would have identified us all," Elijah said. "Whether you believe his bullshit story or not, he still would have gone to the police and put the finger on us."

Taylor snapped. "Damn it, Elijah! You've got to stop making decisions without our consent."

"We already made this decision," scoffed Elijah. "This man tried to kill our people. If he had his way, they would have killed all the Indians at Redtree."

"Bullshit!" shouted Keith. "You heard what he said. Gayland forced him. He had no way out."

"He lied. If he was so concerned about breaking the law, then he shouldn't have been in with such seedy company. He knew what he was getting into."

"My patience is running thin with you, Elijah," flared Keith. "This was unnecessary. You are causing me a great deal of anxiety."

Elijah pointed the pistol at Keith. "I can end your suffering right now," he said.

"That's enough!" Taylor interjected. He reached out and pushed down Elijah's arm. "Everyone stay calm. We have other issues to contend with right now."

"Other issues?" laughed Keith, "what other issues?"

"Jennings recently paid me a visit."

"Who the hell is Jennings?" said Elijah.

"He's a detective with the State Bureau," answered Taylor.

"A detective?" said Keith. "That's it, it's over. I quit."

"He was just checking out a lead. Someone spotted our car when we did Ratcliff."

"So that's it, he was just following up on a lead?" asked Elijah.

"That's right. I don't really think he knows anything."

"He doesn't know anything? Are you crazy? He's been watching you, Taylor. He knows something," Keith said, incensed.

"If he was watching Taylor, don't you think he would have taken him in?" asked Elijah.

"I don't know," Keith said. "But I don't like it one bit."

"I agree with Elijah. He doesn't have anything. I'm sure they're just getting desperate."

"I don't care," Keith said. "I'm still out."

Elijah smiled. "Good," he said. "We're better off without your anal-retentive logic anyway."

"I can't take this anymore. This thing is moving way the hell too fast. We've got to slow down."

"We can't slow down," replied Taylor. "We have to strike when the iron is hot and today, the iron is white hot."

"It's too much. You're both acting like fools. We've obviously made a mistake or Jennings never would have talked to you. We should stop now and let things cool off."

"If Jennings gets in the way," said Elijah, "I'll take care of him myself."

"You will do no such thing," Taylor said, sternly. He grabbed Elijah by the shoulder of his dress. "Under no conditions are you or any of us to harm any of the innocent. Do you understand?"

Angered by his tone of voice and aggressiveness, Elijah merely looked Taylor in the eye and muttered, "Okay."

"Good," Taylor said, releasing his hold. "Now let's get the hell out of here." Leading the way, he grabbed the hem of his dress to wipe off the doorknob.

As Elijah followed, he looked back at Peat and said, "And then there were two."

Chapter 44

Carol shivered as she lightly tapped the idling pickup's horn. Cranking the heater to high, she tugged on her gloves and glanced nervously at her house. The ice cold leather seemed to moan as she twisted to check the backseat to be certain everything was packed for their weekend trip to Ducotey.

Every passing second intensified the hollow feeling in the pit of her stomach. Through the picture window, she could see Jennings pacing as he talked on the phone. His body language screamed of frustration and disappointment. She was certain the call of duty had ruined yet another outing.

Finally, he hung up and hurried to join her. The moment he jumped in the passenger side, she shifted into reverse and said, "Please don't tell me that I'm dropping you off at the office on my way out of town."

"No. Let's get the hell out of here."

Carol excitedly replied, "I was afraid that…"

"Finken walked," interrupted Jennings.

Shocked, she muttered, "Are you kidding?"

"I wish I were."

"What happened?"

"Since the chain of evidence was broken and the judge ruled it inadmissible, the jury didn't feel like they had a strong enough case to convict."

Angry, Carol seethed, "I can't believe it."

"We've seen it before and we'll see it again, I'm sure." Jennings grabbed a cigarette from his jacket and fired it up.

"Are you smoking full time now?"

"Full time for the time being," barked Jennings while he stared distantly out the passenger window.

Carol had never seen Jennings so disturbed. They'd lost tough cases in the past and he always took it hard, but not like this. "Are you all right?" she asked.

Jennings took a deep drag on the cigarette and rolled the window down slightly. Rather than exhaling the smoke, he let it roll out of his mouth slowly. "No," he said. "I really thought we were going to take him down. Now there's a dead kid and that son-of-a-bitch is walking the streets. He'll soon be dealing drugs to children again."

Carol took his hand in hers. "Don't take it personally. There's nothing more you could have done—sometimes the system fails."

"I know. It just seems like it fails more and more nowadays."

"I agree, but it's out of your control. You can only do so much."

"It was the ugliest thing I've ever seen," Jennings said.

"What are you talking about?"

"Finken's face. It was the ugliest thing I've ever seen."

"When? During the trail?"

"Yeah. On the days that I testified against him, he stared at me the whole time I was on the stand. He was smilin' like a shit-eatin' rat," Jennings said.

"It's hard to imagine that he'd be so confident, especially since he was facing the death penalty," replied Carol.

"He was taunting me—silently telling me that he and I both knew that he killed that kid, but it didn't really matter. He knew he was going to walk. He had the money to bring in the big guns and there wasn't a thing anyone was going to do about it."

"I had no idea he was so arrogant during..."

"That image is chiseled permanently into my memory. I saw pure evil," he declared, inhaling a long drag of smoke.

"Honey, you can't let this get to you. It's part of the job. You've got to let it go. I know you feel helpless, but there's nothing more you can do."

"Maybe it's time for me get out. You know, buy a few acres and some livestock. We could get hitched and farm in our retirement."

"We'd be poor, but we'd probably be happier," Carol said lightheartedly.

"I'm serious," replied Jennings. "Maybe this is a sign. Maybe it's time to move on."

"You never know. The Lord works in mysterious ways."

"Indeed He does."

"Mom called this morning," Carol said.

"What did she say?"

"I told her we were on our way. She's very excited. We're having a little party at their house this afternoon."

"What kind of party?"

"The kind where everyone acts like adults. I've invited Quana and he accepted. I hope we can convince Dad to bury the hatchet."

"That should be interesting," Jennings replied with a smile. "Speaking of Quana, has he checked the courthouse records yet?"

"Yes. The records in Ducotey show the government purchased the Redtree land from a man by the name of Arnold Lane."

"I wonder who he is."

"I don't know. I checked the databases and found that he doesn't exist."

"Really?" Jennings said with surprise. He flicked his cigarette out the window. "Not anywhere?"

"Not anywhere. It's very interesting."

"Maybe he's just not in the database."

"Everyone's in the database," said Carol.

"So what are you eluding to?"

"If Gayland's as dirty as we've been hearing, he probably has connections to the underworld. If that's the case, he could have created Arnold Lane as a cover so his name never appeared on any government contracts."

"I wouldn't be surprised, but linking this to Gayland is a problem. Prosecuting him will be just as difficult as prosecuting Finken."

"I agree. We should keep our ears open, though. It won't hurt to find out everything there is to know about Arnold Lane."

"I'm sure it will lead nowhere, but I'll certainly give it a try."

"Lead nowhere? That's a bit cynical, don't you think?"

"Look at our recent track record. We didn't get a conviction with Finken, we have little to no leads in the bizarre cross-dresser murders, and the powers-that-be are stonewalling us on questioning Gayland. We're officially screwed, both coming and going."

"You shouldn't give up hope, my dear. The cross-dress murderers will make a mistake sometime. Sooner or later, they'll get sloppy and leave some evidence."

"But that's just the thing. They've killed several people on separate occasions and haven't slipped up yet. It's almost too perfect. I've thought a lot about it lately and I just can't tie it all together."

"We're just overlooking something. There's a link. We're just not seeing it."

"I sure can't. There's such a range of victims with these crimes. Lawyers, wealthy men from small towns, even a mob hitman—and all we know is that people dressed up like women have been seen near some of the crime scenes."

"Speaking of hit men," Carol said, "did you hear about what they found on Escartes?"

"No."

"Evidently there was a note stuck to him with a small arrow."

"A note? What did it say?"

"It said, 'I buried my heart at redtree.'"

"What the hell does that mean?" Jennings said as he took a drag on a cigarette.

"Beats me. I guess the killers are leaving riddles now." As Jennings watched the smoke roll out the window, he had an epiphany. "Wait a minute!" he shouted. "What did the note say?"

"It said 'I buried my heart at redtree.'"

"Redtree," Jennings whispered.

"Yeah, redtree." repeated Carol. When Jennings took his cell phone out of his pocket and began to dial, she asked, "Who are you calling?"

"The office."

"Why?"

"I've got a hunch. It's the Indians."

"What Indians?"

"The Indians from the Redtree Housing Unit."

Carol clenched her teeth, grabbed the phone and turned it off.

"What the hell are you doing?" shouted Jennings.

"Listen to me," Carol said, wagging her finger in his face. "This can wait until Monday. We haven't had a relaxing weekend ever since we've known each other and by damned, I'm not going to allow this one to slip us by."

"But I might be onto something," he replied in a softer voice. "This might be the break we've been waiting for."

"I don't care! You're letting your job interfere with your personal life and I've had all I can take."

"But honey, it all makes sense. Your father said that some of the Indians were angry that the police couldn't solve the case. That's our motive—especially when you consider what happened at Kickingbird a few years ago."

"So what are you saying? That a group of Indians are out for vigilante justice?"

"It's possible," Jennings said. "Remember when we did background checks on all those victims?"

"Yeah, and?"

"They were all scumbags who'd grown wealthy through shady business deals."

"So?"

"Maybe they were involved. Maybe they were in on the poisoning with Gayland. And remember, Gayland was spotted at the Redtree Housing Unit that day by your father."

"Then why isn't Gayland dead?" asked Carol. "If he's the ringleader, don't you think they would take him out, too?"

"Maybe they haven't gotten to him yet."

"Then tell me this—why did they decide to kill a hit man?"

He shrugged. "I don't know how Escartes fits into this."

"I know why. It's because your theory is a long shot at best, a far and away long shot. You're making all these assumptions based on a note that has thousands of possibilities."

Disappointed, Jennings sighed.

Carol offered him the cell phone.

"What are you doing?"

"It's unfair of me to ask you to choose between me and your job. If you want to call the office, feel free. I'm sure they'll send someone to pick you up at the next rest stop. I'm going to Ducotey."

Jennings reached into his jacket and grabbed a cigarette. After lighting it, he stared at the floorboard, then looked at Carol and smiled. "I'm sorry," he said, "I guess I got carried away with myself. You're far more important to me than my job. And you're right—I guess it is a pretty far fetched theory."

"Regardless, it can wait until Monday," Carol said.

"You're right. And I'm sorry."

"You should be. We're not getting any younger," Carol said. "I know the job is important, but so are our lives."

"You're absolutely right," Jennings said. "I realized that today on the phone when they told me about Finken being acquitted. Even though I've lost faith in the justice system, we have each other and that's all that matters. But I still feel terrible about the Finken case."

"So do I, but I don't really know what to do about it."

Jennings smiled. "Land. Horses. Cows. Maybe the answer has been around for centuries."

Chapter 45

Wendy waited impatiently for her computer to reboot. Due to several unexpected dilemmas, her first day back to work proved more difficult than she expected. She'd spent the entire morning on the phone with the bank's computer technician trying to fix all the problems caused by the temporary secretary. After several frustrating attempts, she felt confident that the computer would work this time.

"Excuse me, Miss," someone said.

Wendy turned to find a young couple. "Yes. Can I help you?"

"I filled in for you while you were gone. I forgot my makeup bag," the woman said. "I think it's in the top desk drawer. By the way, my name's Veronica."

"Nice to meet you. I'm Wendy," she said as she opened the drawer and handed the bag to Veronica.

"This is my boyfriend, Howard," Veronica added with a smile.

Wendy acknowledged him with a polite nod. "Can I ask you a question?"

"Sure," replied Veronica.

"What exactly did you do to this computer? I'm having problems getting it to work this morning."

Veronica laughed. "I didn't do it," she said. "Yesterday afternoon, Gayland rushed in here and told me to get off the computer, that he had some files he had to see. He was acting like a madman, cussin' up a storm. He smelled like he'd been drinking, too."

"That doesn't surprise me."

"Within a few minutes, he managed to crash the whole system. I don't know what he was looking for, but it must have been awfully important."

Wendy heard the sound of the computer launching successfully, so she turned. She was relieved to see that the system appeared to be restored. "That's a welcome relief," she said.

"I'm sorry about the computer. I told him that I would find the files for him, but he insisted that I leave the room."

"That's interesting," Wendy said. "I wonder what he was looking for?"

"Haven't I seen you before?" asked Howard. "You look awfully familiar."

"I was thinking the same thing," replied Wendy. "Do you go to college here?"

"Yes. Wait, I know, you're Taylor's girlfriend. I've seen you at parties."

"That's right. And I remember you now. You're the guy who can chug two beers at the same time through the beer bong."

Howard laughed. "It's a gift."

"How do you know Taylor?" asked Wendy.

"Oh, I've known him for most of my life. I'm from Ducotey."

"We're on our way there now. I'm going to meet Howard's parents for the first time," bragged Veronica.

"Good luck," Wendy said. "I hear there's a big Indian festival there today. There's supposed to be lots of people."

"There's no Indian festival in Ducotey today," Howard said. "That's in the spring."

"Are you sure? I was told it's today and that there'd be people everywhere."

Howard shook his head. "I don't think so. I haven't heard anything about it."

"Well, maybe I misunderstood," Wendy said, knowing full well that she hadn't. Taylor had definitely told her the festival was that day. She was certain.

"Yeah, you must be mistaken. That festival is the only big thing that ever happens in that town—and it's just once a year."

Wendy had no idea why Taylor would lie. Maybe he just got the dates mixed up, she thought. "So you and Taylor went to high school together?" Wendy asked, eager to change the subject.

"That's right. We graduated the same year."

"Other than Taylor, you're the first person that I've met from

Ducotey."

"That's not surprising. Ducotey's a very small town and most of the kids start farming full time after they graduate from high school. Few go to college."

"I see. Were you and Taylor close growing up?"

"Oh yeah. I've wasted many hours of my life drinking beer with him on country roads. Those were some good times."

"That seems to be a favorite pastime down there," laughed Wendy. "Taylor's told me that Keith and Elijah still do an awful lot of it."

"Who?" asked Howard.

"Taylor's friends, Keith and Elijah. Surely you know them."

Howard shook his head. "I don't know anyone named Keith or Elijah in Ducotey."

Wendy was perplexed. Howard must be having a memory lapse, she thought. "I think you've been chugging too many beers with the beer bong," she laughed.

Howard smiled. "Why do you say that?"

"Because Taylor's told me several times that when he was growing up, he spent a lot of his free time with them. They're all best friends."

Howard looked at Wendy and tilted his head like a confused dog. "I don't think so. Taylor and I were very close in school and again, I never knew anyone named Keith or Elijah."

Wendy was baffled. "Are you sure?"

"Ducotey is a very small town; the school's even smaller. Everyone knows everyone. I've never heard of those guys."

"That's impossible. They live in Ducotey now. I've been to their house."

"How long have they lived there?" asked Howard.

"I'm not sure."

"I don't visit Ducotey much anymore, so it's possible they moved in after I left."

"Yeah, you could be right, but I'd think you would know them from your childhood."

"Well, there are dozens of small towns around Ducotey. Keith and Elijah could've attended school in a nearby town. Maybe they hung out with Taylor when I wasn't around. It's possible," said Howard.

Veronica grabbed Howard's hand. "We'd better hit the trail. This is a big day for us," she said with a smile.

"It was nice to meet you," Wendy said as the two left.

Wendy wondered what the hell is going on. Taylor had some serious explaining to do. She dialed his apartment and listened as the phone rang several times, but he didn't answer. Times like these made her wish they could afford cell phones.

"Wendy," Gayland said as he walked past her desk. "I'd like to speak to you in my office."

Wendy rolled her eyes, reluctant to find out what he wanted this time. While Gayland waited at the door, she entered his office and sat in one of the wingback chairs. Gayland closed the door, then walked to the window and stared at the morning sun. "Do you remember when you first started working for me?" he asked without looking her way.

She nodded. "Yes," she said.

"You were ready to change the world. I remember when I was that age and how fresh and new things seemed. I had so much potential back then. Sometimes I'm shocked at how badly I've screwed it all up."

Gayland's words surprised Wendy. He was showing a vulnerable side that she'd never seen.

"You seem to have done all right for yourself," Wendy said. "You have power and wealth. What more do you want?"

Gayland sat in his leather chair. "I know your father forced you to come back to work for me because I pressured him."

"So?" Wendy said. "What does it matter? I'm here, willingly or unwillingly."

"And that's what bothers me."

"You shouldn't let it. Since when did it matter how I feel? Or anyone else for that matter."

Gayland rubbed his eyes, then stared at Wendy. "I'm trying to say that I'm very sorry about all the things that have been happening lately. My actions have been unprofessional."

"Very unprofessional," Wendy coldly replied.

"You're one of the few people that I really care about, Wendy. I've always felt like I could talk to you. Sometimes I do things before I think them through," he said with watering eyes.

Because she suddenly felt a twinge of pity, Wendy looked away. Her emotions were mixed—she wanted to release all the hostility that had been building for years, but she still didn't trust him.

"Wendy, I'm very sorry about the other night when I was drunk. Please forgive me."

Her compassion quickly won the emotional war. He was finally atoning for his sins. When she saw sincerity in his eyes, she sighed and said, "I forgive you."

Gayland smiled. "I knew you would. You're an understanding girl. You always have been."

"I guess it's the curse of being raised in the Midwest."

"There's one more thing we need to talk about," Gayland said.

"I'm listening."

"Yesterday, Detective Jennings from the State Bureau came by the office and asked me a bunch of questions."

"Questions about what?"

"Oh, a variety of things. He was just meddling where he had no business."

Wendy was surprised by Gayland's choice of words. "Are you in trouble?" she asked.

Gayland laughed. "No, no," he said. "Not in the least bit. I'm just warning you in case he and his bully friends come back and start asking you about certain things."

"Oh."

"It would be better for both you and your father's financial well being if you don't cooperate with them if they conduct a witch hunt."

Wendy was shattered. Just moments earlier the man had begged for forgiveness. Now he was threatening both her and her father's livelihood if she talked to the authorities.

Gayland removed a cigar from his desk and cut off the end with a sharp knife. "Do you understand what I'm saying?" he asked.

"I think I understand completely."

"Good," Gayland replied and lit the cigar. "Let's never mention this again." He grabbed his briefcase from the floor, laid it on his desk, and popped open the locks. Turning to the credenza behind his desk, he filtered through a stack of papers.

Wendy stood to leave, but caught sight of the bloody contracts from Taylor's apartment inside the briefcase. Her knees buckled as she collapsed back into the chair.

"Wendy? Wendy, are you all right?"

She opened her eyes to see Gayland leaning over his desk, waving the cigar in front of her face. "Is something the matter?" he asked.

"No," Wendy quickly replied. "I'm fine."

"You look like you've seen a ghost," Gayland said. "Are you sure you're all right?"

"Yeah, I'm fine," Wendy replied, trying to think of a good excuse for her momentary lapse. "I haven't been getting much sleep lately."

"I see."

Wendy looked in the briefcase to reconfirm her finding, but it was already shut and locked.

"I'll be out for the afternoon," Gayland said.

"Where are you going?"

"I'm headed over to Ducotey."

Again, Wendy felt weak. "If you don't mind my asking, what are you going to do there?"

"I'm closing a business deal," Gayland said and puffed on the cigar. "I doubt I'll make it back before five, so be sure to lock up."

"All right."

"If you're feeling better this evening, perhaps you'd like to stop by my house for a night cap."

In her current emotional state, Wendy wasn't sure if she'd rather throw up or scream. She opted for a polite refusal. "Sorry, but I'm busy. I've got some studying to do."

"Suit yourself," Gayland said and walked out of the office.

Wendy returned to her desk and laid her head on the keyboard. As soon as she was sure Gayland had left the building, she grabbed her things and headed for the door.

"Leaving early today?" the receptionist asked as Wendy stormed past.

"Yes. And don't expect me back."

Chapter 46

"What are these things called again?" Jennings asked. "I can't believe how great they taste."

"They're called meat pies," Fred mumbled while devouring one. "It's an old Indian recipe."

"Mom's been making these for as long as I can remember," Carol added.

"Well, Louise, they're mighty good," Jennings said.

"I agree, Mom, these are some of the best ever."

"Thanks," replied Louise. "But your dad's eating them so fast, I'm afraid they won't last long."

"Maybe you ought to spend less time talkin' and more time eatin'."

"You're acting like a wild animal that hasn't been fed in weeks. If you don't watch yourself, you're going to be missing a finger."

"It's all your fault. You shouldn't make these things taste so damned good," Fred said without looking up.

"Here, here," said Carol. "Remember, we've got company."

"Carol tells me that you testified at the Finken trail," said Louise. "Do you think you'll get a conviction?"

Jennings sighed. "Unfortunately, Mr. Finken was acquitted this morning."

"Oh, my. I was sure he was guilty. He's a terrible man, you know. He and his nephew nearly wiped out the farmers in this part of the state."

"I know of his past," Jennings said while eyeing the remaining meat pies on the platter. "He's a pitiful excuse for a man. It's a shame he didn't get what he deserved today."

"Have you two found anything on Gayland?" asked Louise.

"I'll let Carol answer that question," he said, his eyes meeting Fred's. Without saying a word he acknowledged the beginning of a meat pie eating competition.

Both men simultaneously finished their first meat pie. Just as they both picked up the second pie from their plates, someone knocked on the front door. Since Fred and Jennings were engrossed in their feeding frenzy, Carol and Louise went to answer the door. Just as they were finishing off their second meat pies and were eyeing the last two, Louise snatched the platter from the table.

"What the hell are you doing, woman?" snapped Fred with a full mouth.

"We have a guest."

"What? Who?"

"Hello, Fred."

Fred stopped chewing. His arch nemesis was standing right behind him about to eat the last of the prized meat pies. Turning, he muttered, "Hello Quana. As usual, you show up when there's free food."

"Mind your manners, Daddy!" Carol scolded.

"Don't mind him," said Quana as he sat, "his tapeworm is still hungry."

"Good to see you, Quana," said Jennings.

"Likewise."

"Louise, do we have any more meat pies?" Fred asked angrily.

"We sure don't. I never dreamed that you and Jennings would turn a meal into a challenge."

"Don't worry about me, ma'am," said Jennings. "I'm happy. That was one of the finest lunches I've ever had the pleasure of eating."

Fred picked up a piece of celery and forced it in his mouth. "It would have been even better had we not been invaded by the meat-pie monster."

"You hush your mouth," said Louise.

Quana looked at Fred and slowly raised a forkful of meat pie into his mouth. "They're simply delicious," he said to Fred.

"That aggie-lover is taunting me!" Fred replied. "He's up to his old tricks."

Quana laughed and continued to eat. "I heard Finken got off this morning. I'm very sorry."

"Aren't we all," replied Jennings. "We did everything possible. We just got outsmarted."

"That sometimes happens. Best not to dwell on it."

Jennings looked at the table as if he were hiding something. "It's hard not to," he said.

"How 'bout that warm weather," said Carol. "Who would have thought it would turn out so nice today after being cold for so long?"

"It's a welcome relief, that's for sure," said Jennings.

"Daddy, since it is so warm outside, why don't you take our guest out and show him our place?"

"That's a great idea," said Jennings. "I'd love to get out today."

"That sounds fine," Fred said as he watched Quana eat. "Getting out of this house right now would be a pleasure."

Quana smiled at Fred while he munched. "Maybe I'll join you," he said and laughed.

Growing angrier by the moment, Fred jumped up from the table and walked toward the kitchen. "Can I get anyone a beer?"

"Sure," Jennings replied.

"I'll take one, too," said Carol.

Quana winked at Carol. "Fred, bring mine in a chilled glass, please."

Fred mumbled some profanities as he entered the kitchen.

"You're going to give him a heart attack," said Carol. "Just apologize and get it over with."

"I'm just having fun with him. I'll make amends soon, I promise."

While Quana spoke to Carol, Jennings noticed a strange tattoo on his right arm.

"That's a nice lookin' tattoo," Jennings said. "What is it?"

Quana rolled up his shirtsleeve, revealing a small and colorful tattoo. "Remember when I told you that I lived in Kansas City for a while?" he asked.

Jennings nodded.

"Well, I got drunk one night with some other detectives and had the Kansas City skyline tattooed on my arm. My wife wasn't real happy when I got home."

"That's interesting," said Jennings. "You must have really liked Kansas City."

"Oh, I loved it. It's great to be home now, but those years in Kansas City were great. As a matter of fact, all my friends call me Kacey."

"K.C. as in Kansas City?" asked Jennings.

"That's right," Quana replied.

"There'll be no talk of friendship in this house until I get an apology," Fred declared as he distributed beers around the table.

He sat a bottle in front of Quana just as he finished his last bite of meat pie. Quana looked at him with cold eyes and declared, "This is not a chilled glass."

Fred walked to his chair and sat without saying a word.

"I'm joking, Fred," said Quana with a smile. Grabbing the beer bottle, he chugged it in a matter of moments.

"Look, this has gone on long enough," said Quana. "I'm very sorry for painting your front door orange and black. It was a childish prank. Please forgive me."

Fred remained silent and stared at his empty plate.

"Daddy, Quana's offering you the peace twig. I think it only right of you to accept."

"All right, damn it. I accept your apology."

"And?" said Louise.

"He ate my last two meat pies. I accepted his apology. I can only give so much!"

"What else would you like to say?"

Fred took a drink from his beer, then slammed the bottle down on the table. "I'm sorry for painting your car crimson and cream," he said while looking at Louise and Carol. "There, are you two happy that you emasculated me in front of our guests?"

"Thank you," the ladies said in unison.

"Apology accepted," Quana said. "Now go grab me another beer."

Everyone at the table laughed, including Fred.

"I'm so happy to see that we've finally gotten past this," Louise said. "Now you men get the hell out of this house. Get in the truck and go show Carol's man our land."

"I've got a better one," said Fred. "Since I know how much Jennings likes to ride, I've made some special arrangements."

Jennings' eyes grew wide in anticipation. "Don't tell me you've saddled up the ponies," he said.

"That I did," Fred said with a smile. "We're going deer hunting, old west style."

"You're kidding!" said Jennings.

"Of course not."

"I don't know that it's a good idea for him to shoot a high-powered rifle off the back of a horse, Daddy. He hasn't ridden in quite some time and the horses might spook. I'd hate for him to get bucked off and hurt out in the boondocks."

"Oh, I'll be fine. I used to do it all the time when I was a kid."

"Don't worry about the horses," said Fred. "They're plenty gentle. I've shot guns around them many times. They'll be fine."

"It's not the horse I'm worried about," said Carol.

"What about you, Quana? Are you going to join us?" asked Jennings.

Quana looked at Fred. "How many horses are saddled?"

"Three," Fred replied. "I kind of figured that you'd come around."

"But I didn't even bring a gun, or boots," Jennings said.

"I have an extra rifle you can borrow," Fred replied. "But I've got to warn you, it's a 7 millimeter Mauser that packs a hell of a kick."

"A 7 millimeter Mauser? What are we hunting, elephant deer?"

"It'll knock them down, that's for sure. Do you have sensitive ears?"

Jennings laughed. "I'm a cop, what do you think?"

"It's a bit loud. I'm sure you'll get along just fine."

The three men excused themselves from the table and headed for the door while Carol left the room.

"I hate to ride in tennis shoes," said Jennings as Fred opened the door. "My Pa always told me never to do that."

Carol returned with Jennings' boots in hand. "Looking for these?" she asked.

"You're something else," he replied as he swapped the casual shoes for sturdy boots. "You kept it a secret this whole time."

"I just hope you have fun."

Jennings softly kissed Carol. "Thanks," he said. "I really needed this."

"You just go out and have a good time. Mom and I will make some more meat pies for dinner tonight."

Jennings bolted from the house like a little boy rushing to ride a bike for the first time. He caught up with Fred and Quana and walked with them to the barn.

"You guys be home before dark," called Carol. "And Daddy, take good care of my city boy!"

Chapter 47

Rather than battle the impulses of the id and superego, the balanced individual embraces the contrasting voices, then shapes an objective and rational process of thought. Evident in a soldier trained for war, the balanced psyche enjoys absolute harmony among the id and superego. When threatened, the id-fueled tactics of survival are activated while maintaining the superego's duty of sound caution and awareness. Individuals possessing this equilibrium are well rounded and resourceful, but most notably, are the most dangerous prey of all.

Taylor's gaze nervously flashed to the rearview mirror. Relieved that no cars were following him, he let out a sigh, then pressed his foot down hard on the gas pedal. The yellow Plymouth's engine thundered as it sped down the highway toward Ducotey.

"I'm sensing apprehension in you," Keith stated from the backseat.

Taylor spotted Keith's face in the mirror. "The eyeliner from your eyebrows has run down your cheeks," he said while laughing. "You look like an angry clown."

"Pardon me." Keith wiped his cheeks with a handkerchief. "It's quite warm back here. I'd rather take these clothes off, I would."

"Not yet. We're almost there." Taylor looked across the front seat and noticed that Elijah was fast asleep. "We'll soon need to awaken the sleeping giant."

"Can't wait," Keith muttered sarcastically, then leaned forward in his seat. "Are you worried?" he asked in a low voice.

"Why do you ask?"

"You seem much more aware of your surroundings, as if you're expecting the police to appear out of nowhere. You're also driving like a madman."

"I'm driving fast for a reason. We've got to take care of Hempshaw before Gayland arrives. Hempshaw will be difficult enough on his own. I don't want to face both of them together. And yes, I am nervous."

"That's unsettling. During all the things we've gone through together, I've never known you to be nervous."

"Me, neither. I know I shouldn't be saying this, but I don't have a very good feeling about this one."

"You're right. You shouldn't have said that," Keith replied with a sour expression on his face.

"I only tell you for your own good. Our war with the criminals ends today, but I fear we'll encounter strong resistance."

"Then we should stop now! We've made our point; we've disabled them. Turn this car around!"

"You know our partner will never allow that. Besides, Campanow and Kacey have gone to a lot of trouble to setup this meeting with Gayland and Hempshaw. They won't be very happy if we walk away."

"It beats staying here and dying or getting caught."

"We have a job to finish," Taylor said. "You know damned well that if we don't take care of Gayland, he'll just regroup and do it all again."

Keith placed his hands over his head. "I just wish this were all over," he said.

"Me too. But over, it ain't."

Taylor reached to jab Elijah in the ribs. "Wake up. We've arrived."

He pulled into the convenience store and parked on the empty gravel parking lot, just outside the front door. He and Elijah simultaneously stepped outside.

"Wait guys," said Keith. "I'm coming with you."

Elijah laughed. "What're you gonna do? Annoy Hempshaw to death with lethal nagging?"

"No. I thought I'd try to help."

"We're better served if you wait here," said Taylor. "Get behind the wheel and be ready in case we need to get out in a hurry."

"As you wish," said Keith.

"And knit me a sweater, too," laughed Elijah. "If it's not too dangerous."

"Piss off," Keith shouted as Taylor and Elijah entered the store. They found Hempshaw sitting on a chair behind the counter with his legs propped up, smoking a cigarette and reading the newspaper. He was a thin, short man whose skin had been so overexposed to sunlight during his lifetime that it looked like leather. Luckily, Hempshaw was alone.

While Elijah waited by the front door, Taylor walked to the cooler and grabbed a twelve pack of beer, then advanced to the register.

Lost in the newspaper, the fifty-five year old Hempshaw didn't acknowledge Taylor's presence until he set the twelve pack down on the counter. Hempshaw's piercing eyes peeked over his old horn-rimmed glasses to look at Taylor.

"Is the circus in town?" Hempshaw asked as he noticed Taylor's female attire.

Taylor smiled. "A circus of sorts, you could say."

"You ain't from around here, are you, boy?"

"I used to be. I live in Carson now."

"That's where all the weirdos come from," Hempshaw smirked. "You best watch yourself. Folks 'round here don't care much for fellows dressed up such as you are. You're liable to get a good old-fashioned ass whuppin' by the time you reach the city limits."

"Well, thank you for the warning, Mr. Hempshaw. I'll try to go unnoticed."

Hempshaw froze. "How do you know my name?"

"Oh, I know a lot about you," Taylor said. "As a matter of fact, I saved your life not long ago."

Hempshaw's stomach dropped. Something was awry. He had no reason to fear the man who stood before him, but Hempshaw sensed that the stranger wanted more than the twelve pack of beer, which sat on the counter. The fear spiked when he remembered the mysterious string of murders that had recently occurred by men reportedly dressed in women's clothing.

Hempshaw raised his newspaper and pretended to continue reading. With Taylor's view blocked by the newspaper, Hempshaw reached down with his right hand to retrieve the .44 caliber pistol taped to the underside of the stool.

"Saved my life? I reckon I owe you a big thanks, then," Hempshaw calmly remarked. "It's not every day a fellow saves your life. Especially someone you don't even know."

Taylor smiled. "You're more than welcome."

"Pray tell. Just how did you save my life?"

"Well, it wasn't easy. It actually took a lot of planning and a lot of nerve."

"What exactly took a lot of nerve?"

"Killing Joe."

"Joe who?"

"Joe Escartes, the hitman," said Taylor.

Hempshaw was confused, but also somewhat elated. The stranger's claim was outlandish and besides, Hempshaw had never even heard of a Joe Escartes. Hempshaw immediately surmised that the stranger must have some mental problems. He probably picked out names from a phone book and was just trying to get some free beer in exchange for supposedly saving his life. Hempshaw moved his right hand back onto his lap. "If you're looking for free beer, you've come to the wrong place. I'm sorry, but I just can't go giving free beer to people who dress up like women and claim to be life savers."

"I'm not here for free beer," said Taylor.

Becoming annoyed, Hempshaw forcefully stated, "I don't know anyone named Joe Escartes."

"Of course not. You weren't supposed to know him until it was too late. Gayland hired him to kill you."

Hempshaw's fear was tangible as he searched for the pistol. "I'm sorry," he remarked while he felt around for the gun, "but I don't know a Gayland, either. I'm afraid you've got the wrong man."

Taylor laughed. "Kyle Gayland, the banker from Carson. The guy who hired Joe Escartes to kill you and the other investors who tried to murder the Indians of the Redtree Housing Unit. He and his partner, an attorney named Ratcliff, planned to kill all of you, then sell the land to the government and keep the profits."

Hempshaw was dumbstruck. "How the hell do you know about that?"

"'Cause he poisoned my parents a while back. Only they didn't recover. He killed them."

"But you ain't no Injun," Hempshaw said. His right hand finally found the gun. Being careful not to strain or give any indication of his actions, he tugged at the gun until it broke free from the electric tape that held it to the stool.

"I was adopted."

"Well, that's a hell of a story, but I'm afraid I can't help you."

Taylor laughed. "I'm not asking for your help. You see, we've tracked down the investors and killed them one by one. Only you and Gayland remain and I understand he'll be here shortly."

"I suppose I'm next," Hempshaw said with a smile, still remaining calm.

"You catch on quick."

"Let's get this over with," said Elijah, still standing by the front door. "I'm getting hungry."

Even though Hempshaw held the gun freely in his right hand now, he felt black tape around the gun's trigger, rendering it useless. He feared that using his left hand to remove the tape would alert the stranger, so he continued working on it, being careful not to drop the gun in the process.

"Here's where it gets interesting," Taylor said. "I'd like to have your help."

"I'm all ears."

"I'm kind of a scholar, a surrealist scholar, if you will, and I study people, wicked people, like yourself and Gayland."

"I hear you," Hempshaw said while working on the tape.

"My hypothesis states that the level of danger a person is exposed to can alter his or her instinctual impulses. A genuine threat can totally transform conscious reality into a completely different identity, an identity which exists within the framework of the subconscious mind and is inaccessible to conscious thought; an animalistic reaction to conflict."

Hempshaw shook his head. "That's really something," he said. "I feel like I'm watching a science special on PBS."

Taylor was surprised that Hempshaw was remaining so calm. He quickly decided to stimulate the subject of his study. "My purpose is to find your true identity," he said while he pulled out his pistol. "I want to see what instinctual identity you will present when your mind becomes so vexed with danger that it resorts to pure animalistic survival tactics. Sort of like a hunter who is charged by a mad rhinoceros and finds his gun repeatedly misfiring."

Hempshaw's thumb finally broke the tape free from the trigger. Now all he had to do was remove the tape completely.

"We're wasting time," shouted Elijah. "Let's hurry up and get this over with."

Hempshaw smiled and looked at Taylor's gun. "That's a big gun, young man. I reckon you're planning to see just how much I'll squirm before you use it on me."

"I have to admit, you're different," said Taylor. "The rest of the investors were easy, but you, I have a feeling you'll be a bit tougher to crack."

"My mama always said I was the stubbornest kid she ever raised."

Hempshaw smiled as the last shred of tape fell from his pistol. He slowly raised the gun behind the newspaper and tried his best to aim it.

"I've been told that you are the meanest of the mean in these parts. I must be missing something because you seem as docile as a field mouse."

"What you see is what you get. And, for the record," Hempshaw said as he quietly cocked the pistol's hammer back, "poisoning the Indians at Redtree wasn't my idea. Gayland came to me with it. He told me that he'd take care of everything, for me not to worry. But I guess that doesn't matter now."

Taylor shook his head. "No sir, it certainly doesn't."

"Enough of the bullshit, Taylor, take care of him or I will!" Elijah shouted.

Hempshaw's face remained expressionless as he pulled the trigger. The bullet tore through the newspaper, whooshing past Taylor toward Elijah.

Taylor watched as blood began oozing from Elijah's leg. Elijah responded by rapidly firing several times at Hempshaw, knocking him off his stool. Taylor leaned over the counter to confirm Hempshaw was bleeding from multiple chest wounds.

Rushing to Elijah, he asked, "Are you all right?"

"I've been hit! Hell no, I'm not all right! Did I get him?"

"You got him. He's done."

Taylor pulled out his knife and cut the fabric away from Elijah's wound. After a quick inspection, he tore some of the dress and tied it tightly high on his upper thigh.

"How bad is it?" asked Elijah.

"It's just a flesh wound. It was bleeding pretty badly, but I tied it off. That should help."

Taylor and Elijah suddenly stopped cold when they heard a vehicle pulling into the parking lot.

"Who's that?"

Taylor quickly ran to the window and looked outside. "It's Gayland," he said. "Quick, get behind the door. As soon as he comes in, I'll end this."

"No!" shouted Elijah. "You can't end it here, someone will find him."

"What does that matter?"

"They'll find him and give him a proper burial. He'll move on to the spirit world if that happens."

"I'm sure that there will be plenty of justice waiting for him in the spirit world. He won't be able to buy off judges there."

"No," said Elijah. "We can't kill him here. He's the leader. We have to take him to a place where no one can ever find him. I don't want his soul to enter the spirit world. I want his soul to suffer."

Gayland parked the Suburban, turned off the engine, and stepped out of the vehicle. Briefcase in hand, he whistled as he entered the convenience store. Immediately noticing the bullet holes in the display behind the cash register, he warily moved forward to investigate.

When he heard footsteps, he reached into his front pocket to grab his pistol. But before he could pull it out of his pocket, his world faded to dark.

Just as Jennings made his way out of the dense thicket of brush, he bumped the horse's stomach with the heels of his boots, prompting the gelding to lope slowly toward Fred and Quana, who waited directly ahead on horseback.

"Did you see anything?" Fred asked as Jennings neared.

"I saw a lot of tracks, but no deer. How 'bout you?"

"I didn't see anything," answered Quana, "but Fred saw some deer moving north toward the reservation."

"Can we hunt on the reservation?"

"Sure," said Fred. "I'll bet that's where the deer are headed due to the cover. It'll do your soul some good to view the scenery. There's a cliff up ahead that no one knows about except me and a friend of mine. It's truly breathtaking."

"Sounds good to me."

As the three men rode their horses side by side toward the reservation, Quana reached over and slapped Jennings' horse on the rear with his reins. The horse responded by jumping forward, twirling around in a circle, pitching his tail, then bucking a few times. Jennings tightened the reins and quickly regained control of the horse. He stopped and waited for Fred and Quana.

"What are you trying to do? Get me thrown off?"

Quana laughed. "No, I was just seeing if you could control the horse."

"I hope I didn't disappoint."

"You sure didn't," said Fred. "As a matter of fact, you ride pretty good for a city boy."

"Thank you," said Jennings. "Now excuse me while I go find my testicles. I believe they flew off about the time the bucking started."

While Fred laughed hysterically, Quana extended his hand to Jennings. "I'm sorry. I didn't know he'd buck."

Jennings smiled and shook Quana's hand. "Don't worry. I needed to be emasculated anyway."

After laughing uncontrollably for several minutes, the group of men resumed their ride toward the reservation.

"I think this is the most at ease I've felt in years," said Jennings. "This truly is a slice of heaven."

"You can say that again. Sometimes I miss Kansas City, but there's nothing like being out here, one with nature. It's one of the best feelings in the world."

"There they are!" shouted Fred. "A whole herd of 'em, too, straight ahead!"

"Where?" asked Jennings.

"On the reservation. Look through the rifle's scope."

Jennings stepped off his horse and retrieved his rifle from the saddle holster. He pointed the gun directly ahead, toward the reservation. "I'll say," Jennings said as he focused the scope. "I see three big bucks and several does. They're moving fairly slow about three hundred yards ahead of us."

"Think we ought to split up?" asked Quana.

"No," Fred answered. "Someone might get hit in the cross fire.

Let's see if we can sneak up behind them and catch 'em off guard."

Jennings placed his rifle back in the saddle holster. He then led his horse to the barbed-wire gate that guarded the reservation. After all three men walked through, Jennings closed the gate and stepped up into the saddle again.

"Guys," Jennings said with a smile, "I've been wanting to say this for a long time—let's ride!"

Jennings gently kicked his horse and released his grip on the reins. As his horse blazed across the open prairie, he had trouble containing his excitement. Even though he was chasing after deer, he felt just like John Wayne, on a mission to bring order to the Wild West. It was the happiest he'd been in a very long time.

Chapter 48

Lying on his back, Gayland opened his eyes to a foreign world of towering white canyon walls. "What the hell?" he muttered as he sat up to cradle his throbbing head. His hand instinctively felt the huge knot and probed the dried blood caked in his hair.

As his heart started to pound, he realized there were no people, no landmarks, not much of anything to offer a clue as where he was or how he had gotten there. Only one thing was certain—he was sitting in the ravine of a canyon near a huge cliff a few hundred feet away.

Placing his hands on the ground, he struggled to stand. Suddenly, he felt intense pain shoot through his head. He quickly realized someone had hit him from behind.

"I'll bet that hurts," Taylor said as he pushed Gayland back on the rocks.

After Gayland landed, he quickly turned. "Who the hell are you?" he gasped. "And what in the hell am I doing here?"

"You've come to pay for your misdeeds," Taylor said and walked down the ravine, directly in front of Gayland. Previously hidden by a large boulder, Elijah and Keith walked to Taylor's side.

Gayland was incensed. "What the hell are you talking about, son? And why the hell are you dressed up like a woman?"

"I would imagine that you probably have a lot of questions," Taylor said.

"Damned right. Now what the hell's going on here?"

"We're doing the job that you hired Joe Escartes to do."

"What?"

"We've been killing off all those investors for you."

"I don't know what you're talking about," Gayland said. "Who's Joe Escartes?"

"Well," Taylor said with a gleeful look, "he's the gentleman that you hired to kill the Indians and your cohorts."

"That's ridiculous! I don't know any Joe Escartes."

"I think you do. You hired him to kill Perkins, Simonson, Peat, Johnson, Hempshaw, and a few others."

Gayland instantly turned angry. "Who told you about the investors?"

"Let us just say that I have some good connections."

After a few moments of processing his thoughts, Gayland suddenly realized the gravity of the moment. "So, it's you," growled Gayland. He quickly jumped to his feet and took a step toward Taylor. "Why in the hell are you meddling in my business?"

Taylor walked up to Gayland and stood toe-to-toe with the banker. "Because you've made it my business," he replied, then sucker-punched Gayland in the stomach, sending him to his knees.

The winded Gayland struggled to stand again, but Elijah was quick to kick him in the chest, sending him back to the ground.

"What do you want from me?" Gayland groaned.

"Four years ago, you poisoned my parents. Today I'm going to take from you what you took from me."

"That was an accident," Gayland said in a much friendlier tone. "I never intended to kill anyone. I was just trying to get them out of those wretched houses."

"Bullshit!" Taylor roared. "You were disposing of them so you could sell land to the government at an inflated price. Don't lay that shit on me, Gayland, I know who you are."

"You got it all wrong, kid. I had nothing to do with killing Indians. I was just trying to make their lives better."

Taylor expelled a deep breath. "Since you won't bear the burden of your responsibility, there is no point in continuing this conversation. I know what you've done; I've seen the paperwork in the safe of your office. Throughout your life, you've made a fortune misleading others; you won't mislead me now."

Gayland's mind raced as he looked around and tried to find a way to escape. Even though his head still throbbed, he was slowly regaining his memory.

"Now I recognize you," Gayland declared. "You're Wendy's boyfriend! I had lunch with you at the Italian restaurant."

"You're catching on."

"And I'll bet that little bitch let you into my office when I was gone. That's how you found out about everything."

Taylor kicked Gayland in the chest. "I'd appreciate it if you didn't call her that."

While he writhed in pain, Elijah pulled out his pistol and aimed it at Gayland.

"So what are you gonna do? Kill me like you killed the others, out here, in the middle of nowhere?"

"That wasn't my idea," Taylor said, "But I kind of like it. I wanted to end all this back at Hempshaw's store, but my friend wants you to die out here where no one will ever find you. This way, your soul will drift aimlessly in the spirit world forever. I think it's rather fitting."

Gayland realized that his brash tactics weren't helping, so he decided to try another tactic. "How much do you want?"

Taylor smiled. "How much have you got?"

"Millions, most of it offshore. Just name your price."

"I'm sorry, but that isn't quite enough. I'm not in this for money; I'm in it for justice."

"Every man has his price," Gayland said. "Tell me yours."

"I came for your blood. That is my price."

Gayland laughed. "Then you're no better than me. You're a killer, just like I am."

Elijah pulled the hammer back on his pistol. "We end this now," he said.

Taylor nodded.

"You'll never get away with it," Gayland huffed. "You have no idea of my power."

"Nor you of mine," Taylor said.

Elijah pulled the trigger several times, striking Gayland's chest. He fell on the rocks.

Taylor grabbed the pistol, wiped it free of fingerprints, then placed it in Gayland's right hand.

"In the event he's ever found, the police will at least be able to link the gun back to Hempshaw. That ought to confuse 'em."

He shook his head as he looked at Gayland's fallen body. "Wealth buys no favors in the darkest chasms of hell," he said.

Taylor turned and walked down the ravine, toward the cliff. With a huge sigh of relief, he said, "It's over. It's finally over."

Chapter 49

"Did you hear that?" Jennings asked. "It sounded like a gunshot."

"Yeah. Sounded like it came from the cliffs," Quana said.

"What cliffs?"

"Over the hill in front of us, about three hundred yards from here. It's a big rock canyon with a river running through it. I suspect there's hunters down there."

"I don't think so," replied Jennings. "That didn't sound like a rifle, more like a pistol."

"They best not be hunting deer with a pistol," Fred announced.

"Maybe we should check it out," said Quana.

"Lead the way," replied Fred.

"It's finally over," Taylor said again as he walked down the ravine. As he approached Running Bear Cliff, he heard a loud shriek, much like the sound of the eagle he'd been hearing in his dreams.

Out of curiosity, Taylor walked to the edge of Running Bear Cliff and looked down. He was taken aback as he watched the blood-red river churn and move rapidly in its banks. After searching momentarily, he found a wounded eagle sitting atop the rocks of the opposite bank, staring directly at him.

"Well I'll be damned," Taylor said to himself. "That's odd."

The eagle's high-pitched shriek pierced the neon-green atmosphere surrounding Taylor, sending chills down his spine. "I'm dreaming," he said. "I must be dreaming."

"Go over," a voice whispered in Taylor's ear.

Startled, Taylor quickly turned to find Elijah standing directly in front of him.

"What's the matter?" asked Taylor.

"Go over," Elijah whispered. "It's time."

From the nearby blue canyon walls, Keith walked to Elijah and stood by his side. "It's time, old boy," he said.

"What in the hell are you guys talking about? We can't go over, it's too far. We'll fall to our deaths."

"Go over," Elijah whispered. "It is time."

"We're not going over, goddamn it! We're going to walk to our car and we're getting the hell out of here. Our mission has been accomplished."

Taylor winced when he heard the eagle shriek again from the bottom of the canyon. The sound was so sharp, it echoed violently in his head.

Elijah smiled and bent to grab something from the ground. By the time Taylor recognized it was a gun, Elijah had already cocked the hammer.

"Would somebody please tell me what the hell is going on?" demanded Taylor. "The war is over. We won. They're all dead now. Our mission has been accomplished."

"There's just one more little thing," Keith said.

"And what is that?"

"We've all got to make it to the other side."

"If it's so important that we make it to the other side, let's find a way down safely, swim the river, then crawl back up."

Elijah trained the gun firmly on Taylor.

"We're not talking about the canyon," said Keith. "We're taking you to the other side of eternity."

"What?" screamed Taylor. "Are you out of your damned minds?"

Keith laughed. "No, Taylor. I'm afraid you are."

"Since when did this all come about?" asked Taylor while he slowly stepped away from the cliff.

"Since the beginning," said Elijah. "We've always known that this would be a mission of no return."

Taylor continued stepping backward. "It would have been nice if someone told me," he said. "I think I have should have a vote in this."

"You're outnumbered two to one," said Keith. "Now come on, it's time to go over."

Satisfied that he'd moved far enough, Taylor stopped walking. Keith and Elijah now stood between him and the cliff.

"I'm not going over," Taylor declared as he pulled out his pistol. "I don't know what the hell has come over you two, but this bullshit is going to stop right now."

Elijah aimed the pistol at Taylor.

"Elijah, I'm not kidding you. This doesn't have to happen. Just put the gun down and we all walk away. It's that simple."

Elijah smiled.

"Why are you smiling!" Taylor screamed. "This isn't funny. Put the gun down, now!"

Elijah raised the gun and braced his feet. Taylor knew he was moments from pulling the trigger.

"Put it down, Elijah."

Elijah smiled and steadied the gun with both hands.

Taylor shook his head. "Damn it, Elijah," he shouted and began firing. Elijah continued smiling as the bullets threw his body backward, down into Running Bear Cliff.

"Oh my God!" Taylor screamed and looked at Keith. "Why in the hell did he make me do that? What's going on? Tell me, damn it!"

"Killing Elijah doesn't solve anything," Keith said as he bent to retrieve the gun that Elijah had dropped. "You're still going over."

"You can't shoot me," Taylor said. "You couldn't hurt a piss ant."

"Times they are a changin'," Keith said as he took aim.

"But I took up for you. I defended you all those times."

"That doesn't matter," replied Keith. "You're still going to the other side."

In anger, Taylor fired his gun several times. The apathetic look on Keith's face never wavered as he fell off the side, into the abyss.

Taylor cried and dropped to his knees. "My God, what have I done?" he screamed to the heavens. "What have I done?"

Chapter 50

T aylor, wake up. Come on, wake up!"
Taylor's eyes opened to the sweetest sight he'd ever seen. Wendy's face looked so soft and beautiful that he gently reached up to touch it.

"It's all a dream," he said with a joyous smile on his face. "It's all been nothing more than a dream." Taylor closed his eyes. He'd never felt so at peace. His world was perfect.

"Taylor, you really need to get up," said Wendy.

Taylor opened his eyes. "Let's sleep in," he said.

"No, Taylor, you really need to get up," she replied with a troubled look on her face.

When Taylor looked at Wendy's face again, he noticed something unusual—a camera was hanging around her neck. After he closed his eyes, he wondered why she wearing a camera in the bedroom. Absolute shock rocketed through Taylor's body. "I'm not lying on my bed at home, am I?" he asked.

"No, and you'd better get your ass up. There are three men on horses riding this way."

Taylor slowly stumbled to his feet. After he glanced at the white canyon walls, he immediately knew that it was no dream. "Oh my God!" he shouted.

Wendy started to cry. "Taylor, what the hell's going on?"

Without replying, he grabbed his throbbing leg.

"Good Lord!" Wendy exclaimed as she saw the bullet wound. "You've been shot."

"How long have you been here?" demanded Taylor.

"A while. Who were you talking to when you fired the gun?"

"Elijah and Keith. I didn't want to do it. They made me!"

"Taylor, honey, we've got a serious problem."

"You don't say?" Taylor sarcastically snapped. "I just murdered my two best friends."

Tears ran in streams down Wendy's face. "While I was at the bank today, I ran into your friend Howard. He told me that no one by the names of Keith and Elijah went to school with you in Ducotey. When he said that there was no Indian festival here today, I came to find out what it was that you didn't want me to see."

"I told you to stay away from this place," Taylor said curtly.

Wendy struggled to maintain her composure. "I went to your house at Kickingbird. I saw a man from the water company down the street and so I asked him some questions."

"He wasn't there to cut off Keith and Elijah's water, was he?"

Wendy ran her hands through Taylor's hair and started softly crying. "No, honey," she said. "He told me that the house had been condemned. It hasn't had water for the last four years. Nobody's lived there, Taylor, it's all in your head."

"Bullshit! That's bullshit and you know it!"

"It's not bullshit, Taylor. It's all in your head."

Taylor stared at Wendy in silence.

"Before I came here, I went to your apartment and read your thesis again. Taylor, the id and the superego, they're you. Elijah and Keith are only in your head."

A weak, forced smile made its way across Taylor's face. "That's just absurd," he muttered.

"They don't exist, Taylor! Howard confirmed that they simply don't exist."

The smile faded. Speechless, he stared at the ground.

"I've been watching you, Taylor. I just saw you shoot that man."

"I didn't shoot him, Elijah did."

"Damn it, Taylor, I watched you shoot him. Then you walked down here to Running Bear Cliff and started talking to yourself and shooting your gun again."

"But I killed them. I killed my best friends."

"No you didn't!" Wendy snapped. "You were shooting rocks. No one was there!" Wendy buried her face in her arms and cried uncontrollably.

Remaining silent, Taylor stared at Wendy with cold eyes.

"We've got to get out of here," said Wendy. "There are three men coming on horseback on the other side of the ravine."

After several moments of silence, Taylor asked, "Did you recognize the men on the horses?"

"No," she replied while she wiped her eyes. "I don't know who they are."

"Get out of here. It's probably the law, just like in my vision. You don't need to be involved in any of this. Get out of here before they see you."

"Come on," Wendy said and grabbed Taylor's hand. "We'll go together."

With no time to think, Taylor followed Wendy's lead toward some nearby trees. Before they made it very far, however, a bullet ricocheted off a nearby rock. Taylor and Wendy turned to see Gayland, his shirt soaked in blood, firing a pistol from the ravine.

"It's that man you shot," said Wendy. "He's shooting at us."

"I must have just winged him," Taylor replied.

"Is that...Gayland?" she asked.

"Look, there's a lot you don't know about and I don't have time to tell you," Taylor said. "Run to the woods and never look back. Drive to Carson and forget what you saw."

Wendy's face turned white. "It was you. You killed all those people, didn't you?" she asked in a sobering voice.

"They were killing my people. The law would do nothing."

Wendy was dumbfounded as she stood and stared at Taylor.

"Get out of here!" Taylor shouted. As he limped toward the gun that sat on Running Bear Cliff, he looked back to see Wendy running into the woods. By the time Taylor reached the gun, Gayland was less than fifty yards away.

"Come over here, you little sumbitch," Gayland called as he waddled toward Taylor. The first bullet he fired bounced off the rocks by Taylor's feet.

When Jennings heard the shots coming from the canyon, he kicked his horse and rode hard to the entrance of the ravine.

"Something's wrong," he said, pulling back on the reins. "I heard someone yelling and then shots were fired. We'd better move carefully."

"Grab your rifle and follow me," Fred said as he dismounted.

All three men shouldered their rifles and walked in a crouched position to a huge boulder by the ravine. They quietly crept around the rock and saw two men in the distance, not more than fifty yards away.

Jennings pulled out his rifle and scanned the area using the scope. "There's a man with a gun walking toward another man who just picked up a gun. It looks like the first man has been shot. He's covered in blood."

"Who's been shot?" Quana frantically asked.

"Oh my God," said Jennings. "The guy who just picked up a gun has a dress on. This might be…"

"Who's been shot?" shouted Quana. When Jennings didn't reply, he pulled out his rifle and aimed it toward the two men.

"The cross dresser looks like he's going to shoot," Jennings said and aimed the rifle at Taylor's chest. "I've got a clear shot. I can take him out right now."

Quana grabbed the barrel of Jennings' rifle and pushed it away.

"Look closer at the man covered in blood," Quana said.

Jennings repositioned the rifle and looked through the scope.

"Do you recognize him?"

"My God," Jennings said. "That's Kyle Gayland."

Taylor placed the pistol behind his back as Gayland neared.

"You thought I was dead and that you were gonna get away, didn't you?" Gayland taunted.

"I thought no such thing," Taylor responded. "Trying to kill a man like you is like trying to kill a cockroach."

"You're damned right," Gayland said. "I'm a survivor. And guess what? I survived again."

"So be it," Taylor said and threw his gun at Gayland's feet. "I am free now. There will be no more killing."

"Taylor!" someone shouted from the trees. "Pick up the gun, Taylor!"

He turned to see Wendy running toward him. "Go back," he shouted, motioning with his arms.

"She's a persistent little bitch. A traitor, but persistent," Gayland said with a wicked grin.

"She had nothing to do with any of this. I'm the only person responsible for dismantling your Gestapo."

"I'll deal with her later."

"You've lost a lot of blood. You'll never catch her."

Holding the gun steady in his hand, Gayland cocked the hammer. "I've got you, though, and that's all that really matters."

"No," said Taylor. "Whether you kill me or not, today you'll die and you'll never kill the innocent again. That's all that matters."

Gayland smiled. "I've got to hand it to you, boy. You're pretty sharp to put all this together. Linking me to Kickingbird and Redtree was brilliant. I guess my big mistake was that I didn't kill all the Indians when I had the chance." With both hands on the pistol, he took aim at Taylor.

"No!" Wendy screamed in the distance.

"Goodbye," Gayland said. "You've certainly been a royal pain in the ass."

As Taylor looked straight into Gayland's eyes and braced himself, a thunderous roar echoed through the canyon walls. Gayland reeled from the impact, twisting in agony as he stumbled to the edge of Running Bear Cliff.

Looking over his shoulder, he spotted smoke coming from the barrel of Jennings' rifle. Still alive, Gayland grabbed the pistol and struggled to his feet. When he pointed it at Taylor, another blast cut the eerie silence. Even as the bullet ripped through his flesh, Gayland's defiant gaze never left Taylor. With a violent shudder, he fell off the cliff to the rocky creek bed at the base of the canyon.

Wendy was suddenly at Taylor's side, wrapping him tightly in her arms. For several moments she held him in silence. Finally, Taylor softly said, "I'm sorry I put you through this. But I knew you wouldn't understand. Someone had to stand up for the innocent."

"I know," Wendy replied, wiping away her tears. "I heard what he said."

"I'm just glad it's over."

Wendy could see Quana and Fred talking to Jennings, who seemed agitated. After several minutes of discussion, Jennings walked away from the other two men to stand alone.

"If that's a policeman, I'm afraid this is just the beginning," she said.

"Don't worry, the truth will set him free," replied Taylor.

"What makes you so sure?" Wendy asked.

"Long story. I'll tell you about it sometime."

A loud shriek tore through the air. Taylor and Wendy both turned to see the previously wounded eagle soar into the sky from the rocky ledge above the water. The eagle floated high above the canyon walls, then dove near the water below Running Bear Cliff.

"I guess the eagle is finally free," said Wendy.

The eagle touched the water with its talons, then flew to the top of the cliff. For several moments, Taylor watched it circle. Each time it passed, it shrieked and seemed to look directly into Taylor's eyes. Finally, the magnificent bird coasted to the rock base where Taylor and Wendy stood, making a final pass just inches in front of Taylor before following the canyon's majestic path. Taylor sighed as it flew out of sight.

"As is my spirit," said Taylor.

Wendy heard footsteps and turned. "The policeman is coming," she whispered, firmly grasping his hand.

As Jennings approached, he looked directly into Taylor's eyes, then reached into his pocket and pulled out a slim leather wallet. With a slight nod, he passed them on his way to the edge of Running Bear Cliff. After a moment's pause, he threw the wallet high in the air. As it plunged toward the water, it opened to reveal a gleaming badge. Once it sank to the bottom of the narrow creek, Jennings silently returned to Quana and Fred, mounted his horse and rode away.

"I guess that settles that," said Wendy.

"I suppose it does," Taylor replied.

"Well, we'd better get on back. You have a new thesis to write."

Taylor smiled. "I guess I do."

Jennings laughed as he watched Quana slap the flank of Fred's horse while the three men rode through the pasture back to Fred's place.

After Fred steered his horse out of Quana's reach, he laughed.

"You just don't stop with the trickery, do you?" he asked.

"It's just my nature," Quana said.

Jennings laughed. "How far away from the house are we?" he asked. "It's getting pretty dark.

"Not too far," said Fred. "Hang in there, we'll be eatin' meat pies before you know it."

"What're we doing tomorrow?" Jennings asked Fred.

"Nothing in particular. You got anything planned?"

"Yeah," Jennings said. "As a matter of fact I do. I think I'm gonna take Carol out to look around. Maybe find a few hundred acres with some horses and cows."